Marry Him

MARINA FORD

RIPTIDE
PUBLISHING

Riptide Publishing
PO Box 1537
Burnsville, NC 28714
www.riptidepublishing.com

Marry Him

Cover art: L.C. Chase, lcchase.com/design-portfolio.html
Editor: Carole-ann Galloway
Layout: L.C. Chase, lcchase.com

ISBN: 978-1-62649-935-5

Second edition
March, 2020

Also available in ebook:
ISBN: 978-1-62649-934-8

Marry Him

MARINA FORD

RIPTIDE
PUBLISHING

To the tourists who, when they saw my then-boyfriend on one knee before me on Ha'penny Bridge, cheered "Marry him!" at me. And to Will, who didn't lose his cool at all.

Table of Contents

Chapter One
THE BIG DAY

Things to avoid on your wedding day:
1. Don't even think about stealing your best man's leg. Seriously. Don't be that arsehole no matter how much he provokes you.
2. Don't set fire to anything. Should be a no-brainer.
3. Don't pour your future sister-in-law's urine all over yourself.
4. Don't lose your groom.

For a moment, I stand there, trying to take it all in. The vision of carnage before me is so remarkable that time slows down for me: Frank is shaking his prosthetic leg at me to emphasise the point he's making. "Marriage is murder!" he yells. Though, in his thick Scottish accent, it sounds more like "Marriage es merder!" He's desperate to get his point across. "You don't know what you're getting yourself into! It's absolute fuckin' wank, is what it is! Do ye hear me, pal? These are all signs that it's the biggest mistake of your life!"

Chloe is dancing on the hotel room curtain, which she's torn off the window, trampling down whatever the fire extinguisher missed, spraying white foam all over the carpet.

"It's all right now," she announces, her breathing strained. "Not to worry! I'll just open the window and it'll be like nothing's happened!"

Siobhan is sitting in the armchair by the wall, weeping.

My mother's poodles are making a cacophony in the bathroom.

The hotel staff is banging on the door, demanding to be let in.

And here I am standing with my shirt covered in a yellow splash of Siobhan's urine, in my boxer shorts and socks, with my wedding suit trousers singed to the ironing board. My mobile is in my hand, the message, *I messed up, Joe. I'm sorry*, on the display.

All I can think, as rage and fear boil up inside of me, is how I want to grab that bloody prosthetic leg of Frank's and chase them all out of my room with it.

Chapter Two
HOW WE MET

Five Years Before the Big Day

In my dreams I meet the perfect guy by looking across a crowded room. Our eyes lock, there are sparks, we smile, moments later we find each other by pretend-accident at the buffet or champagne table. We talk, there are more sparks, and then one thing leads to . . . well, shagging. And the rest becomes history.

This is not that story.

Frank had just met the "most amazeng gerl" of his life. His words, not mine.

"She's a bloody marvel!" he told me, while I tried to locate, in the mess that was Chloe's and my flat, the prints I made for a new job I'd been hired to do. It was a commercial thing—not my finest hour, I will readily admit—but it would pay the rent (something our landlord kept reminding us was the appropriate reaction to having housing offered to one by a kind stranger with a lawyer and little patience).

"She sings, she dances, she dresses like an angel . . ." Frank went on.

"What's her name?" I asked, out of politeness.

"Gabriella," he declared, much like another man might say *Excalibur*.

"Pretty."

"Oh, it's beautiful!" he said. "And the way she pronounces it. Gabriella. *Gabriella* . . ." he went on. If she pronounced it anything like him, she sounded like David Tennant on mushrooms, but I didn't say that.

"Have you seen my portfolio?" I asked. "It's black and large and it's overdue on the other side of the river five minutes ago."

"Normally dating sites are shite." Frank continued to ignore me. "The girls on there are never what they say they are. You think you're going to meet an Audrey Hepburn lookalike who reads Tolstoy in the original Russian, and then you're presented to someone who works in the local chippy, misses her front teeth, and thinks Britney Spears is a valid form of music."

I rolled my eyes. "*You* worked in a chippy, and her teeth were fine and as to Britney . . ."

I saw the laugh in his eyes—he was teasing me—and so returned to searching my flat.

"I'd given up hope! And then . . . *Gabriella*! Just like that!"

"Yes, it's marvellous," I said, without conviction. "You're sitting on my portfolio. Please get up."

I dragged the thing out from underneath his barely lifted arse, and then pulled on the first T-shirt I could get my hands on.

"We talked for hours," Frank went on. "And then later she rang me to say good night, and we talked for hours more! I never had this much to say to a lass in my life!"

I'd already gone for the door, but he suddenly snapped out of this Gabriella-induced trance, and cried, "Oi! Hang on! Come back!"

I turned around.

"What? I'm late!"

"Take that off, ye tit," he said with a laugh. "Ye can't go like that!"

I glanced down at my chest and then burst into a chuckle. It was my *I pooped today* T-shirt, which I was meant to bin ages ago. I took it off and grabbed another.

"Better?" I asked.

Frank shook his head at me. "Marginally. Good luck."

I nodded, waved, and headed out. It wasn't my usual sort of gig. Normally, I worked for galleries, for independent shops and fairs. Once in a while, however, it became necessary to make some actual money, and that was when I looked for commercial jobs. Usually this was also small scale—an indie rock concert wanting leaflets, posters, and flyers designed, or small businesses wanting their interiors decorated with flair. This time was different, though. This time a chain of restaurants needed a marketing campaign, and the marketing firm they hired wanted local artists in each region to come up with local-flavoured imagery to advertise it.

I lived in Harlesden, which had a shitty connection to the city. You either took the always-delayed (and if not delayed, then always painfully slow) Bakerloo line, or you took the number 18 bus, which meant the exercise in patience that was the driver change around Willesden Junction—it was like those people had a special Japanese tea ceremony to conduct before they could get us places.

So I was late when I ran into the lobby of the high-rise in which P&B Design Agency had their offices. Panting from all the running, I threw myself into the sofa, waiting for someone to come and fetch me or to be told to piss off, expecting the latter more than the former.

"Mr. Byrne isn't in at the moment," the receptionist said, putting the phone down. "You might have to wait a little."

I expected that as soon as this Byrne chap showed up I'd be told to go home again, but until that happened, I could cool off in the air-conditioned foyer. As I sat there, it was also beginning to dawn on me, watching the people coming in and going out of the building, that even in my non-poo-themed T-shirt, I wasn't appropriately dressed. Everyone wore suits—insanity in this weather, I thought—and many of them stared at me like I'd got lost or was perhaps about to stretch my hand out and ask for spare change.

Then, a man, followed by a young woman, burst into the building, exchanging sharp words with someone on the mobile phone pressed to his ear.

"Do you know what?" he asked the unfortunate person on the other side in a sharp, cultured voice. "How about you fuck yourself? I have no intention— No! I'm going into the lift now . . . No. Absolutely not. Goodbye."

The woman following him was tall and willowy, with a cream-coloured hijab around her head, and enormous purple-rimmed glasses, which made her face look tiny. She saw me, and while the man had entered the lift, she stopped in front of me and said, "Mr. Kaminski?"

"Yes?" I rose to my feet.

"You're late," she said, blinking up at me and then at one of the two watches on her wrist. "He's not in a good mood today. I'll have to make up an excuse for you, and you'll just have to play along, all right?"

"Sure," I said, shrugging. If she meant the bloke who'd just left in the lift, then the chances I'd still have the job by the end of the day were close to nil. She could do her worst, I thought. We waited for the lift to come down again.

"Something of a character, your boss, eh?" I asked.

She smiled. "He's all right, really. Going through a bit of a rough patch."

"Sounded brutal."

"Don't worry, Harry's very professional."

Upstairs, she led me down a corridor and into her office, where she poured me cold water in a plastic cup from one of those enormous water dispensers, and then set off to inform her boss of my arrival. She came back moments later, and said, "They'll be in the conference room with you in about half an hour."

I wasn't sure who *they* were or why we needed a whole conference room for this. But whatever floated their collective boats was fine with me.

"And if anyone asks," she continued, "you were at the A&E helping your grandmother after she fell in her bathtub."

"Oh," I said, full of admiration at this lie. "I haven't got a grandmother, but sure, I'll stick to that. And thanks."

"No worries." She pushed her glasses up her nose. Then she leaned forward and admitted, "The other guy they wanted kept suggesting I wear fewer clothes."

I startled, dismayed. "Well, that . . . You don't have to worry about that with me."

She smiled in a knowing way, as though my preferences had been obvious from the start. I never knew what it was that tipped people off, because I don't think I'm exactly camp, but yet the only surprised reactions I got when coming out to people were sarcastic.

"I'm Maya, by the way," she said.

"Joe Kaminski." I stretched out my hand. She took it, examining me with renewed curiosity.

"I know," I said. "I don't look much like a Pole, do I?"

She tipped her head sideways, taking me in from my hair, down to my tawny, beige arms, and shook her head. "Maybe Poland via the *Pirates of the Caribbean*?"

This made me laugh. "My birth parents were Jamaican, actually."

"W-well, it's a nice name, anyway."

When the time came, Maya walked me through to the conference room, and asked if I needed her to set up PowerPoint for me. I didn't. I hadn't prepared anything beyond the prints in my portfolio, and I didn't expect that I was going to have to present anything besides handing the contents of my bag over to whoever made decisions around there. I made no opposition to sitting down and seeing how this was going to unfold. At worst, this would be something to laugh about later with my friends, who already found the idea of me in an office environment amusing.

They would have been in stitches if they could have been flies on the wall that day when all the suits poured in. There they were: middle-aged men, red-faced from all the heat, their ties looking as though they were choking them, and women with professional bob haircuts, thin lips lined with fading red lipstick, and mascara that clumped on their lashes from tiredness, stress, and heat.

Positioning himself at the head of the table was their boss, the one whose name made up the B in P&B Design Agency; the one who told someone to fuck themselves earlier when I saw him go into the lift. Presently he stood, with his hands on his hips, his sleeves rolled up, his steely eyes scanning me, waiting for his employees to take seats around the table. He was young for a guy with a letter in a company name. Grey-eyed, brown-haired, he looked like the coldest motherfucker in town.

And there I was in my khaki shorts, my slightly too tight T-shirt, leather bracelets around my wrists, my ears pierced in several places, unshaven, with my hair tied back in a ponytail. I wasn't nervous, but the whole thing was unsettling and unfamiliar enough that when Harry Byrne said, "Mr. Kaminski?" I responded without thinking, "Yo."

This made some of the people around the table smirk. Not Harry though.

"All right," he said. "We're going to have to keep this short since I'm on a call in about half an hour. Mr. Kaminski, the floor's yours."

He sat down, and all eyes turned to me. My immediate reaction was to gape, because I really had nothing to say, and the conference room, with its ash-coloured walls and a horrible wall clock ticking away time between now and death was depressing to my spirit and creativity. I didn't feel like Harry would tolerate any prevarication, so I stood, opened my portfolio, and said, "Er, well, I prepared some designs."

I handed the prints over to the person on my right to pass on to the others. I explained, briefly, that the colours were vibrant and attention-grabbing; that since the location of the restaurant was between Belgravia, Pimlico, and Westminster, it played on themes of the history of the region. I told them how the font hinted at it being a sort of upscale place to dine, but the plants and the use of wood would indicate that it had warmth and was welcoming. To be perfectly honest, half of it I pulled out of my arse right then and there, but I thought it sounded good and the people around the table nodded, made notes, and examined each picture in turn very carefully.

Harry looked at them too, expressionlessly, and then passed them on. I had the feeling he wasn't really listening to me. When I'd finished, he let his people give feedback or, as I like to call it, tear my work to shreds.

They decided that it was too "plant-y", too green and yet not "green" enough; too London specific ("What about tourists?" someone asked). They didn't like the orange tones, but they liked the blue, though they worried the blues might be too cold, and someone had to google how cold blue was.

Most of the things they said were contradictory, and Harry (whose opinion I thought would settle which way we would proceed) seemed to not be listening to them at all, and instead only snapped back to attention when one of the women asked him, "What do you think?"

He then shifted in his chair, turned to me, and said, "I've got a call to get to. Mr. Kaminski?"

I followed him to the door, half-expecting to be told never to come back. He was texting as we walked down the corridor together, and didn't say anything.

"So," I said, feeling a little awkward following him around like that, "do you want me to make any changes?"

"Yes," he said, impatiently. I'd never seen anybody text so quickly and so angrily.

"Which of the comments—" I began, and his head snapped up, suddenly, as if remembering I was there.

"I've got a meeting," he said. "My colleagues have explained to you what we want, I expect you'll know what to do."

This last he said like an accusation. As though, if I couldn't make out the contradictory mess of non-instructions his colleagues discussed in the conference room, it would mark me as a poor artist.

"I'm not clairvoyant," I said, a little defensively.

"Clearly," he muttered. His phone buzzed in his hand and he frowned down at it. Without lifting his head, he said, "Maya will help you set up another meeting. Next week, no later."

He was texting again, frown lines deepening with every thumb tap. Then he hit Send, finally looked up, and dryly added, "I hope your grandmother recovers well."

Maya was not a convincing liar, apparently. He turned into his office without shaking my hand or even saying goodbye.

I hated, hated, *hated* the guy.

Chapter Three
TELLING PEOPLE

Six Months Before the Big Day

Things to avoid when telling your parent you plan to get engaged:

1. Don't tell your mother while she's holding a hot beverage in her hands and her poodles are crowding around her feet.
2. When you tell your mother while she's holding a hot beverage and her poodles are crowding around her feet, don't try to kick the poodles away, hoping to rescue your mother from getting burned by hot beverage.
3. While your mother is screaming in shock and agony, don't take it personally when she calls you a bumbling idiot.
4. Don't then tell her, dramatically, "Fine! No grandchildren!"
5. When you do upset her, don't then compound the problem by begging her forgiveness, promising her a small country worth of grandchildren, when you haven't discussed children with your SO at all.

My mother is the first person I decide to tell. There are many reasons for that, the main one being that my former flatmate and one of my closest friends, Chloe, doesn't like Harry, and my best friend, Frank, is going through a rough separation. It seems sort of appropriate, anyway, to tell one's parent first.

The reason I decide to confide in someone, instead of just popping the question, is that I'm equal parts scared and excited about this, and I need someone to get excited with me, to make it more parts excited than scared, so that I have the courage to actually go through with it.

"Are you serious?" my mother asks, when at last she sits, putting her tea on a coaster and telling her dogs to calm down.

"I think so."

"Well, do you think so or are you sure?" she asks. "There's no *if*-ing and *but*-ing in marriage."

"I hope there's butt-ing in *my* marriage," I murmur. She slaps my hand and tells me to be serious.

"Okay, I *am* serious," I say. "I *do* want to marry him. What do you think?"

She sighs heavily.

"I never thought about it." She sips at her tea. "I never thought you'd get married at all, after— Well, you know."

It's not something we ever discuss—a situation in which actions have always spoken louder than words—and so I put my hand on hers and say, "You don't hate the idea, do you?"

I really want to get married, but I couldn't do it without her on board. Not after all she's done for me. I don't even mean just the fact that she adopted me (contrary to the wishes and advice of all her friends and family). Not to brag, but she alienated her entire community and divorced her husband for me. We were Jehovah's Witnesses at the time when it became clear that I would never live up to the standards of the religion. You can't be a gay Jehovah's Witness. At least, you can, and some probably are, but in our case our elders strongly believed you shouldn't be, and when everybody found out, we were shunned (we call it D-ed, meaning disfellowshipped).

"I don't hate the idea," she says, turning her hand in mine and pressing back. "You know I love Harry."

When I brought him home (and it was the first time I'd ever brought a bloke home to introduce to her), she was in love with him almost from the moment he stretched out his hand, smiled, and said, "Nice to meet you."

Harry is the sort of guy all parents hope their children might bring home one day.

"Joe," she says earnestly, "marriage is a very serious thing. It changes everything, you understand? Your relationship with Harry, your relationship with yourself, *everything*. And you're not the most—how do I put it?—you're not the most *together* person there is.

You have a way of throwing yourself at things . . . recklessly. I want you to think deeply about this. Is this really what you want?"

"Yes," I say, without skipping a beat. "I want to be with him forever."

That makes her smile, which makes me sigh in relief, because her gravity was starting to get to me.

"Well—" she sips at her tea "—I can't blame you."

I roll my eyes. For some reason, Harry is very popular with women.

"Do I ask for your blessing or something?" I ask.

"I suppose if you want to be traditional about it, you'd have to ask his father for permission," she says, with a twinkle in her eye. Then she bites her lip and, repressing a laugh, adds, "Maybe you can make him cry again?"

I sink my face into my hands. "Don't remind me."

"Maybe this time don't wear a skirt. That might help."

"It wasn't like that! It was a—"

"I liked it. I'd kill for legs like that."

This was when Harry first introduced me to his parents. In fairness, I *could* have chosen a different time to pioneer skirts for men. And I could have, come to think of it, not made things worse by arguing forcibly that Harry's dad should wear them too, armed with a bunch of information about testicular health.

Harry's dad is a "traditional" man. This makes it funnier for my mum that, as legend has it, I am the reason Harry's old man cried for the first time in his life.

"Well, don't despair," she says, laughing. "He accepted that ex-boyfriend of Harry's once. He'll come around to you too, eventually."

I groan. "I don't think I can de-evolve fast enough for that to happen!"

She chuckles. "You're pretty charming when you try to be, Joe. Don't underestimate that."

"I think I'll go ahead and skip the 'ask the father of the bride for permission' bit anyway, thank you."

"So." She leans back from me again. Her glasses have patches of steam on them from her tea, but I can see her big, blue eyes looking at me with concern from behind their thick lenses. "Sort of sudden, isn't it?"

"We've been together over four years. What do you mean 'sudden'?"

"I didn't mean I expected you not to stay together, but . . . to be frank, I didn't think you'd do so conventional a thing. Not like you."

I ruminate over this. It *is* terribly conventional. Perhaps this is what she meant earlier, when she said she never thought I'd get married at all. After all we've been through together, throwing off the shackles of an oppressive religion, why would I bend to tradition now?

"I think . . . I think Harry would like it," I say. Watching Harry eat breakfast, or brush his teeth or sort his ties, or frown over his iPad, reading the news—it came to me recently that I'd be devastated if that ended one day. And once in a while a mate of mine would describe some girl he's been seeing for a few weeks as *my girlfriend*, and I thought how strange it was for me to use the words *my boyfriend* to describe Harry. The terms are the same, and yet the realities are so different. Harry and I live together. I can't get a good night's sleep if he isn't in bed next to me. There are whole TV shows I have never seen because Harry doesn't have time to watch them, and it would be sacrilege for me to watch them without him. *Harry and Joe* is one of those sets of words that just go together, like *bread and butter* or *rock and roll* or *Adam and Steve*.

"And I think it's time," I tell my mother, saying but a small part of the whole truth.

Chloe, my former flatmate, a fellow artist, an activist, and a bullshit detector now in her late sixties, is not pleased when I eventually do tell her. She didn't like Harry at the beginning, and while she accepts that we are together ("For now," she says), she holds as an absolute truth that people are better off outside of stable relationships.

"Marriage is nothing but patriarchal horseshit," she tells me. "It's a device used by men to subjugate and enslave womankind."

"We're two men," I say. "It doesn't apply."

"Oh but doesn't it?" She rolls a furious eye at me. "Let me tell you something: equal rights are all well and good, and I will fight for them to the death, you know I will, but you gays are well out of matrimony, mark my words. Why tie yourself to someone legally for eternity? Why, but to prevent someone from leaving, no matter how royally shitty a bastard you become? Eh? Answer me that!"

I can't answer her, not because I share her opinion, but because she's spent decades debating in various political and social organisations, including feminist, atheist, and socialist groups, for the rights of women, labourers, homosexuals, transgender people, and various other causes, and has therefore got a counterargument for anything. Arguing with her is like playing tennis with one of those machines that spits balls at you. You might become a better arguer, but you won't win.

"Let me tell you about Henry VIII—" she continues.

I interrupt her by grabbing her arms, looking her in the eyes, and saying, "Don't. It's no use. I'm *going* to do it."

She stares at me.

"I'm going to go on one knee . . . or, no, I won't do that, that's tacky, isn't it? Maybe I'll just do it over dinner . . . No. No, it's got to be something special. Either way, I *will* do it. I don't know how, I don't know when, but by God I will do it!"

Her expression is sour as I make my declaration.

"Your funeral," she says darkly.

Neither does Frank receive the news with any degree of pleasure. Granted, I could have found him at a better time. He just finished moving into his mother's attic room, living like, he claims, Bertha bloody Rochester, after Gabriella left him.

"Have ye learned nothing, man!" he demands of me. "Are ye looking on at what is happening to me, and thinking to yourself 'I want that'? What is wrong with you? Don't do it! Don't! Do! It!"

With this lack of enthusiasm from my friends and family, I am reluctant to let anyone else in on it, lest they make me lose my courage altogether.

In the end, I involve one more person. I ask Siobhan, Harry's twin sister, to come with me to the workshop of a friend of mine to pick up the engagement bracelets I designed and ordered to propose to Harry with. At first, I don't tell her what they're really for, and say they're for our anniversary. But it doesn't take me long to crack.

We sit together in my friend Freya's living room while she finishes up with another client in her workroom. Siobhan swipes through her phone looking for a new hair style.

She eyes a pixie cut with a mixture of curiosity and dismay.

"How moon-faced am I? On a scale from one to moon?" she asks.

"You have a lovely face, darling," I say, "but that would look like arse on you. That Katie Holmes one, though . . ."

"Yes!" She beams, delighted. "Do you think I should change colour? I was thinking ginger, but I don't know. Ollie says redheads are hot."

She shows me various shades of red hair dye so we can determine which would look best on her. I honestly want to keep the engagement from her, but the way she speaks to me, the angle at which she holds her head, something about the way she smiles at me, the shape of her eyes maybe, *something*, so reminds me of Harry that I blurt it out.

She says, ". . . and this one is Christina Hendricks-red, which would make me look awfully pale, don't you think?"

I nod. "I want to marry your brother."

She startles. Her eyes go wide. "What?"

"I want to marry your brother," I repeat, my heart hammering in my chest. I love Siobhan, and if she's against this, if she piles on with a list of reasons why I'm being stupid, I don't think I'll ever be able to go through with it.

"Oh!" she says, blinking rapidly. "Do you mean it?"

That's when Freya comes in to present me with the two bracelets each in a separate box. Siobhan's blinking stops, and tears spill out.

"The— Is that— Do you mean— Oh my God!" she whimpers.

The bracelets are exactly what I wanted. Braided leather straps with a silver clasp, and on the clasp the letters *J* and *H* intertwined.

"This is so beautiful!" Tears are pouring liberally down her cheeks. "Harry is going to love it!" She throws her arms around my neck and hugs me, hard. "It's going to be so beau-u-u-utifu-u-ul!"

"Thank you," I whisper. Freya, sensing a personal moment, smiles and leaves us.

Chapter Four

FIRST TIME

Five Years Before the Big Day

For a while, I wasn't invited to present in the conference room again—a move I chose not to interpret as a verdict on my first performance there—but instead handed my work in to Harry directly. Usually this meant that I visited Maya's office, dropped new prints off at her desk, and spent a half hour or so chatting with her over coffee. Once in a while Harry burst in, demanding irritably whether or not Mr. This-And-That had called or whether or not some email had arrived. When he saw me, his reaction was usually frosty but polite, mostly verging on the sarcastic.

"Ah, Mr. Kaminski," he said, dryly, "how's your grandmother? All better, I hope?"

"Oh yes," I said, ignoring his tone. "Not a pleasant thing, hurting your hip at that age."

"And what age is that?"

I don't have a grandmother. I didn't know what ages they naturally come in.

"Ninety-four," I lied bravely.

"Ninety-four," he said, suppressing a smile.

"Yes. Ninety-four," I enunciated. When lying, always stick to your story.

"She must have been very fertile into a very old age to have a grandson your age."

"Well . . . you know what they say about her generation."

"No, what?" he asked.

"They—they were very fertile into an old age."

"I never heard that said of them," he said, and then smiled at Maya. "One learns something new every day."

Maya maintained her gravity with difficulty.

"So that's quite an age to hurt her hip and recover so quickly," Harry went on. He'd seemed in a hurry before, but now leaned with his elbow against the counter of Maya's desk, content to dig deeper into the matter. "But if she's all better—and thank God for small miracles—then what is the reason, I wonder, for you being late today?"

"Am I late?" I asked, innocently. "I'm sure I arrived on time. Didn't I?"

Maya nodded and lied solemnly, "He arrived an hour ago. We just got to chatting."

"Must be nice to have so much time to spare," Harry said to both of us, a slight humorous glint in his eye, and then left.

Once he was gone, I said to Maya, "I don't know how you put up with him. If I had to work for that wanker, I'd put a bullet through my head."

She laughed and shook her head. It was true, though, that despite being an enormous dickhead, the people in his office seemed to like him. Maya seemed fond of him. His employees greeted him cheerfully. They even, to my surprise, celebrated his birthday with a party in the pub across the street from their building. I knew this, because Maya invited me to come along. I wanted to refuse, for obvious reasons, but she insisted.

"Be my 'date,'" she said, putting *date* in air quotes. "It'll be so much fun, I promise."

"Not my style," I said. "Although it makes sense that he wants to celebrate the day some coven spawned him from the entrails of dead birds in the circle of people whose wages he pays."

She laughed and made me promise to think about it.

"Of course ye should go!" Frank told me over the phone, when I asked him. He sounded tired. "It's called networking. By the way"—here he lowered his voice and sounded at once proud and amused—"I'm at Gabriella's right now. Her father is an I-shit-ye-not vicar. He doesn't know I'm in the house. I have to sneak out of here like a fuckin' Shakespeare character."

"What? Where is *she*?"

"Went to work. Just left me here," he said, laughing. "I'm telling you, she's one in a million."

Yeah, like Charlie Manson was one in a million.

I investigated my wardrobe for clothes appropriate for a networking event, but found that I had no idea what networking was and how one was supposed to appear when attending the process. In the end it didn't matter, because when the day of the party arrived I completely forgot about it, and was, in fact, in the middle of painting when Maya rang and asked me where I was.

Then I had to quickly shower (and let me tell you, quickly showering is not an option when you're covered in oil paint) while Chloe, instead of helping me, critiqued my work.

"Derivative," she said, examining the painting through her glasses, while I rushed around searching for a clean-ish shirt.

"Derivative of what?" I demanded, indignantly. "Does this have holes in it?"

She eyed the T-shirt I was holding up. "Well, no, but that's because it's mine."

"Ah." I dropped it.

"Rauschenberg," she said.

"What?" My face was swaddled in a different T-shirt that seemed way too small for me, my hands tangled above my head.

"Derivative of Rauschenberg," she said.

I pulled the T-shirt down my chest. It didn't belong to me or Chloe, I decided peering down at it, but it would have to do.

"This is not a bloody pop art collage!" I shouted, before turning to the bedroom and flipping my bed over in search of socks.

"The colours," she said. "Besides, I like Rauschenberg."

"That's because you know nothing!" I hopped one-legged out of the bedroom, putting on my shoes. "Do you know where my wallet is?"

She found my wallet, phone, and keys.

"We really should clean up in here," I said, heading for the door. That sentence could very well have been our anthem. My mother liked to "joke" that my and Chloe's flat was how they invented penicillin.

At the pub, Maya spotted me before I spotted her. The people from P&B, all still in their shirts and ties and pencil skirts, were well into their libations, roaring loudly at each other, clinking glasses, clearly delighted to not be working.

"You came!" Maya was more pleased than I deserved. "Come, let me find someone to get you a drink. Wait, let me find Harry..." And with the best of intentions, I have no doubt, she went off, and I didn't see her again until much later.

I got my own drink therefore, and since I didn't know anybody there besides Maya, I contented myself with drawing caricatures of them on the pub napkins. Networking, I decided, was a very strange thing indeed.

It was one of those historic pubs with dark, low beams and roaring fires, evoking memories of bewigged gentlemen demanding satisfaction from their red-faced chums for some imagined infraction. At least, looking around, I had the impression that they were all roughly drunk enough for that sort of thing to happen. But they were good-humoured, laughing at each other's jokes, patting each other's shoulders, and loosening their ties.

They were, for me, conveniently absorbed, so that I could watch them, and draw them, at my leisure. I'm particularly fond of an interesting profile, and I caught one or two romantically lit by the fire.

This would have been quite an entertaining way to pass the evening—a pint of lager in front of me, and some paper napkins and a pencil for my drawings—if I hadn't been accosted by a man I hadn't met before, who glanced over my shoulder and said, "Ha! That's good!"

"Thank you."

He was gawky and skinny, with a copper-and-gold moustache, old-fashioned glasses, and intense dark eyes.

"Hit it to perfection!" he said, laughing. "Marvellous. Who's that, then?" He pointed at one of the napkins.

"No, let me guess," he said, before I could open my mouth. "That's Sophie, isn't it?"

He pointed her out, and I confirmed that it was indeed the woman I had drawn—I liked the sharp line of her jaw and her Roman nose.

"Great!" He laughed. "Is that Harry?" Here he laughed harder still. "Oh this is perfect!"

He laughed at some of my other drawings. I didn't know who he was, but since I was there to network, I thought I'd buy him a drink.

"Oh no," he said earnestly when I offered. "I don't drink. Water, from time to time, but I try to avoid it."

At my surprise, he eyed my pint and said, "That stuff's poison, you know."

I shrugged. "It's okay once in a while. Water's not poisonous, though, is it? I mean, clean water? Tap water?"

His expression was full of pity. "You are putting something foreign in your body. It is . . . unnatural, shall we say."

I was sure he was having me on. Nobody, surely, believed that. "Are you serious?"

"I'm a practicing breatharian."

Living in London, especially in art circles, you meet people who want to tell you about their strange diets all the time (ever heard of the werewolf diet? I have), and yet I'd never heard of breatharians before.

"A what?"

"Breatharian," he said. "It's the belief that you should live without eating and, in advanced stages, without drinking."

"You're having me on."

"There used to be Indian gurus who lived their entire lives like that. Nowadays it's more difficult because our parents fill our bodies with toxins from a very young age." He shook his head solemnly. "They don't know the damage they do."

"Wait, hang on." I put out my hand to stop him. "You mean you don't eat *anything*?"

"Well, I'm not as advanced as all that." He laughed with false humility. "But I try."

"Why?"

"To live a spiritually pure life of course! I couldn't bear to do *that* to myself." Here again he nodded at my pint. "Filthy stuff!"

"You can't live without eating. That's insane," I insisted.

"Well, excuse me!" he said, offended. "I am not insane. It's a valid belief and a practice that would—"

"If people could live without eating, mate, there'd be no starvation," I maintained. "You're pulling my leg."

"I am not pulling your leg, young man," he said, indignantly, even though he couldn't have been more than a decade older than me.

"It's a scientific impossibility."

"Science, you know, doesn't explain everything."

"Yeah, maybe, but it does explain that. You can't live without eating. It's impossible."

"Then explain to me"—he was flushed and bright-eyed with anger—"how this woman I once met lived without eating for five years! And scientists tested it and couldn't explain it."

Perhaps I shouldn't have reacted, but I'd spent a lot of my life arguing with religious people who wanted me to control my urges and needs on the basis that godlike beings were real, and who offered as proof precisely such statements: *I knew someone who knew someone who definitely saw this miracle with their own eyes.* It goaded me.

"Any scientist worth their salt," I said, "would have locked her up for a week without food or drink, and seen how she coped. And they'd have found her ill and possibly dying, and then they'd have sent her home and told her to find something useful to do with herself instead of wasting everybody's time."

His brows furrowed and his lips thinned and quivered. I knew I'd said too much.

"Your ignorance," he said, "is extremely disappointing."

"It's just common sense," I persisted. "Like, you'll agree, probably, that we need nutrition, right? Well, where does that woman of yours get her nutrition from if she doesn't eat?"

"The sun," he said slowly, as though *I* were stupid. "The sun is the source of the purest energy."

I shook my head sadly. "Mate, if you don't know the difference between humans and plants, you shouldn't be allowed to decide your own diet."

"You—!" His nostrils flared. "You dare—!"

"What?"

"Do you take me for an idiot?" he enunciated furiously.

"Well, yes." I was surprised he had to ask. He stared at me, speechless. For a moment there, I thought he was going to punch me. Instead, a familiar voice said, laughing, "Okay, okay. Easy there."

Harry stepped in. I didn't know he'd been standing nearby, but apparently he'd heard the conversation, and now put his arm around the man and said, "Come on, Malcolm, walk it off, mate. Maya, I think Mal needs a bit of fresh air, it's getting stuffy in here . . ."

Maya walked the guy named Malcolm away, shooting worried glances in my direction. Then Harry turned to me, his eyes brimming with amusement. "Do you know who that was?"

"The village idiot?"

Harry stifled a laugh.

"He's Malcolm Peppard," he said. "The *P* in P&B Design Agency"

Well. Fuck.

"He's not very bright, is he?" I said, defensively. "That's not my fault."

"No, he's not very bright, but he is the heir to a large fortune that helped start the agency and kept it afloat throughout the financial crisis," he said. "So we don't tell him that he's an idiot to his face."

"Well, maybe someone should."

Harry stepped forward to take Malcolm's place, and gave me a look of mingled amusement and reproach.

"Is that supposed to be me?" He nodded at the napkin next to my pint.

"Oh, that—" I reached forward to put my hand over it, but he was quicker. Networking was new to me, but I was pretty sure that insulting your two bosses wasn't a recommended approach. He examined the sketch for a few moments, before handing it back.

"What a fierce frown I have," he said.

"You could smile more."

"You think?"

"Sure. You know what they say about frowning and smiling."

"Enlighten me."

"Stop being an arsehole and smile," I said.

He laughed. "And you know what they say about the virtues of not being a prick to your employers?" he asked, though he was still smiling.

"I don't know, the same thing they say about being a grumpy old git?"

"Old!" he said with a laugh. "I take exception to that."

"You accept 'grumpy' and 'git,' then?"

He turned to the bartender, who walked by just then, and ordered two more pints.

"For me?" I asked, as he pushed the one pint towards me.

"Sure, that should shut you up." He lifted his glass. "Cheers?"

We drank our beers, and he turned the conversation to the people on the napkins, explaining who was who, and giving his opinions on how well I'd captured them. Mostly, his judgement was critical of my skill, but he spoke in his usual dry, teasing way, which I was starting to realise was his way of being friendly.

I didn't immediately notice that it was slightly odd he should bother socialising with me, rather than with his friends and colleagues. What I did grudgingly notice, though, was that when he was smiling, his eyes were less like steel and more like liquid silver; and his features, when they weren't stiff and unyielding from anger, fell into handsome, manly lines. Perhaps he'd had a better night's sleep too, because he was less pale and worn and the bags under his eyes were gone, which made him seem ten years younger. Why mince words? He was looking fine.

"Two pints," I said to the bartender. At Harry's surprised expression, I added, innocently, "Your birthday, right?"

He thanked me, we clinked glasses. One of the other people from the office, standing nearby, addressed him about some movie they both liked and then tried to convince a third person to see. Harry turned slightly away from me.

"Do you like card tricks?" I said, interrupting his colleague. My heart picked up a little, but fuck it, I wanted Harry's attention back.

Harry's eyebrows rose in that familiar, bemused way. "What?"

I turned to the bartender and asked if he had a deck of cards. He found a fresh pack, and I showed it to Harry.

"What do you say?"

He lifted his pint glass slowly to his lips, keeping his eyes on me. "Why do I have a feeling of foreboding about this?"

There was something about the angle of his smile or the arrogance in his voice that made my pulse go a little faster.

"Hey, want to see something?" I asked the other people from the agency who stood nearby.

They turned and eyed me with interest, and Harry explained, in his drawling voice, that I was going to perform a trick.

"I forget," a man in a hipster beard said, "are we supposed to find magicians lame, or are they so lame they're ironically cool now?"

"Oh, no, mate," I said. "You've not seen anything like this, I swear." I looked around me. "Do we have any pens?"

Some of them had pens in their pockets. The bartender lent us two. I made sure the people nearest me each had one.

"Okay," I said. I had slid the cards out of their packaging and began to shuffle them with, I like to think, some skill. "I want you all standing around me here. You go here, you go here . . ." I spread my audience in a semicircle around me.

"So," I said. "I want each of you to, you guessed it, pick a card, any card—" I fanned the deck out, facedown, and let each of them pick one "—and write your card down on your hand. Don't show it to me, just write it down so that it's legible. Wouldn't want anybody accusing me of fraud, here, all right? This is serious business, people, my reputation is on the line."

Harry watched me, amused, but picked a card when it was his turn.

When they were done—and they struggled mightily with their sweaty palms and the often ill-functioning pens, I went from person to person, giving them a once over, tilting my head, pretending to mind read them.

"You," I said, standing in front of Sophie with the great profile, "you picked . . . Check in your breast pocket."

Sophie reached for the little pocket and, amazed, withdrew a card. Her eyes wide, she showed the card and her palm—the seven of clubs—to us.

"What the— How the— How did you do that?"

"Ah, you know what they say about magicians and their tricks," I said, a rush of excitement running through me. "Now, you, sir," I turned to the man standing next to Sophie. "Your card . . . your card . . ." I massaged my temple, making a show of concentrating. "Check under your left shoe."

The guy lifted his foot and stepped off an ace of spades. He showed us all his palm.

"Ace of spades, everybody!" I cried and there was a resounding cheer, as most of the taproom was now watching.

"Either I'm really hammered," the bearded hipster said, "or you're actually really good at this."

I turned to Harry. He'd been watching me with eyes narrowed.

"Now let me see," I said, scanning him slowly head to foot. "Here's a tricky one."

His colleagues were laughing. One or two said his name, teasing him.

"He's the enigma!" someone shouted.

"You won't get Harry!"

"Go, Harry!"

"We'll have to try something else to get to your card," I said.

"Try what?" Harry asked, warily.

I put my hands to my mouth in the shape of a prayer, breathed in, and closed my eyes as if I were concentrating.

"All right, I've got it," I said. "I know where your card is."

The others in the room were all aflutter with giggles and whispers, their eyes intently fixed on me. I didn't care about them. Harry's eyes were on me, which was all I wanted.

"Well?" Harry said, with a tone that implied *Astonish me*.

I said, "First, let me guess . . ." I lifted one finger. "Your card was . . . the jack of hearts?"

Harry's eyebrows rose in surprise, and he showed his hand. It was indeed the jack of hearts. There was clapping, and in one or two corners of the room I heard a gasp. Harry didn't seem impressed so much as suspicious. Oh I was enjoying this. A tingle of exhilaration passed between my shoulder blades.

I grinned. "Oh boy. I'm so fucking glad you picked the jack of hearts, mate."

"Why?"

"Because I get to do this." I, saying this, turned around, bent over, and mooned him. The jack of hearts was stuck to my butt cheek.

The laughter in the room was now uproarious. One or two of his colleagues toasted me. I pulled up my trousers quickly because the bartender, though amused, had a job to do, and keeping everybody in the place clothed was one of them.

I got patted on the shoulder. Someone bought me a drink.

I turned to Harry. "I owe you a beer, I think."

Harry rolled his eyes in a gesture of amused exasperation. "I think you owe me a lobotomy."

"Well"—I grinned—"you know what they say about magicians."

"What?"

"Always lobotomise your audience afterwards."

He laughed.

"So, you walk around with a card stuck to your arse?"

"Oh, it's too early in the night for me to tell you what I do."

I liked the way he was smiling at me, and how, in this light, his light-brown hair had a greenish tinge, and his grey eyes looked very dark. I could smell him, could feel the heat beating off his body.

"Shouldn't you be talking to your friends, rather than staying here with me?" I asked, with my elbow on the bar, leaning my chin on my hand, gazing at him.

"I don't know, do you want me gone?"

"I know I wouldn't spend my birthday this way," I said.

It was very loud and crowded around us. He leaned in a little, and there was a small, pregnant pause. In a lowered voice, he said, "What would you be doing, then?"

"Celebrating." I grinned at him.

He eyed me with amusement and, I thought, interest. I hadn't heretofore considered that he might be gay. Now I tried to imagine what he'd be like naked, and the urge to see it myself was coursing through me with a warm buzz.

He was smiling, his eyebrows lifted a little, his eyes shiny and his cheekbones slightly rosy. He'd loosened his tie and opened his collar by now. He glanced down at my mouth, and then met my eyes.

"And how would you celebrate?" he asked, gently.

"There are no words to describe it. I'd have to show you."

This shocked a laugh out of him. Then he scanned the room and turned to me again. "Let's go."

We took off. He told no one he was leaving.

"Jesus, you're better guarded than a fucking medieval princess!" I laughed. To get to him, I had to pull off his suit coat, under which he wore a shirt, with a tie, and underneath that he had a white T-shirt. Then there was the belt, then his trousers, and then the boxer shorts. I wore a T-shirt and jeans, under which I had absolutely nothing. I'd never understood ties, so I let him handle that, but I dragged his T-shirt off over his head, and then dropped his trousers with boxers to the floor. At last, kissing, stumbling, and tripping, we fell onto his bed.

One-night stands, in my limited experience, involve a lot of hard elbows, don't-touch-thats, and awkward tension rising usually from the doubt of whether this was going to work. The surprise of how smoothly Harry accepted my weight on top of him quickly gave way to a glow of warmth from how good he felt under me, how clever he was in response to every move I made. I shifted my leg, he pulled me in by my hip. My cock, rigid from the moment he pawed on it when we burst into the flat, glided against his warm skin; my eyes rolled up in my head, and in return he sighed against my neck and rocked his hips up against me.

My lips traced his collarbone and his breath hitched. I kissed down his chest, his warm belly, until I was on all fours.

"Oh my God," he muttered, winding his fingers into my hair. It gave me a thrill to hear the shocked little sound at the back of his throat. "Oh God!"

I loved it. I loved the feeling of him in my mouth, I loved the taste and the scent of him, and the sounds I could make him let out. Using my tongue, lips, throat, and hands, I made him mutter oaths to the God and saints, until his breath became so ragged I was sure he was skirting the edge. I came up to kiss him.

"You're good at this," he said, breathing hard.

"Happy birthday . . ."

"What are you— Oh . . ."

I'd taken us both in hand and, holding him close to me with one arm, I stroked us. He let out helpless sighs, short and abrupt, clinging to me, his hands and mouth urgent, insistent, hot. He jerked, an "Ah!" escaping his lips, and his hot spill was all over my fingers. I let go of him; my head fell down onto his shoulder.

"Did you . . ."

I could barely hear him over my pulse drumming in my ears. I was still hot and hard and very close. He lifted me up and turned around to drop me on the bed, onto my back.

"What—" I didn't finish, his kiss stopped me. I should have warned him that I was still covered in his come, but blood was pooled away from the part of my brain that helped with speaking, and then he was there, warm mouth, sucking, deep and wet and warm . . .

After, we lay, breathlessly, side by side, staring up at the ceiling. The backs of our hands were brushing together. My heart was racing. That had been . . . wow.

I rubbed my face.

I'd had good sex before. This wasn't the first time I'd felt like I couldn't get enough of a guy. But I hadn't expected Harry to be that good. Or rather, I hadn't expected him to *feel* this good. Where'd he learn to kiss like that?

He turned to his side, smiling at me. My eyes had adapted to the darkness enough to have my heart stutter a little at the way he was looking at me.

I don't want to go home yet, sprang to my mind.

"So, how did you do it?" he asked.

"What?"

"That card trick."

I started to laugh, returning to reality. It came back to me now: the napkins, Malcolm, the cards . . .

"I mean, how did you know? You can't actually read minds; I know you can't. But bloody hell!"

"It's a thing between magicians. We're not allowed to tell," I said, my voice trembling with laughter.

He reached for my face and kissed me, saying against my lips, "I couldn't convince you?"

"You can try."

He deepened his kiss, then moved abruptly away, sucking in air as if resisting extreme temptation. It made something warm settle in the depths of my chest.

"I need a shower," I said. *Come with me*, I meant. Moving up, I reached for him and he followed, reading my intention with a pleased bemusement.

His flat was small. We went by moonlight across to the bathroom, barefoot, our bodies bathed in silver light. He ran the water in this almost darkness. Let it go warm.

"Come here," he murmured.

"You come here."

He grabbed for the back of my neck, pulled me to him. "Can you not always," he muttered, then kissed me. We walked into the cubicle, still kissing.

We kissed the way two lovers might when one of them is about to go to the front. Like we would never see each other again for some tragic reason: his arms about my neck, pressing his whole body to me, eyes closed, mouth open, sighs deep from his throat echoing through all my nerves in a hot shiver. I wanted to bury myself deep inside of him, claim him in some primal way.

I turned him around, pressed him close to me.

It seemed to surprise him. I held him close to my chest, my heart beating a riot. His body, tight, muscled but spare, felt so good against me, his bottom pressing up against my quickly hardening cock. Wild thoughts of sliding into him, of taking him, of what that would feel like, raced through my fevered brain.

I kissed his neck, sucked on his earlobe. Looking down his body, I watched soap and water gliding down his chest, his flat stomach. He was stroking himself, waiting for me to decide what I'd do next. There was so much I wanted to do, but I didn't want to scare him away. Men didn't sleep with me for my pleasure. They slept with me for what I could do for them.

Soap slick, I pressed my rigid cock between his thighs and reached around, taking him in hand. I stroked him slowly along with the rhythm of our rolling hips, alternating pressure and lavishing his neck with kisses where he seemed most sensitive.

His arousal was quickly reaching its tip, his moans echoing off the shower walls. I stopped, releasing him to the sprinkle of the shower water and running my hand up his stomach. He grabbed it, pulled it down to his straining erection, wound my palm around him and thrusted into it, insistently.

Our actions became frantic, racing, thrust for thrust, groan for groan, in clouds of steam, sweat and water mingling, until we came together in copious bursts.

Harry turned, wound his arms around my neck and, pressing my flushed back against the cool, wet wall, kissed me again, accepting my arms around his waist as if that was where they naturally belonged. Suddenly, I felt sick at the thought of letting go. Our embrace tightened, as if loosening it would mean we'd both dissolve and slip down the drain together. Instead, as his embrace tightened, it was as if the rest of the world had slipped away, and it was just the two of us, together, our hearts pumping violently against each other.

I woke up to a bright, rather Spartan room. Next to me, Harry was asleep, on his front, with the side of his face pressed deeply into a pillow turned away from me, snoring gently. His flat was a studio apartment on Carnaby Street in Soho, so from my position on his bed, I could see the flat in its entirety, and noticed for the first time that all of his belongings were in boxes. The night before, we hadn't bothered to switch on the lights. As soon as we had entered his flat, he'd pulled me to him and kissed me, and then we'd stumbled straight onto the bed. Now it was daylight, and it was clear that Harry was moving either in or out of this place. The sight of boxes and empty shelves and counters disoriented me for a few moments, and it was a while before I identified the sounds that had woken me up: someone was trying to fit a key into the lock of the door.

Whoever was trying to get in finally found the right key; the grind of metal in the lock resonated with an echo in the room, and then the door opened and a man walked in.

I had lifted myself up onto my elbows and had on nothing but the leather bracelets around my wrist and the rings on my fingers. The man was staring at me in wide-eyed astonishment, all colour drained from his face. He was soldierly in appearance—short-cropped hair, a flat nose, and eyes set wide apart.

"Who the fuck are you?" he said. Not the sort of thing you necessarily want to hear from a man who, over six foot tall and quite wide, in a black biker's jacket, looked like a person who could handle New Zealand's All Blacks all by himself.

"Who the fuck are *you*?" I demanded back, nevertheless.

"Get the fuck out of here," he said, advancing.

"What the—" but before I could say anything more, he grabbed me by my arm and dragged me out of Harry's bed.

"Hey!" Harry said, at last waking up. He was squinting and rubbing his jaw. "Kieran? What are you doing here? What— Let go of him!"

"Is this what you do when I'm not around?" Kieran, the guy who was now painfully holding my arm in one of his enormous hands, demanded. "You go off and sleep with the first homeless hippy you find?"

"Hey!" I cried indignantly.

"Let go of him." Harry sat up in bed. "You're making a scene."

"This is exactly what I'm talking about!" Kieran shouted. "You never understand the important things! All you want is fucking ceremony and—"

"This really isn't the time—"

"The fuck it isn't! When it comes right down to it, all you want is—"

"Will you let him go? You're embarrassing yourself."

"*I* am embarrassing *my*self?"

"Mate . . ." I tried, delicately, to intercede.

"Shut up, you!" Kieran shouted at me. Rude.

He glared at me with a measured menace, a snarl on his lips and a warning in his eyes that said, *Careful or I'll snap.* Presumably, big guy that he was, he expected me to turn away in submission, but he miscalculated. Adrenaline was boiling up in my blood, my muscles were hardening with every second, and though he had several inches on me, I'd fought before. He probably never had to. I fixed my eyes on him squarely, and I could tell when he became conscious that I wasn't afraid.

Harry stood from the bed. He was entirely naked, which stunned both me and Kieran into silence, because, boy, he looked fine. At night I hadn't seen that much of him, though he had felt good, and in the shower we stood too close together for me to really take him in fully, but now, in bright daylight, he took my breath away a little.

Calmly, he walked over to Kieran and touched his hand where it held my arm. Like Moses parting the Red Sea, Kieran's hand loosened and then he stepped away from me in a huff. Harry turned to me and said, quietly, "I'm really sorry. The bathroom's right behind you." He picked my clothes up from the floor and handed them to me. Evidently, he tried to do this as delicately as possible, but it still felt like he should have stuffed a tenner into one of my pockets for my services.

I walked off to get dressed in the bathroom. Cold tiles against my bare feet, my nipples puckered against the chill. It wasn't just the temperature in the room that made everything inside of me tighten.

The bathroom, like the rest of the flat, was almost entirely empty, save for a cardboard box on the floor where all the shower gels, shaving foams, and toothpastes were. Last night, I hadn't noticed any of it. It was like a completely different bathroom from last night.

I dressed quickly, and then saw myself in the mirror. I suppose I did look a little rough, with my hair loose and half my face shaded by dark stubble, but *homeless hippy* was an unjust description.

Outside of the bathroom, Harry and Kieran were quarrelling. I couldn't make out the precise words, but the tone said it all, and it was clear that the sooner I was gone, the better it would be for everybody.

I hoped to sneak out straight to the front door, but that hope was dashed as soon as I peeked out from the bathroom.

"Joe?"

Harry had his dressing gown on, a navy blue one with red and white stripes, and he was able to carry this off as if he were wearing one of his suits.

I came out then, ignoring Kieran altogether. Not that I was particularly keen to talk to Harry either, now that I realised what he'd done last night.

He walked me to the front door, even though it was only a few steps from where Kieran stood by the kitchen counter, glowering at me from underneath thick, dark brows.

"I'm really sorry about all this," Harry said, in an almost whisper, his hand rubbing my arm where Kieran had held me moments earlier. I nodded, eager to get out already.

"Thank you for last night," he said.

"Yeah, no, totally," I said, abstractedly, reaching for the handle. He said something else, but I didn't hear him—as soon as the door opened, I dashed downstairs and out onto the streets.

This had been a bad idea. I mean, sleeping with your boss was a strategy that rarely worked out for anybody, but in this particular case, I really ought to have known better. Christ, he had a boyfriend! Has anybody ever kept their job after being discovered with their boss by their boss's partner? I cursed myself and my stupid impulses.

My heart was heavy. It wasn't the job I'd probably lost that was making me feel so . . . let down. It was the memory of him embracing me with both arms, kissing me like I had just returned, having been thought missing presumed dead for the past three years. I considered myself a fairly experienced man, but that had been a first. It'd felt dirtier and racier than anything else we'd done.

It was disappointing to know that all he'd wanted was to use me to cheat on his troglodyte boyfriend.

Chapter Five

THE PLAN

Six Months Before the Big Day

When I get excited, the excitement often takes over, and sometimes (read: always) I get carried away. Usually, this means I burst into action and do whatever it is that is exciting me. But not now. This proposal, I vow to myself, will be all about Harry.

I start planning.

This I do for Harry's benefit, because Harry is a planner and I'm not, and so I know that if I plan something—as in plot, organise—he'll be impressed.

As I draw a map of the different plot elements I am putting together, Chloe sits next to me, with a glass of wine the size of an infant in her hand, drinking and criticizing in turn. With her thick, long grey hair frizzed up into a beehive, she looks like Frankenstein's bride.

"Do you know," she says thoughtfully, as she leafs through the various schemes I discarded, "these would make for great slapstick comedy."

"I told you, I'm not doing any of those."

"Yeah, but what a shame! I'd quite like to see you dangling from a hot-air balloon by a rope tied around your ankle, with a hundred doves in cages that won't open rattling underneath, and Harry, panic-stricken, trying to drag you back in."

"Thanks."

"Or this one!" She enthusiastically points to the bottom of another page. "Where would you even get a Chinese emperor from nowadays? I mean, honestly, Joe . . ."

I grumble in response.

"Or this one!" She turns to another page. "Where you get sawn in half by a magician on stage and the magician pretends that the trick didn't work and you were *really* sawn in half. I mean, you could carry that one all the way to a fake funeral. Comedy gold."

"You'd like that, would you?" I mutter.

She laughs hoarsely. Then she attaches a cigarette to her ridiculous, old-fashioned cigarette holder, lights up, and continues her reading.

I won't deny that I have a few crazy ideas at first before I come up with the viable one. But that's the creative process in a nutshell.

The central idea behind the Plan is that the engagement is going to be a complete surprise to Harry. He will expect nothing. He is to be knocked off his feet. I want him to first be shocked, then say yes (naturally), and then in the days that follow I want him to slowly assimilate the lengths to which I've gone to do this for him. It's going to be like a slow-release art piece.

Phase One of the Plan begins a few days later while Harry and I are at home.

It's the evening: as far as Harry knows as ordinary an evening as any other. We are cooking. Or, to be more precise, he's cooking, while I'm distractedly waiting for the first plot element to arrive. He talks about the away day his firm had, and the team-building exercises they've gone through, while I intermittently stare at him and then the door wondering if the whole plan will collapse on this first step.

"I mean, in the end, I suppose they must serve a purpose," he says, chopping vegetables like a TV chef, "because you do have to work as a team, and the exercises are sort of fun. Not that I would ever praise any idea of Malcolm's, but there you go. Although—" he laughs "—Sophie was telling us about this retreat she'd done with the firm she worked for some years back, and— Pass me the parsnip, will you?"

I start at being addressed. "Hm?"

"Pass me the parsnip?"

"What parsnip?"

"Bob," he says, dryly, "Bob the Parsnip. Could you please pass him over so that I can acquaint him with Betty the kitchen knife?"

I relax and laugh, and pass him the parsnip.

"What's with you today? You seem distracted," he says.

I shake my head and go to the fridge.

"Want some wine?" I ask, very casually. Like a man who has nothing to hide.

"Beer."

I open a bottle for him and hand it over.

"Thanks."

"So what did Sophie say?"

He looks at me curiously, and I avert my eyes because I'm a terrible liar and a worse actor, and I know that if he realises something's up, he'll get it out of me without any difficulty at all. Luckily, before he can ask anything, the doorbell rings, my heart jumps, and I say, "I'll get it."

I run to the door.

It's Chloe, as arranged. My heart is pumping so hard, my chest aches. It's happening. I did it. I am doing it. Oh God.

"What took you so long?" I hiss at her.

"Thought I'd give you time to think the better of it. Has it worked?" she whispers.

"No!"

Harry's voice comes from the kitchen: "Who is it?"

I make desperate gestures at Chloe. She rolls her eyes, clears her throat, and begins.

"Oh, Joe!" she cries, loudly, theatrically, so that Harry can hear. "Had a call from the Temple! They said your exhibition has been moved forward!"

"What's that?" Harry, wiping his hands on his apron, comes around to see what the noise is all about.

Chloe smiles at him.

"It's Joe's exhibition in Dublin. The one I'd arranged for him with my contacts in Ireland? Had a call from Orla, the curator. She said they had to move Joe's pieces forward."

"When?" I ask, pretending to be worried.

"This weekend."

"What, *this* weekend?"

"Yes," Chloe says. "Told them you'd be there."

"What? Why did you do that?" I ask, giving Laurence Olivier a run for his money. "I can't just— I mean, Harry and I have plans. And besides, you should've told them to ring me directly."

"She tried." Chloe looks at me pointedly.

I smack my forehead. Everybody knows that my phone is always discharged or on silent. This is all part of the Plan. One of the little intricate things that Harry will notice later on. Little winks at our foibles. Or my foibles. He has no foibles.

"Well, can we call her back?" Harry asks, visibly concerned. "Maybe she can move it again."

"I don't think so," Chloe says. "She sounded very firm on the phone that it had to be this weekend or they'd have to say no to your pieces altogether. They've had a scheduling disaster. They're fully booked for the year otherwise."

"You have to go, then," Harry says to me. "I'll book your flight and—" He pauses. As I predicted, he remembers that this weekend is our anniversary. "Maybe I could come with you? I could stay out of your way during the day, and then at least we'd have the evening together."

I sigh in pretend frustration.

"I suppose we'll have to."

"Well, I'll call her to confirm, then," Chloe chimes in.

"Do you want to come in?" Harry motions her towards the kitchen. "I'm making duck and roast vegetables."

"Sounds lovely," Chloe says, "but I have to be somewhere."

She kisses my cheek, waves at Harry, and then leaves. I make a play of my disappointment: I toss a kitchen towel, despondently, onto the counter, and I pour more wine out for myself, like a man who's just had a bit of a blow.

"Hey." Harry nudges me, amused. "You know, Dublin's not the worst place to be for romance."

I shrug. "I know," I say, in the tones of a martyr.

"It's got castles, culture, and cuisine. Hell, I'm glad we're going. What else were we going to do? I'd plan an itinerary of activities and you'd take pleasure in keeping me from fulfilling it by putting your hand in my trousers."

This does make me smile, because it makes me think of our last anniversary. I'd prevented us from going to a really boring, fancy party by giving him a blowjob in our car.

"Come on." He reaches for the plates, sets them on the table. "It'll be great. We'll make a thing of it."

"I'll have to work."

"Not all the time."

"I'll be away most of the day."

"Well, and so what? Hand me the cutlery. We'll make the evening count."

I let him warm me to the idea.

This is the Plan.

On Saturday, since the exhibition thing is entirely fictitious, I am going to spend the whole day hiding from him (to maintain the pretence), preparing for the grand evening, while he explores Dublin. Then, in the evening, I am going to take him to dinner at a traditional Irish restaurant. His family is Irish, hence the whole Dublin idea.

At dinner, I'm going to flirt with him until he tries to drag me back to the hotel room to do dirty things to me. Between the restaurant and the hotel there's the Ha'penny Bridge, which Google Images assures me is gorgeous at night. I'm going to stop him from dragging me to the hotel by insisting we have a look at it first. We will go on the bridge, look at the river, and then, somehow, if by some miracle my heart doesn't explode beforehand, I'm going to ask him.

Even Chloe approves of this idea, because it's demonstrative without being over the top.

"That's the most romantic thing I ever heard," she says, grudgingly. "Now I kind of hope he'll say yes, the bastard."

I even go so far as to ask Siobhan, because she knows Harry better than anybody, and she's bound to know if anything in that plan isn't to Harry's taste. She bursts into tears.

"Oh, it's going to be so beautiful!" she sobs. "I want to be there! Can I be there? Can you at least take a picture of it?"

"Well, no," I say. "That—that would defeat the whole purpose of the surprise."

The conversation, which we have over the phone, lasts maybe five minutes, of which four and a half are purely snivelling sounds from her, and my manly attempts at soothing her emotions.

I tell Frank, out of loyalty, as well. His reaction is somewhat different.

"Two words, pal," he says furiously. "Prenup agreement."

Cynicism sounds harsher in a Scottish accent.

"I don't really have a whole lot of money," I say. "Besides, don't you think Harry'd find it a little unromantic if I dragged him to a lawyer right after he said yes?"

"Romantic schmomantic," Frank insists. "It's the Wild West, pal, and ye better be a gunslinger or else ye'll be one of the corpses the gunslingers have to step over."

Not, as I said, a particularly helpful perspective.

So, with my friends and family braced, with the bracelets in my bag, the hotel booked, and a firm plan in my head, Harry and I set off on Friday afternoon for the airport.

In the cab, Harry is texting, because he had to leave work early to make the flight, and he's not easily detached from his many responsibilities there.

"Can you believe it?" he says to me, frowning at his mobile. "Malcolm wants to introduce compulsory morning yoga to the office. He wants to be a yogi."

"I'd pay to see that."

He smiles to himself, amused, as he continues to text.

During all the planning, the person I most wished to confide in was Harry himself. For the past four years I haven't really done anything major without first consulting with him. It feels wrong to have a secret I can't share with him. In fact, the whole Plan is a set of a thousand little secrets, each one equally painful to keep from him.

His phone rings in his hand. He freezes, suddenly—I can feel his whole body stiffen.

"Are you ok?" I say, surprised.

"Ah, yeah." He picks up, putting a finger to his free ear and leaning away from me. This is odd. He speaks in a quiet, rushed voice. "Yeah? No, I can't talk right now . . . Sorry . . . Yes, okay, bye."

He hangs up.

"Who was that?" I ask.

He looks at me, smiles a perfunctory smile, and shakes his head. "A very intrusive client. Do you have our tickets?"

"I do. What client?"

"It would take too long to explain."

He puts his phone into his pocket, the one farthest away from me, and then reaches for my hand and smiles at me. "Don't worry. I won't let her disturb our romantic weekend. I wouldn't want us to have to turn around and spend our anniversary in bed."

"No, that would be awful," I agree, remembering to smile.

"Intolerable."

"Ghastly."

"I wouldn't know what to do," he says.

"You never did," I confirm.

He laughs and presses my hand. The cab driver glances in the rearview mirror at us, but Harry cheerfully ignores him. My thoughts wander, between his face, turned to me with a warm smile, the bracelets in my backpack, and the phone in his other pocket.

Harry's never been shy about unburdening himself about work before.

Chapter Six

HOW I FELL FOR HIM

Five Years Before the Big Day

It had been two weeks since I'd stormed Harry's castle and come out of it as the jester. Two weeks during which I'd hidden my disappointment well. That is to say, Chloe, Frank, and I were unanimous in our opinion that despite my initial willingness to admit that Harry was not all bad, it turned out that he was, in fact, the worst.

If my insistence on reviving the topic whenever possible gave either of my friends a hint that perhaps I cared more than I was willing to admit, they were both kind enough never to tease me about it.

"Corporate wanker!" Chloe would cheer, wine in hand, whenever we went out and I wanted to go over it again.

"Bloody scoundrel!" Frank would toast with his pint of ale.

These were two weeks during which I avoided the agency as much as possible, sending my designs to them by post or dropping them off at the lobby—Harry hadn't fired me.

Chloe's newest work involved sculptures of derrières, and since she'd finished them all at home (making something of a mess involving clay, sculpting powder, and various forms of paint all over our bathroom, kitchen, and sitting room), I had to help her pack them in boxes so she could move them over to her studio.

"Why butts?" I asked as I lifted a particularly voluptuous example, complete with short, wiry hairs stuck in tufts to the provocatively rounded cheeks.

Chloe laughed. Her smoker's voice made the laugh sound particularly lascivious.

"Love them," she said. "Can't help it. There's so much expression in them. It's like your second face."

"As someone who's seen his fair share of butts, I beg to disagree," I said, wrapping the one in my hand in bubble wrap and placing it tightly next to the others in the cardboard box.

"You're not looking properly, then," she told me. "And it's fascinating, because even though it belongs to you, you probably wouldn't recognize it if it were shown to you in a photograph or, say, in a sculpture."

I stopped mid-motion. "Hang on . . . You didn't—you didn't make a sculpture of *my* butt, did you?"

She laughed. "Would you know if I had?"

It's not implausible. I do walk around naked a lot.

"Chloe . . ."

"Relax." She reached for her pack of cigarettes and lit up. "You know how I feel about consent."

Relieved, I continued on with my work.

"I notice that most of these are men's butts," I said. "Personal preference or are men just more eager to moon you?"

She grinned and wriggled her eyebrows at me. "What happens in this flat when you're not here is nobody's business but my own." Glancing at the clock, she moaned. "Shit, it's late. Got to go."

She kissed my cheek, grabbed her handbag and, before she left the flat, threw over her shoulder, "Be a darling and wrap the rest for me, will you? We'll drive them over when I get back." For a few moments, there was nothing but the sound of my laptop playing Nelson Riddle's "Lisbon Antigua," (because sugary orchestral music from the 1950s cheers me up) while I continued to wrap fist-sized sculptures of men's buttocks in bubble wrap—officially the gayest thing I'd ever done.

There was a knock on the door. I shouted, "It's open!"

Maya popped her head in meekly and said, "Joe?"

There I was in nothing but my boxer shorts with two male butts, one in each hand, listening to the sort of music Disney's Cinderella used to encourage critters to help her tidy, and all this in the midst of what, even to my eyes, seemed like the sort of place a tornado would leave alone, assuming its job here had already been done. Maya's eyes travelled around the place with obvious awe.

"Wow," she said, stepping in. "Wow."

"Er, sorry" was all I could think of responding. "This . . . I have an explanation for this." I lifted the two butts up.

Her eyebrows rose high. "I'm not judging."

"They're not mine, they're . . . Okay, er, come in, have a seat— Wait." I put the butts away, cleared a chair of old clothes and cut-up magazines, and then rushed to the laptop to turn the music off, before hunting for a shirt to put on.

"Oh you don't have to—" she said, watching me run around.

"No, it's fine, it's all right," I said. "D'you want a drink?"

"No, thanks," she said, which wasn't exactly a surprise considering that all our glasses were, at this point, set out on the kitchen counter, each hosting misty, dark-grey water and soaking a different-sized brush.

She did sit down, however, and when I turned to her at last, mostly dressed if a little chaotic, she smiled and said, "I haven't seen you around, so I came to check on you. Are you all right?"

"Yeah, fine, fine," I said, waving my hand around to show her that I was indeed fine. Crikey, but was my heart beating fast. Had Harry sent her?

"You cancelled the last meeting," she noticed, giving me a speaking look.

"Oh yes, well," I said, and then turned my gaze away from her searching eyes. I had no right to be disappointed, really. Harry hadn't made me any promises. I never asked him whether he was single. He never technically lied to me. In any event, this wasn't a subject I would ever raise with his personal assistant. "I sent you the new prints, didn't I?"

"You did," she said, mildly, and the way she looked from side to side, it was clear that she had some unpleasant news.

"Why? What's the matter?"

"Okay, don't be cross," she said. "There's a small chance that Malcolm might have hired another artist to take over your job."

"*What*?"

"Yeah, he seems to think—"

"Wait a second. I have a contract."

"Yes, but if you look at the fine print, it does say that if your work is rejected by the client, then the agency won't be held liable," she said.

"Why would the client reject me?"

"If he were given a competing design, for example. Look, I've spoken to Harry, and he likes your work, but you need to come to the office and keep his people on your side. You need to convince them that yours is the work they should hype up for the client when the time comes."

Bloody Malcolm. I knew nothing good ever came of networking.

"I'll pop around next week," I said, grudgingly. "Is there— Is there a time I could come when Harry wouldn't be there?"

I had turned my attention to the butts in the box so I wasn't looking at her, and it was my intention to sound casual, perhaps humorous, à la *You know, Harry and I don't like each other, wink, wink, nudge, nudge.* But she was silent for a few seconds and then, delicately, said, "I think he really wants to see you."

"Oh?"

I continued to focus on the rearranging of the butts in the box.

"Yeah, he asked about you," she said. "I don't think anybody saw you two leave together the other night, but even if they did, they wouldn't suspect anything, you know. And even if they did, we're not that kind of office. Everybody loves and trusts Harry, and nobody would think to suggest that you slept your way into your job or anything like that."

"What?" I was shocked. It hadn't occurred to me that, on top of everything else, I would have to endure that sort of speculation.

"I'm just saying," Maya smiled. "Harry really likes your work, and that's all that matters to us."

A thousand things sprung to my mind. I wanted to ask her whether this amazing good opinion Harry had earned among his colleagues would be at all impacted by knowing that he was a cheating scumbag. Or whether they caught young artists for him to fuck on purpose. What sort of organisation was this, anyway?

I didn't say any of that.

"I'll come around next week."

Maya beamed at me. "I'll set up a meeting."

"Thank you," I said. "And I'm sorry I made you come all the way to tell me in person. My phone is habitually discharged."

Although I really didn't want to see Harry again, I did need this gig, and I'd already done too much work to simply give it up for someone Malcolm chose. *Especially* for someone Malcolm chose. It would have been one thing to have been used as a sex toy by a gorgeous-yet-evil suit, and another to have then lost the job.

I rang Frank.

"I need your help," I said, and explained the situation.

He came over with his laptop, ready to walk me through the intricacies of doing a competent presentation for a corporate client.

"First," he said, "you need to know that these fuckers love a good PowerPoint presentation."

"Excellent," I said, eagerly. "How do I get me one of those?"

With the help of a few pints of beer, he guided me through the process almost painlessly. It wasn't difficult in and of itself. In fact, interlaced as his tutorial was with salacious stories about his sex adventures with Gabriella, the whole evening was painless enough.

Her parents didn't mind her dating Frank, but since she still lived with them, there was the small problem of premarital sex—in that Frank and Gabriella wanted to have it, and her parents thought that it would be neat if instead Frank practiced some prayer-fu. So the way this relationship worked was that Gabriella and Frank violated some commandments in her house, mostly while her parents were away. That's because Gabriella, like all normal human beings who'd been forbidden something, enjoyed that something all the more for it. And wildly.

"Sometimes," he said, leaning in confidingly, "she scares me a little." The twinkle in his eye didn't suggest she was anywhere near scaring him off, though.

"She sounds nuts," I said.

"Oh yes." He laughed. "Nuts like a fox! Have you ever just sort of meshed with someone? You know what I'm talking about? It's like everything suddenly fits."

"It happens. It doesn't mean anything," I said, my heart giving a sick leap.

But Frank was in his own world and barely heard me. Dreamily, he went on, "It isn't just the sex. Sometimes I feel like I want to burst; I want to do everything, go everywhere, all at once until my head spins. She has a way of *looking* at me, and suddenly everything inside of me goes calm."

I cleared my throat. "Hm, yeah, so how do you put in another slide again?"

I worked tirelessly for days, and after one last sleepless night of putting all my material into a long and elaborate presentation, I went to my meeting with the P&B Designs team, determined to both win the client and show Harry that I wasn't to be fucked with (figuratively speaking). I was in battle mode.

When I entered the conference room, everybody had already gathered there.

Harry was sitting at the head of the table, as usual: cool, composed, and in charge. It had been sort of sexy before I'd seen him naked. Now it was infuriatingly sexy. Steadfastly, I avoided looking at him at all.

I greeted everybody in conference room A of the P&B Design Agency very properly with a solemn "Good morning" and then went to the other end of the table, and began setting up. I was slightly regretting the amount of alcohol I had consumed with Frank when he'd been teaching me. My memory of what I was to do, the different keyboard shortcuts that did things quickly and professionally, was hazy. But I managed to find the presentation, and it showed up behind me on a screen.

Pleased with myself, and still absolutely refusing to meet Harry's eyes, I passed the prints around the table. Malcolm entered, pulled a chair from the wall, and sat next to Harry, with his arms crossed and self-importance radiating from his entire person.

"Right," I said, in an attempt to project confidence and command. Calmly, I tried to recollect Frank's advice about how to make the slide go full screen. I pressed the control key, because I remembered that often did stuff when pressed with another key, but I couldn't remember which. I could feel Harry's eyes on me. They were like torches or something very bright at the edge of my vision. I tried the A key. But that hadn't done what I wanted it to do. The slides on the left all lit up in yellow. I wanted to make it go away, so I hit backspace.

Magically, the entire presentation was now gone. It just vanished. I pressed backspace again. *Go back*, I willed that stupid computer, *go back, goddamn you!* It wouldn't listen to my thoughts.

All of it gone, from slide one all the way to slide twenty-six. The screen behind me, which showed everything I could see on the screen of the laptop in front of me, gave my audience a real-time update on what happened. I grabbed the back of a chair, clenching my jaw.

There was a moment's heavy silence while I let the truth sink in, and gaped at the now blank, grey space where my beautiful presentation had been seconds before. Everybody around the table was staring at me aghast. Everybody, that is, except for Harry. With his eyebrows raised, he just appeared surprised.

"So," I said, pulling my shoulders back and clearing my throat. "I am not here to give boring speeches with PowerPoint. My work . . . speaks for itself. It is bold and striking, attention-grabbing and—and interesting."

Harry had his lips clinched, as though he were trying not to laugh. Wanker.

"Er, I invite you," I said, lifting my chin, "to, er, examine my prints from the point of view of not a marketing expert, or an artist, or a critic, or even the client."

Malcolm raised the corner of his lip in a sneer, which was all the more pronounced for the moustache that twitched with it.

"Perhaps we shouldn't examine them at all," he muttered audibly enough for me to hear at my end of the room.

"Please, examine them instead," I continued, ignoring him, "from the point of view of . . . of a single man thinking of a nice place to take a date. Look at them from the point of view of a husband and wife who want a place to spend their monthly date night. See them, if you can, from the point of view of needing somewhere to take a friend or family member, to celebrate the new job they got, the promotion, the engagement, the birth of their first child . . . in short, if you wanted to go someplace nice to eat, what would these images signal to you?"

I spoke about each image in turn, passing the prints around the table, feeling Harry's gaze on me the entire time. I continued to pretend he wasn't there at all and maintaining an air of competence and composure. I would be the first to admit that this wasn't a strength of mine, but at the end Malcolm's moustache was droopy, from which I gathered I had done a better job than expected.

When I finished, the team clapped and I, relieved, remembered to take a breath.

After the meeting, I was left alone with Malcolm and Harry.

Malcolm said, "So this PowerPoint thing, was that supposed to be an homage to *Dead Poets Society* or . . .?"

"Sure," I said, shrugging.

"Very effective," Harry said, glancing down at the laptop. "You went to some effort to make it look like a genuine presentation too. I was worried there for a minute." He was no such thing.

"Seems like so much hogwash to me," Malcolm said. "And these prints, do you mean to change them every week?"

"As long as it takes to find a set that pleases you," I said. "I go by the feedback you give me."

Harry whistled. He'd somehow, by some computer magic, managed to retrieve my presentation. There it was again: the pictures, the graphs, the statistics. Twenty-six beautiful slides had abandoned me and returned at his command. Traitors.

"Look at that," he said to Malcolm, as though in wonder, "you can't say he's not dedicated." He flicked through the slides where I had infographics showing how different people perceive different colours, how different fonts are associated with different moods, and how localised aspects of the design could be made to feel inclusive for people not in the know. Now that all the material in the presentation was before me, I realised how much of this I had meant to say, and how I hadn't.

"Could you forward this to me?" Harry asked. "While I liked the little show you did, this seems quite interesting, actually. I'd like to read it, if I may."

"Yes, of course," I said, meekly.

Malcolm scoffed.

"We'll see" were his parting words, before he waltzed off, head held high. The door fell shut behind him. Harry and I were left in momentary silence.

"You didn't make a friend there," he said, nodding in the direction of the door. "It might have been that time you called him an idiot. Subtleties like that don't escape him, you know."

I smiled reflexively, but then remembered I was angry with him, or at least extremely disappointed, made my smile fall, and busied myself with putting my stuff together to leave.

"So," he said, watching me place the prints in my portfolio bag. "Do you have time to grab lunch?"

"No," I said. Then, remembering myself, I added, "Sorry, I'm busy."

"Coffee, then?"

I looked up from my bag. "I really don't think that would be a good idea."

He was clearly taken aback. Examining my face, he seemed to seek an explanation. "Oh. Of course. Sorry."

I don't know what it was in his surprise that touched me, or whether it was the flattery that he should be so taken aback by my refusal and even hurt by it, but I said, "I could grab a cup of tea, I suppose."

"There's a kettle in the common room, if you like. That would save us some time."

I agreed to that, especially since it meant we wouldn't be alone. As it turned out, we made our coffees and teas in the coffee-making area of the common room, but then he led me over to his office, where he closed the door behind me so that we were, in fact, very alone—more alone than we would have been had we gone to a coffee shop as he'd initially suggested.

Still, I was determined to carry this meeting out like a professional. I sat down in the chair on the other side of his desk, and he, seeing this, pushed his chair up to sit nearer me, without the desk dividing us.

His office was well-ordered. Floor-to-ceiling bookshelves were filled with books of every size and colour: books on design, albums about architecture, art, media, film, cartoons, literature. In front of the books, crowding the little space there was, were little ceramic figurines. They were colourful and depicted a large variety of subjects from roosters to two boxing gentlemen facing each other in nothing but breeches with their fists cocked, to young women riding on what looked like zebras.

Harry followed the line of my gaze and said, "I had to move in with my sister and she has nowhere to put them, so they're here for the time being."

"What are they?"

"Staffordshire figurines. Quite old. Some of them go all the way to the seventeenth century."

"Christ." I stood to examine them more carefully. They were crudely painted, I discovered up close, and seemed to be depicting ordinary scenes of daily life.

"Some were coloured by children," Harry said, coming to stand next to me. "They were used to decorate middle-class homes centuries ago."

I picked one that featured a tree and in front of the tree two lads, in Regency costume, embracing. Underneath it said, *Friendship*.

"Do you think that was nineteenth-century code for 'roommates'?" I asked.

He laughed. "You have a one-track mind."

I put it back. There was another one, of a milkmaid and a cow. Underneath, it had a mark that said, *Love, KJ*. I showed it to Harry. He smiled self-consciously.

"Kieran Jones," he explained.

I put the figurine back because I didn't want to go down that track.

"You moved in with your sister?" I asked, picking up on what he'd said earlier. "So that's why all your stuff was in boxes?"

"Yes."

We sat down again. It felt strangely formal.

"After Kieran and I split up, I didn't feel like I could stay in that flat by myself," he said. I stared in surprise. He and Kieran had split up? When? Because of me? No, the boxes had already been packed by the time I entered the picture.

When I didn't respond, he continued, "That morning . . . I really owe you an apology for that. I had no idea Kieran had any intention of coming back. He just popped by to pick up some of his stuff, even though I told him I was going to drop it off with him later that day." He smoothed his trouser leg with one neatly manicured hand.

"He flipped out when he saw you," he said, visibly uncomfortable. "But you have to understand, we'd been together for seven years. I wouldn't have been any kinder to any bloke I found in his bed, to be honest. But he's sorry for what he did, and he'd tell you so himself if I hadn't begged him to leave it to me. I didn't think you'd want to be accosted by him again."

He smiled apologetically. I nodded, though I understood little more than half of what he'd said. What I did hear was that he and Kieran were split up. He was single. Had been single when he went to bed with me. I couldn't help but smile back at him, my heart lifting.

He reached out his hand to touch my arm, the same place where Kieran had held it.

"I hope he wasn't too rough with you?"

"It was nothing," I said, now feeling quite generous-spirited towards the man. Truth be told, Kieran hadn't really frightened me. I used to box when I was younger, had been quite good in fact, and so he'd only managed to do what he had because I'd let him.

Harry smiled. His hand lingered, warmed on my arm, and then he let go.

"So, er," I began, feeling as if I'd suddenly lost a great amount of weight. "You live with your sister now?"

"My parents live too far away, in Harpenden. Siobhan's flat isn't exactly comfortable, but it'll do for now while I look for somewhere else to rent. If you know of any place . . ."

"I'll let you know."

"Thanks."

We fell silent once more. He sipped his coffee. I reached for my tea.

"So," I began again, because the silence wasn't doing anything helpful to my peace of mind. "Seven years. That's quite a bit of history you two have, huh?"

It was a silly gambit. I had no desire to hear about him and Kieran.

Harry nodded. "It's been a long time coming. The break up, that is. He has a lot of issues, and we couldn't ever quite work them out. He wouldn't introduce me to his family up in Doncaster; he kept telling everyone I was his best friend, his flatmate . . . Hell, once he introduced me as his 'compadre' which— Don't laugh." He was smiling, though, so I wasn't too bothered about offending him.

"At first you just swallow it as part and parcel of who he is," he went on. "But after a while it wears on you. Eventually, we fell out over wanting to buy a place together. That's to say, *I* wanted to buy a place together, and he panicked and lost his temper, because apparently it was easier to explain to people that you lived in a studio apartment with another bloke, than that you bought a house with him."

He rolled his eyes.

"Anyway"—he smiled self-deprecatingly—"I'm sure you don't want to hear all this nonsense."

"I don't mind," I said. "I've never been with anyone that long. It sounds tough."

Harry shrugged. "It shouldn't be. I believe that with the right person, it should be easy. At least, it shouldn't be like pushing a pile of shit up a hill with a fork."

I laughed. "Well, thanks for that image."

There was a knock on the door, and Maya's head appeared.

"Duncan Webb is— Oh." She stopped when she saw me.

"Ah yes," Harry said. "I'll be right there, Maya, thank you."

She sent me a quick smile, and then ducked out of the room. Harry turned to me.

"I've got a meeting," he said. I rose to my feet.

"I should go too."

As we approached the door, he raised an arm towards me. Pleasantly surprised, I put my arms around him. He felt weirdly stiff in my embrace. Then I realised, he'd just been reaching past me to open the door. I shut my eyes in embarrassment.

But his frame relaxed, and he exhaled and his one arm returned a mild squeeze. God, he felt good. How did he still smell so good too? It was fifty degrees out there. I was still holding him. He leaned back from me, with an amused smirk.

"Okay, bye," I said, my mortification swiftly returning, and rushed out of the door. The lift had just appeared at the end of the corridor, and I dashed for it, ducked in, and then wondered why it was that when you needed a sinkhole to open up underneath your feet and swallow you whole, the ground remained firm and you were a goof for the world to admire.

The feel of him stayed with me. For some reason, his scent, the warmth of his arms, the angle of his smile as we let go of each other, they all stayed with me. Who knows why some people do this to us, and others don't. I'd hugged loads of men in my time, and most wore off as soon as I turned my head.

When I came out of the Tube, my phone buzzed, alerting me to the arrival of new text messages. One of them was from Harry.

You had to leave so quickly, I forgot to ask. Would you like to go out some time?

I was nearly hit by a cyclist as I stood there, staring at the text message, grinning like a maniac.

Chloe eyed me with suspicion and displeasure while I dressed for my date with Harry. To be fair to her, she had plenty of reasons. I'd never in my life worn a shirt and dress trousers or leather shoes where you had to think about what belt went with them. I drew a line at wearing a tie. But the restaurant Harry had picked was fancy, and I didn't want to look out of place.

"So this Kieran person," Chloe said from her Danish wicker chair, "he's out of the picture now, is he?"

"Yup."

"And this Harry person is single now?"

"Yup."

"And you believe that poppycock?"

"Yup."

"So, what happened to 'lying, cheating son of a bitch'?"

"I was wrong," I said. "He explained it. It made sense. He's going through a rough patch."

If I sounded like Maya now, I didn't choose to admit it to myself.

Chloe stared at me horrified. "What are you doing?"

"Brushing my hair."

"*Why?*"

"It's what people do!" I said, defensively. Usually I kept it in a ponytail and forgot about it. It occurred to me that Harry probably liked neat men, with neat hair, clean-shaven and all that. I'd clean-shaved for the date. I'd showered very, very thoroughly. I was as polished as one of those weird figurines he collected. Chloe had reasons to be worried.

"I don't like it." She narrowed her eyes.

"I'm not asking you to like it," I said, spraying my deodorant in the air and walking through the cloud of scent. Note to self: buy cologne like an adult.

The restaurant Harry had chosen was Italian. I checked it out online and it struck me as a little extravagant. On the other hand, he wouldn't be taking me to a nice restaurant if this were just a friend-date. This surely was a date-date. In my excitement, I barely ate anything all day, playing imaginary scenarios over in my head, in which we always ended up on the table, wrestling our clothes off, while making imaginative use of that olive oil they always serve with bread before the meal.

Unfortunately, this resulted in my standing in front of the restaurant that evening waiting for Harry, ravenous and dressed like an overgrown man-child (because the whole ironed shirt, dress trousers look only works when you're wearing your own suit, rather than one borrowed from your friend whose limbs aren't as long as your own).

Harry arrived in a cab, dapper in his suit, with his hair clean-cut and parted at the side as usual. I was a little envious how he could pull this off so well, and keep it looking sharp even after a cab ride. I don't know how it was, but in my case, it was always a toss up between appearing like I'd just escaped a terrible accident or being somewhere on time.

He forbore to notice this, however, and greeted me with a smile and a pat on the arm. I thought this was a bit of a cold greeting for a date, but then I remembered what he'd said about Kieran, and guessed that he probably wasn't used to PDA.

"Have you been waiting long?" he asked.

I told him I hadn't, and even stopped myself from bragging that I had, for the first time in my life, arrived on the dot. We went inside and let the waiter seat us at a table by the window. It was a nice sort of place, with warm colours and muted piano music contributing to the "ambience."

Unfortunately, it was the sort of place that served things like calf liver sautéed in onions—what the living hell is that anyway?—and it was the sort of place that, despite alleging to be Italian, did not serve pizza. Harry seemed to have no trouble picking out his own dinner at a glance and spent the bulk of his menu time examining the wine options.

"What's an osso buco?" I asked him.

"It says right there," he said. "Veal shank. It's a Milanese dish, usually served in a sauce of white wine and broth."

Smart-arse.

"Why is the only meat here veal?" I asked.

"This one's got sausage in it." He pointed to a place on my menu.

"Ah, I sort of skipped over that one, since it says 'rape'. Didn't want any of that."

He laughed. "It's a type of broccoli."

I picked that since it was the only dish on the menu that didn't have veal in it or wasn't vegetarian, which would have been worse.

"What's your problem with veal?" he asked. "You don't like it?"

"Never tried it."

"You don't like trying anything new?"

"At the moment, no," I said. "At the moment I'm trying to focus on the fact that since you're talking to me, you're not actually a giant ham."

He thought this was vastly amusing, like a man who'd never starved a Joe Kaminski before.

The food came and, though it was tasty enough, it was not nearly enough for me. I didn't want to seem ungrateful though, so I said it was great, and he believed me.

Throughout the meal we chatted as before, and he never mentioned Kieran once. In my imagination, I'd hoped there'd be some signal, some sign he'd send me to let me know he was available and interested, but he did nothing of the kind. He asked me a million questions about the installation I was showing at the Independent Artist Fair in the Rag Factory, which made me conclude that perhaps the whole meal was meant as a sort of job interview—perhaps he had another client who might use my services. But if that was it, he never mentioned a client or a job offer.

I was conscious of a feeling of disappointment.

When we'd finished the main meal, desserts, and drinks, he insisted on paying. Outside, there was a moment's pause, as we were slowly coming towards a goodbye. We let each other know which way we were going, and then he suddenly hugged me and blurted out, "Let's do that again some time."

Startled, I returned the hug and said, "Okay."

It felt odd and abrupt. I wished he wouldn't go. Having waited for this date—if one could call it that—with anticipation for days, I was quite keen to take him home with me. But he'd already turned away and walked up the street.

Still hungry and with my head in a whirl, I headed into town. There was a marketplace, quite close to the restaurant, which during the night was empty of stalls and instead full of revellers. There was a pub or two on the way, which I thought I might investigate once I found a chippy or some other takeaway place that was open till late.

Eventually, I stumbled upon a burger and kebab place. Besides me, there were two young women there, both of them giggly. I ordered a large donner kebab and some chips. I sat down in the red plastic seats near the window and waited for my order. My foot was tapping. I couldn't fix on a single, coherent thought. I needed a distraction. I asked the girls, who were dressed skimpily enough to suggest they were going somewhere fun, what they were up to this evening.

"We're doing a pub crawl," the blonde told me.

"Sweet," I said. "Is it for a challenge or something?"

The blonde looked at me like I was daft. The redheaded one liked me, I thought, because she was laughing at pretty much everything I said.

"You should come with us! Meet our mates. We're doing a pub quiz later. Are you clever?"

I shrugged. "I can do a pub quiz. Or at least I can drink while you do a pub quiz."

The redhead found this hilarious. The blonde told me how many pub quizzes she'd won in the past. We were in agreement that, putting our minds together, there was no way anybody could beat us.

We went out of the takeaway place together, and I immediately bit into my kebab, because holy shit was I hungry. We made it barely three steps out of the place, with the redhead complaining about her pinching shoe, when I stopped short and the girls did as well. I was standing, my cheeks packed with donner kebab, in front Harry.

He was as startled to see me, as I was him. I don't know why, but immediately, like a bloody child, I put the kebab behind my back.

"H-Harry," I said, spitting lettuce. This tickled my new friends to no end. Harry, when I first saw him, had seemed pale and miserable, but now his mouth was twitching and his eyes had that attractive glint of amusement in them.

"Hungry, were we?" he asked.

"Er, no!" I said. "It's, er . . ." I swallowed hard and tried to think of a reason why I should be out on the street with a kebab behind my back.

"Kebab-tasting competition?" I ventured. The girls toppled over each other in laughter.

Harry smiled. "I see. And, er, are these the judges?" He nodded at the girls.

"No, that's . . . Emma and Bev. We're going to do a pub crawl."

There was a moment's pause while he looked at me in a strange, assessing way.

"All right, then," he said, breaking the silence. "Have fun."

He waved at the girls and then went on past me. Feeling like a right twat, I ran after him.

"Sorry about that," I said, catching up with him. Showing the kebab in my hand, I said, "I didn't mean to— It's just— I was famished."

He smiled. "That's all right. I'm sorry about the restaurant; I thought they'd have a larger menu."

"No, it was a lovely restaurant, honestly. It's me. I hadn't eaten all day, because—" I stopped, my face warming, and cleared my throat. "I didn't have the time. So I was ravenous coming in, and then I didn't want to behave like a complete peasant ordering everything on the menu and—"

"It's all right," he said mildly. "You don't have to keep apologising; I'm not cross."

"Oh, okay."

I realised, for the first time, that he hadn't gone home after our dinner either. Intrigued, I asked, "So, where are you heading?"

"I fancied a walk."

I thought I saw, or perhaps I hoped I saw, something lurking in the depths of his silver eyes. It was like he wanted to tell me something but couldn't.

"Want company?" I asked.

He seemed pleased I'd asked. I held up my finger and rushed back to Emma and Bev, who'd been watching us with great interest.

"So . . ." Emma began, "who's Mr. Darcy over there?"

"What?" I laughed, a little embarrassed.

"Oh my God, he's blushing," Bev teased. "How cute! Oi! Handsome!" she cried at Harry. "You want a piece of this?" She and Bev collapsed into giggles when Harry frowned at them, bemused. Amidst their hoots of laughter, Emma said to me, "Sh-sh-sh, we're helping."

"Thank you and please stop," I said.

"Go to him," Emma urged in a loud, conspiratorial whisper.

"Make beautiful babies," Bev gave us her blessing. They stumbled away together, into the night.

When I returned to Harry's side, he seemed more amused than annoyed.

"Harvard alumni reunion?" he asked, dryly.

"Shut up," I said, laughing.

We set off together, he with his hands in his pockets. I with a wilting kebab in mine. We walked in an ambling pace.

"So…" I began, hoping to distract him from the girls' performance. "You're not keen to get back to your sister?"

"Not really," he said. "It's a strange time. You don't get used to being suddenly single again easily. You find yourself with all this freedom—nobody to tell where you're going or what time you'll be home. It should feel freeing, but actually it's depressing."

I nodded as though I had any idea what that was like.

"Do you know what I mean?" he asked.

It felt like he was asking me more than just whether I understood him.

"Not really," I said. "But I can imagine."

"You feel guilty about things you shouldn't feel guilty about. You want things you feel bad for wanting. You do things you didn't think you wanted to do, and experience things you didn't know you'd like." He glanced sideways at me as he said it. I hoped he meant me.

"You'll get used to it," I suggested.

"I haven't been entirely honest with you, Joe," he said, after a small pause. "And I felt guilty for that as well."

I didn't say anything. I knew what was coming. Regret. He would tell me that our night together had been a mistake. A one-off. A freak occurrence in his well-ordered life. He would ask me to understand.

My kebab was cooling in the night air and my appetite for it died entirely, so I chucked it in the nearest bin. My hands were greasy and sticky. Harry stopped in front of me and, ever the gentleman, took out a clean tissue and wiped my hands for me.

"I had fun that night," he said, quietly, his head bent, his eyes fixed on our hands, as he carefully dabbed my palm. The street was entirely empty, and in the darkness of the evening, this felt private and intimate.

"Yeah, me too," I said, my throat a little tight.

"And I suppose," he sounded cautious, "I suppose I wanted to maybe do it again."

I stopped myself from picking him up and running home with him.

"Sure! Where do you want to go?" I said coolly.

He laughed. "Er, no, that's not—that's not what I wanted to say. Hear me out." He scrunched the tissue and binned it.

"I know this is probably nothing to you," he said. "You probably hook up with people all the time. And I know rebound is a thing, and everybody knows about it, and it's probably the most natural thing in the world for me to do at this point. But I have to be honest with you: I'm probably not the sort of guy who can do that. I get attached."

"That's cool," I said with a grin. He could get attached to me all he liked. I could be the eucalyptus tree to his koala. I'm attachment's enthusiastic amateur.

He smiled and gently shook his head. "I just want you to know what you're letting yourself in for."

He looked at me in a way that made my mouth go dry.

"I mean," he said, his eyes flicking down to my mouth and back, "that night was . . . that was something. For me, at least. I'm not usually like that. I didn't know it was possible to—to do that with someone I barely knew. I felt like I'd known you for years. Like I knew you better than some people I *had* known for years. It was a very—" His breath caught, and he dropped his gaze to the ground, where he kicked lightly at the paving slab. "It was an intense experience for me."

"Yeah, me too."

"Was it?" He sounded surprised.

"I was there that night, remember?"

The miserable air he'd carried with him when I met him outside the kebab shop lifted entirely, and his smile was bright and happy. We walked on. I realised we were going in the direction of a Tube station. The subject of taking the Tube somewhere, together, was looming before us, closer with every step. I didn't want to be pushy. I did, however, want to get him out of that suit.

Finally he asked, "So, would you like to . . . go somewhere?"

I slid my hands down his back, pulling him to me, our bodies melded together, all friction coming from our tight embrace alone. I felt him coming against my skin, shudderingly against my abdomen— he was hot, cheeks blazing, eyes glowing.

When he leaned back, bee-stung lips and flushed cheeks, he brushed his hair back before reaching down to stroke me, slowly, deliberately.

"Look at you," he said, his eyes caressing my face. I'd forgotten how good he was with his hands.

"God, I like looking at you," he sighed, as he bent down to kiss my neck. His arm was working, his fingers tight around me, gliding smoothly in rhythm with my hips. I tilted my head back. He remembered me well. He remembered where I was sensitive, where everything felt like hot, burning, tingling sensation.

"Harry . . ."

He found my lips with his. Long, lingering kisses turned into deep, passionate ones. When my breathing fell in with the rhythm of his pulls, he went down to his knees and began to kiss and then lick me, sucking me into his mouth. It was all too much. I came with a cry, saw white, my eyes rolled back in my head, and it was a while before I could catch my breath and remembered where I was.

He was in my arms again, kissing my shoulder, embracing me by the waist, running his hands over my body. When I was with him again, he sought out my eyes, as if checking if I was still ok with this, checking for regrets.

Our limbs worn and soft as jelly, our hearts relaxing slowly into a normal rhythm again, half-sleepy, we lay in my bed, his head on my chest, my fingers in his hair. They use words like *crush* or *smitten* when they talk of this feeling, but I felt curiously light and full, like a balloon.

He wasn't asleep; his fingers were brushing over the sprinkling of hair on my chest.

When he spoke, it was in a low, thoughtful murmur. "Do you think it's true that we take breakups so hard not because we mourn the person we're losing, but because we mourn what we thought our life was going to be?"

That brought me down to earth.

"Probably," I said, after a moment.

He sighed. "I wish I could go back in time and never have met him."

Ah yes. *Him.* Harry hadn't mentioned him all evening. Yet Kieran lurked behind every corner.

"Then you'd be a totally different person," I said. "And I—" I stopped myself.

He glanced up at me, a question in his eyes.

I like you, I wanted to say. No, I wanted to say more. *I like you a lot. You smell good and your smile makes me go warm inside, and—*

"Why is there a picture of you here dressed as a dog?" he asked me, frowning.

I twisted my neck to see the pictures I'd stuck on the wall over my bed and found the one of me dressed as an Alsatian puppy. "Oh, there was a convention."

"A convention?" His voice trembled.

"They call themselves furries, and I'd just met this bloke in this pub, right, and he told me about going and so me and a few mates decided to go along too and check it out."

"You seem to be, er, enjoying yourself . . ."

"They were nice people," I said, defensively. "My owner and I exchange Christmas cards every year."

"Owner?" He laughed.

"What? He said I made a cute puppy."

"And that's all it took?"

I grinned at him. "I'm easy to please."

"Clearly."

I flipped him over onto his back while he laughed. We didn't talk again that night.

Chapter Seven

IRELAND

Six Months Before the Big Day

Things to avoid when proposing to the love of your life:
1. Don't plan anything elaborate. Just. Don't. You'll want to. You'll want the whole of the world to bathe in your success. It's a bad idea.
2. Remember that there's a reason why nobody entrusts you with planning anything.
3. Make no radical changes to your appearance. Things your lover won't want to see: you grinning like a maniac through fifty layers of makeup and bursting out of a skintight full-body leather costume. Things your lover will want to see: You. Just you.
4. As best you can, try to remain clothed. At all times.

We arrive in our hotel late. The flight was delayed, and then, for some unfathomable reason, a rainstorm meant that there were no cabs to drive us into the city, so we end up taking a bus. Harry doesn't have a problem with this. He still texts his colleagues, his friends, tries to cheer me up by pointing out of the window at the passenger of a car driving next to us, who is eating cereal out of a bowl. But when I see the hotel itself, I really do cheer up. I want this trip to be perfect, and taking a stinky bus isn't part of any vision of perfection anybody's ever had. The hotel is beautiful, though, and at last, my plans are back on track.

Harry asks for our keys at the reception while I look through the brochures, hoping to find something touristy for Harry to do while I try to arrange everything for the big moment tomorrow evening.

"Come on, sunshine," he murmurs near my ear when he's done. "I'm too knackered to go and see the castle right now."

"Oh yes, of course." I take one of the bags off him and follow him to the lifts.

When we reach our room, I am even more pleased. I'd rung the hotel in advance to ask for one of their better suites—as good a one as I could afford—and now Harry's reaction is priceless.

"Holy shit!" he says, when he switches on the light. "Joe, this must be some mistake."

"Nah, it's all right. The gallery has a deal with the hotel."

"Really?"

"What?" I laugh, dropping our bags next to the built-in wardrobe. "Stick with me and you'll live the high life, baby."

He raises a dubious eyebrow. "That old man's garage last time . . ."

"Was a one-off!" I say, defensively.

"And that cholera-infested water foundry?"

"That's a historical landmark. And did you get cholera? No."

He throws me a laughing look and then switches on the bathroom lights to do his usual hotel room inspection.

"Besides," I remind him as I throw myself on the biggest bed I've ever seen, "you didn't complain when I got us balcony seats for Ian McKellan's King Lear. Or backstage passes for The Killers after I had to make up those posters for them."

Harry just shakes his head in amused exasperation and walks over to the window. I get out of bed to switch off the light, so he can see a panorama of Dublin at night. I am, if I may say so myself, a genius. Everybody knows cityscapes at night are romantic.

"I should probably give my uncle a ring," he says.

I'm a little disappointed that that's where his thoughts go when he sees so much beauty, courtesy of *moi*.

"Your uncle?"

"My dad told him I was going to be in town, and I've got an army of cousins I should probably go and see while you're at work."

"Oh, sure, yeah, that sounds fun."

Since it's imperative he's out doing something all day (because I will need the hotel room to put all my plans into action tomorrow), I got one of Chloe's many friends to take him around some castle for half the day—I can't show too much preparation or he would get suspicious. So I encourage the idea of cousins, while pulling him to me and towards the bed.

"Aren't you tired?" he asks, returning my kisses and unbuttoning his shirt.

"Nah." In fact, I'm electrified, restless, and in need of some activity to release all this excited energy that's tingling in my muscles. I take his hand and push it down my jeans.

"Flatterer," he murmurs against my cheek.

We fall asleep two hours later, naked. There's nothing like hearing your lover sigh in contentment after you've exerted yourself for him using all the skills in your repertoire. Nothing like feeling him glow at your side, his hand holding your hand to his chest.

Everything goes calm inside.

Sometime in the middle of the night—maybe two or three in the morning—his phone buzzes. I jerk awake. He picks it up and goes to the bathroom. Weird.

I can't hear what he's saying, but the conversation is short and tense. It sounds like he's reassuring someone. I lean back against the pillow. *What the hell?*

He comes back a few moments later, plugs his phone into the charger, and then lies down.

"Who was that?" I ask sleepily.

"Oh, sorry, did I wake you up?" He reaches for my hand again, kissing it and putting it where it was before, against his heart.

I'm tempted to get up and look at his phone to see who it was. But I can't. He's holding my hand.

"Seriously, Harry. Who'd ring you at this hour?"

A pause. "A client who's moved to Australia and forgotten about time zones."

I have more questions, but his eyes are closed and his breath is going steady. His pulse is a little raised against my hand.

I'm being paranoid. Paranoia has no place during a perfect engagement weekend. So I snuggle closer to him and force myself to think of tomorrow.

We have a peaceful breakfast at the hotel restaurant. Harry drinks his usual black coffee while checking the news on his phone, and I bask in how successful the Plan is so far. In fact, planning is not so hard, after all. I think I should do it more often. Harry is right when he says that planning makes everything easier because you're prepared. That's what was missing from my life—I'm never prepared for anything. But I will have a new life, soon. A life with Harry. Well, it will be largely the same, except I will be better. I will listen to him more, and I will plan (no more crappy PowerPoint failures—this time I mean business), and he will be happy with me.

I watch him as he frowns over the latest in politics, the referendum, elections somewhere. He cares about so many things, I sometimes wonder how he finds the time or the space in his brain to do it. When I look at the news, all it makes me want to do is take a nap. He knows the details of each party's manifesto; he doesn't just get pissed off with politicians who deny the veracity of climate change research, no, he reads scientific articles about climate change, and there's a whole shelf in our flat dedicated to the subject, as though the future of the world depended on him being able to argue his case at a moment's notice. He gave most of our savings (his savings, really) to the charities dealing with the refugee crisis, and then organised fun runs for his office to raise more money for the cause. He's as close to a superhero as you can get nowadays, short of wearing a fetching cape.

When he hears me sigh, he looks up and smiles apologetically.

"Sorry, bad habit," he says, switching his phone off. "Are you nervous about today?"

"Nah, it's all right."

At the beginning of our relationship, he used to come to every exhibition, and every show, because he imagined that's what being a good boyfriend to me was. But soon we established that it's not worth it. After I set my pieces up, I just wander around, answer questions, sometimes I sell a piece or two. It's the dullest thing in the world for guests, which is why I never invite any.

"What time do you want to meet up?" he asks.

"I reckon I should be done by six. I'll find a place for us to have dinner."

"I can do that," he says. "You shouldn't have to think about—"

"No, no, that's all right, I'll do it," I say, quickly. His eyebrows rise up in surprise. I clarify, "Orla told me of a cool place last time we spoke. Don't remember the name, but I'll find out and see if I can book us in."

He agrees to this, but elicits a promise that if I'm too busy, I should just send him a text and he'll take care of it. Siobhan calls him "Mr. I'll Take Care Of It" in fond mockery. If I'm perfectly honest, it can get a little much sometimes, because his natural instinct is to assume everybody is a little bit incompetent and if he doesn't have a hand in something, it will probably fall apart. *Well*, I think to myself, *we'll see about that, Mr. Byrne.*

"What are you smiling about?" he asks.

"Oh, sorry."

"I've never seen you look so smug." He laughs. "What's up?"

"Nothing." I wipe the stupid smile off my face. Really, the last thing I need now is for my goofy face to betray me and spoil everything.

We part in front of the hotel.

"Good luck," he says. "Let me know how it goes."

"I'll probably be run off my feet, so don't expect any texts or anything."

"Okay."

"I'll meet you in our room six-ish, all right?"

He smiles, and I know he's thinking not to expect me before seven. Well, we'll see about that, won't we! His taxi is already waiting for him, so I watch him get in. We wave at each other like the sappy creatures we are. The cab merges with the traffic, and I head into town. I've a busy schedule to keep.

First, I have to buy a suit. All our relationship I've been trying to smarten up for him, because I know he likes it. Well, he says he likes my style, and never actually asked me to change anything about it, but I've seen the way he looks at suits: the way Chloe looks at ice cream sundaes, and the way my mother's poodles look at my mother.

The problem so far has been that even the few times I'd procured a fancy set of trousers and a shirt to wear (one time for Siobhan's wedding, another time for Harry's grandfather's funeral), they always get crumpled and stained within the first hour of me wearing them.

It's like someone put a curse on me. I try so hard to keep them neat and clean! Well, tonight I'm determined it's going to be different. Tonight, I'm going to look so fucking sharp, he won't recognize his own boyfriend.

I've saved up for the occasion, and though I didn't have time to research places to buy suits (or, in fact, buy one before we got to Ireland), I have my phone on me, and a few minutes on Google produces all the information I need. The suit is going to make me look like one of those men in men's magazines, which Harry pretends not to drool over. And it's going to fit me, and it's going to stay clean, goddamn it, if it's the last thing I do.

The shop assistant, an elderly Indian man, is very keen to help me. I am open with him.

"I know nothing about suits, but I have to look like James Bond tonight," I say.

The look in his face informs me that this is not the first time someone has tasked him with this. To his credit, he doesn't give any indication that he's tired of the dumbasses who do. We decide that black suits wouldn't look good on me, what with my dark complexion, but that the grey and the navy blue would. In the end we go for the grey. He gives me different sizes to try on, because I haven't the least clue what my size is—most of my clothes come from discount bins in Tesco, and they're all either too large or too small. While I try them on, he brings an array of matching shirts, ties, belts, and shoes, and then comments dryly on the fact that Bond would probably wear matching socks. I ask him to find me socks.

When I emerge at last from the little curtained booth, I realise that with hair as long as mine, I look like a mafioso, or perhaps an undertaker's son. But there's time, and I can still pop into a hairdresser's and get my hair done. Fuck it, I've got so much time in my Perfect Plan, I could get a manicure while I'm at it.

The price of the ensemble makes me gulp, but then I think of Harry, and how impressed he will be, and charge it all to my credit card. After all, a man gets engaged but once, right? Best to do it properly. Besides, even I have to admit that the suit makes me look good, minus the hair of course, and I think Harry will be both impressed and aroused by it, which really decides the matter.

The salesman packs it all up for me. "Keep the receipt, in case you want to return anything."

"Sure." I beam at him, though in my head I'm already thinking of the sharp new haircut I will get.

Chloe rings me as I leave the shop.

"So, have you done it yet?"

"No, this evening," I say. "Why?"

"I just thought maybe you thought the better of it. I've been sending you vibes. Did you receive anything?"

"No, weirdo, and stop spoiling my perfect day."

"Is it?"

"Oh, you wouldn't believe. I've got a suit now—a proper one, with cuff links and a tie and everything. And shoes. And a fucking belt. That's right, I said a belt."

"Wow," she says, singularly unimpressed. "A belt, you say? You mean that thing prisoners use to hang themselves with? Very apt."

"Shut up. I'm going to a hairdresser now. I'm cutting my hair."

"Your *hair*?" she sounds astounded. "That wasn't part of the Magnificent Plan, was it?"

"It is now."

"Joe . . ."

"Why are you calling me? Are you trying to spoil this for me?"

"No, actually. Just calling to check on you. Turns out it's a good thing I did. Don't do anything to your hair. Just go and tell that man how you feel."

"My hair doesn't go with the suit. It's got to go."

"Who cares about that stupid suit, you maniac?" She laughs. "Harry won't care. He always gazes at you like you're art anyway. It's the most annoying thing in the world."

I feel a little warm under my collar. *He does?* I want to ask. It only determines me on my course. "I'm doing it. I'm going to look like James fucking Bond. That's right."

She groans. "That misogynistic, imperialist—"

"I'm going to do it!"

She sighs, resigned. "Let me know when it's done, so I know when to put on my black clothes."

"You're lucky I love you, weirdo."

When we say goodbye, she says "good luck" once more, and I know she means it.

The first salon I pass is closed, but two blocks down there is one with enormous posters of beautiful people in the display window. With my heart in my throat, I enter.

The hairdresser, a chipper Irish girl, ruffles through my hair with her fingers and asks what I want.

"Er, I—I don't know," I admit. "Honestly, I never cut it."

She smiles. "Never?"

"Well, I cut it to keep it this length, when I remember to, but I don't, er, cut it short. Ever."

She ruffles my hair again, interested. "Are we cutting it short now?"

I feel an enormous gulp in my throat.

The Elders kept insisting my mum cut my hair short.

"I'm proposing today," I tell her. She meets my eyes in the mirror and beams.

"Aw," she says. "Then we have to make it special. Does she not like your hair?"

"Oh, er, no, he—he does." She looks surprised and then, giving me another glance, stops looking surprised.

I've seen his ex-boyfriends. I've seen the men he fancies, the celebrities he thinks are hot. None of them have hair longer than a few centimetres. Not one. Except for me. Now, I don't mind being different from the lot he's liked/dated before. That's fine by me, because I mean to keep him, so they can all go and suck it. But I'm different from those guys in every way. And it would be nice to conform to at least one standard of beauty Harry holds. One thing I could point at and say, *That's why he wants to be with me.*

I show the hairdresser what I want—the sort of cut that would be sharp and sexy and amazing, and knock Harry off his feet: buzzed short at the sides and a styled pompadour on top. The model I point to in the magazine she offered me for inspiration looks really hot.

The girl's chatty. Which is good, because as she plugs in the clippers, I start getting nervous. It's my hair. It takes ages to grow back. My lovely, lovely hair. My long, signature hair. My ponytail. When she switches the clippers on, it's like I'm at the dentist's and she's about to drill into my teeth.

I swallow, hard, but try to smile encouragingly at her, because she starts eyeing me with apprehension.

"Yer sure you want to do this?" she asks.

"Oh yes, totally."

Last thing I need is for her to get nervous. Still, when she puts the clippers to my skull, I have to close my eyes. *Think of Harry. Think of Harry. Think of Harry.* I can't think of Harry. I think of my hair, and of prison, and of belts, and of the bracelets I got for him. No, not bracelets. Shackles. That's what they are. Shackles. *Oh God. Oh God. Oh God.* The sound of clippers diving into hair. The feeling of my locks falling down onto to my shoulders. The feeling of cool air tickling the now bare skull around my temples.

It's not so bad, I tell myself. It's quite freeing, actually. And hair grows back, anyway. In a year or two, this will be but a memory. Now it becomes easier to think of Harry. I imagine him laughing at me, but being secretly delighted with the change. I imagine how touched and happy he will be, and how much he will laugh later, when the lengths to which I went to for tonight will become apparent to him.

"It's not so bad, is it?" the girl says, seeing me relax. "I'll make it look a treat, I promise, and I—ahchoo!"

She sneezes, violently, with the clippers still against my scalp, and her hand slips and runs over the top of my head. A long strand of deep-brown locks falls over my forehead, down my face, to my lap. My eyes are wide. Her eyes are wide. We freeze, the clippers still buzzing.

"Oh," she falters. "Oh no."

Her eyes slowly travel to meet my own in my reflection in the mirror. I don't know what to say. I want to scream, but this day is going to be fucking perfect, so I can't scream. People don't scream when they are having the most perfect day imaginable, right?

"Sorry?" she says, in a squeaky, meek voice, with that hint of a tremble that informs me she is ready to burst into tears any moment.

"It's all right," I say. My voice is strained, but I try to smile. "It's fine. Really."

Three of her colleagues rush to her side, eyes wide, horror in their faces.

"Oh no, what happened here?"

"Are you all right, sir?"

I assure them I'm perfectly fine. The girl is hyperventilating. There's a bald spot on the top of my head.

"Ah . . ." One of the older women casts a critical eye over me. "I don't think we'll be able to do anything with that. Shall we shorten the rest?"

I contain myself. I do not scream, *No! Leave that bald hole on the top of my head like I'm a fucking medieval monk, why don't you, Edwardina Scissorhand!*

"Sure," I say, placidly. "That . . . that's probably wise." For the benefit of the girl, who is shedding copious tears now, I add, "It's been a chore to wash, anyway. Really, it's all for the best."

So then her colleague makes me bald.

There's a large audience by this point; they all try to be positive. "Oh doesn't he look handsome," they say. "Like a young Barack Obama!" they gush.

I tip them, generously, because I'm running out of money, they just ruined my perfect day, and all my days for the next year or so, and so that deserves special recognition.

I'm numb with shock.

I walk out of the salon and immediately feel the chill on my head. Walking past shopping windows is an exercise in dealing with panic attacks, because every time I glance at my reflection, I feel like jumping in shock, horror, and disgust. Briefly, I consider a wig. Then I realise that it's already one o'clock, and I still have to iron the suit and shirt, and then make a booking at the restaurant for tonight. A part of me wants to delay the proposal, for maybe another year or two when I bear a resemblance to me again. But I'm here now, and I went to great lengths to make this happen tonight, and one trigger-happy hairdresser isn't going to change this!

With renewed determination, I head back in the direction of town, where the restaurant is. In an effort to keep my cool, I pull up my hood to hide my head both from general view and from the cold. Still, my nerves are a wreck and when I arrive at the door of the restaurant and see how nice it is, with an elegant stone-framed entrance in a red-brick Georgian style terrace hotel, I lose some of my courage and think of drawing back. I'm not a fan of fancy restaurants, but Harry is, and now that he has a bald boyfriend, he really deserves it more than ever. So I pull down my hood, run my hand along my skull, shudder at the feel of it, and then head in. The waitress who stands at the little counter with the reservations book open smiles politely when she says there are no tables available today.

"None at all?" I ask. "Not even later in the evening? Or earlier?"

"I'm sorry. We have bookings from weeks and months ago, sir."

I know this isn't personal, but now that I'm hideous, it *feels* personal. I feel like Julia Roberts in *Pretty Woman* except I'm no longer pretty. I feel like curling back into my coat, hissing at the lot of them, and dramatically crying: *A pox on all your houses!* But I leave like a normal person. It occurs to me after all that Orla does have a lot of contacts in the city, and she could get me a table either at this or at another equally good restaurant.

So, struggling to stay optimistic, I head out and ring the gallery. Orla's assistant, Aiden, picks up, and tells me that Orla isn't in at the moment.

"Just tell her to call me back when she's available," I say. "As soon as possible. It's kind of urgent."

He takes down the message and promises to deliver it. With this done, I go to a store, buy a pair of scissors to deal with all the tags on my newly purchased outfit, and then, while passing the cosmetics counter, decide to buy an exfoliator and a bunch of other beauty products. God knows I need them now.

I decide to go back to the hotel and calm myself by taking a bubble bath and preparing my suit before showtime. When I reach the hotel doors, I see my reflection again. "Ah!"

I make the doorman jump. "Sir! Are you all right?"

"Yes, yes, I'm fine," I say. "Sorry. Sorry."

I apologise to the pair of old women who were just passing out of the hotel, and then rush to the lifts. Once in the room, I feel calmer. I see the shirt Harry had prepared this morning to wear this evening. He ironed it while I watched TV, because he's good at this and I am, er, less so. But no matter, I can still catch up. After all, I've given myself plenty of time for a reason—I'm a novice at this.

I unpack the suit, cut off all the tags, and lay it out on the bed. The suit itself, I realise after reading the tag, shouldn't be ironed. One learns new things every day. This cuts my workload in half, which is another win for me. So, once the clothes are laid out, I undress and draw myself a bath. I'm a little hungry, so I order room service. I know better now than to go to a fancy restaurant hungry. I check my phone, but there's no news from Orla yet. But it's not even three, so there's plenty of time still, and no need for me to panic. I put on the TV, draw on the dressing gown, and then let the waiter in with my lunch.

I wonder if all men in the history of the world went to this much trouble when preparing to propose. Something tells me that if they did, the human race would be long extinct.

I watch *Horrible Histories* while eating my lunch and that helps me relax. It's going to be fine. It's going to be great. The whole hair incident—an anecdote we can tell our friends for years afterwards.

I throw the dressing gown off and climb into the bath, now a pleasant warm temperature. I examine the different products I bought today. I'm not into beauty products, and neither is Harry, but maybe I should be. The first one is a lotion that promises radiant skin. Sign me up! Hopefully it's so fucking radiant it blinds everyone at least until some of my hair grows back.

There's an exfoliating gel, which I rub all over my face and which makes my skin sting. Once out of the tub, I pat myself dry and put the radiant lotion on. Then I remember the face mask I purchased, and dab blobs of it onto my face, before realising it's four, and I still haven't got a table booked for tonight.

While the mask dries on my face, I wash my hands and get on with ironing the shirt. I haven't ever done this before, but I've seen Harry do it a million times, and he makes it look easy-peasy. I can't find the iron, though there is an ironing board. A quick call to reception and I put on the dressing gown again, though now that I've had my bath the whole bathroom and room is steamed up and humid, and when the iron arrives I wait for the guy who brought it to leave so I can slip out of the robe again.

I know that it's imperative to heat up the iron first. Harry always puts it on, and then leaves it to stand on the little holder at the side of the board while he arranges his shirt in portions. First the sleeves, then the front, then the back. Not forgetting the collar. As I said, easy-peasy.

At least, on paper it seems as though it should be, but actually, even though I let the iron stand for a bit, and even though I portion the shit out of that bloody shirt, and even though I glide through its snowy whites with the bloody iron, it seems to do absolutely nothing. Harry's shirt, the one he somehow ironed this very morning, is hanging off the wardrobe door, mocking me. Where the hell did he get the iron from? Or, perhaps more pertinently, where the fuck did he hide it afterwards? Did he know I was going to need it? Did he try to tell me, in this subtle way, to keep away from the iron because I wouldn't know the magic spell to make that tool of the devil do anything useful?

Frustrated with my negligible results, I start to press down onto the shirt really hard, grinding my teeth, thinking warm thoughts of the suffragette movement, which worked tirelessly to liberate womankind from this slave work, when I notice that I haven't plugged the iron into the socket. I touch the underside of it, and it's stone-cold.

The door to my room bursts open. My heart jumps as seven enormous men spill in, freezing mid-chatter in the entry way as they see me, naked, teeth grinding, wielding an iron, face covered in mud-green goo. They stare at me. I stare at them.

"Yes, can I help you?" I ask, holding the iron up to show that I am armed. The expression on their faces informs me, however, that they're more scared of me than I'm of them.

"Oh, sorry, mate," says the ringleader, a round-faced, round-eyed, pudgy fellow, with short cropped ginger hair and watery blue eyes. "We thought this was Harry's room."

"Wh— You mean Harry Byrne?" I lower the iron.

"Yes," says another of the lot. This one is slightly taller, slightly less pudgy, and younger looking. "He said to come here. He said to drop this off." He raises a heavy jar of something.

A third, dark-haired lad pipes up, "Are you Harry's boyfriend, or is this, er, something else?" He eyes me up and down with a dubious expression on his face.

"What?"

I remember now that I am in fact naked. The thing is, I am naked a lot. I grab the dressing gown and wrap it around me.

"Who are you?" I ask. "Where is Harry?"

"We're Harry's cousins," says the pudgy one, waving his thumb at himself and at the blokes that crowd behind him. "We just came to drop this off for him." Again the jar is shown to me.

"It's Grandma's coddle," he says, setting it on the table, reluctant to come farther into the room than this, and retreating to the entryway as soon as the jar is firmly placed. I don't know what to say. This is all very unnerving.

"Where is Harry?" I ask again.

"He's been trying to get hold of you," says the pudgy one.

I remember my phone—it's discharged. I curse. Harry's cousins watch me as I hunt for a charger, stumble, nearly pull a lamp down, straighten in a very dignified way and plug my phone in. It powers on leisurely, as if unaware of its own importance. My temples are throbbing.

Ten missed calls. Six from Harry. Four from Orla.

Great, I think. The restaurant. I can't forget about the restaurant.

I go to my contacts, my favourites, look for Harry's number at the top. The phone flashes up, vibrates in my hand. It's Orla. Shit.

My finger is a little shaky as I try to pick up. "Hello?"

It's her assistant, Aiden. "Er, Joe?"

"Yes?"

"Er, small matter, nothing alarming, but, er, well, ah, this lunatic came in, claiming to be your boyfriend, and is kicking up a stink. Thought you might know something about it."

My stomach drops.

"My— Do you mean— What does he look like?"

"Er, tall, well-dressed, he's giving Orla the dressing down of her life? Do you know him, by any chance? He seems to think that your exhibition was meant to be today, and—and he seems to think that, since it isn't, we've scammed you?"

"I'll be right there. Sorry about that. I'll sort it out, just give me a few minutes, okay?"

Bugger, bugger, *bugger*!

I hang up, slip off my dressing gown, and reach for the new suit trousers to put them on, before I realise that the room door is still wide open and that seven grown men are standing there, staring at me.

"Well?" I ask, impatiently. "Do you want to come in to have a better look?"

They all vigorously shake their heads and retreat. One of them meekly says, "Nice to meet you," as though he can't help his own politeness, as he leaves. I ignore them, throw on the crumpled shirt and the suit, leaving the tie and belt behind.

Then I run out of the hotel. I have a feeling that everybody is staring at me. Cars slow down. Children plaster their faces to the car windows to look at me. People stop and stare in the street. A woman turns the corner and then cries out and drops her shopping.

What's with everybody?

The gallery is two blocks away, which is not a comfortable distance to run, especially in new clothes I swore I wasn't going to get dirty. I find myself praying, as I haven't done in years, that this business Aiden spoke of isn't about Harry after all, that it's an actual lunatic who just randomly decided to ruin my life.

But when I reach the gallery, I find that prayers, as usual, go unanswered. There is a small crowd gathered around the reception desk to the left of the main gallery room. I can see Harry, with his fists on his hips and a stern expression in his face.

Orla is saying, "But it isn't our fault!"

"What kind of organisation is this? Do you call yourself the manager of this place or do you not?" Harry demands. "Because if you do, then you have a duty not just to your customers but also to the artists who sacrifice precious hours of hard work to—"

He spots me, and the words die in his mouth. Everybody spots me. They all look horrified. Harry most of all. First his eyes widen, then he frowns, and then, narrowing his eyes, as though barely recognizing me, he says, "Joe?"

"Harry."

I don't know what else to say. I can see my reflection in the enormous mirror that hangs behind the reception desk. I forgot to wipe off the facial before leaving the hotel. I look like the actual Mask from the movie *The Mask*.

"What happened to your hair?" Harry asks. "And your face . . . what are you wearing?"

Orla, indignant, says, "Oh good, you've come. Maybe you can explain to me what the meaning of all this is?"

"I—" I begin, but there's too much and, frankly, I'm a little in awe of how much can go wrong in one day.

The door to the gallery opens, and a man walks in.

"Harry? I found a parking space . . ." he says, before pausing and realising that something isn't as it should be. "What's the matter?"

It's Kieran.

Chapter Eight

KIERAN

Five Years Before the Big Day

I sat in our wicker chair and stared at my phone. Chloe eyed me suspiciously from above her reading glasses. The silver beehive on her head was particularly frizzy this day, little bits of wiry hair limned by the light of the lamp next to her head. She was carving a tiny wooden figurine for her goddaughter.

"Should've thrown that phone in the loo when I last had the chance," she muttered.

I sighed and leaned back. Harry hadn't called. It had been two weeks. Two weeks since we'd been on an uneven but ultimately amazing date. The following day he'd had to leave for a business trip to Berlin. That trip had ended two days ago. I knew this, because four days ago I'd submitted my final portfolio to Maya, and Malcolm had come in, irate, demanding to know when Harry was landing at Heathrow. Maya had told, and I'd been like a wasp in a jar ever since. I couldn't sleep. I couldn't eat. Honestly, I'd looked up my symptoms online, and the things I found there were not cheering.

"I think I've got cancer," I told Chloe.

"You'll have my slipper up your bum if you don't calm down soon," she grumbled.

I looked at my phone again. It was definitely on and charged. I'd texted Frank to see if it was receiving. Judging by the lengthy phone call from him, in which he went into incredible detail about how he and Gabriella had had sex on her boss's desk at her Christmas party, my phone was working just fine. My memory needed wiping, but that was another problem.

Chloe rolled her eyes. "You do realise this isn't Victorian times, right? Your mother and his mother are not going to come to an arrangement over you two."

My cheeks heated. "I know."

"What are you waiting for, then? Text him already."

Perhaps this would have been slightly less difficult for a man of nearly thirty if he'd had a less religious and restrictive upbringing and normal romantic experiences. I'd never asked a man out before—it was easy enough to wink at someone and suggest hanky-panky. How did one wink and suggest a relationship?

I looked up at Chloe and wanted to ask, but I knew what she'd say. Relationships were bogus, unnecessary, and she avoided them at all cost. Asking Frank would have been equally useless. He didn't choose his relationships. He tumbled into them, heart first.

I went to the kitchen, took out a bottle of wine, and hid in my room. It took several swigs before I had the courage to even pick up my phone.

With a feeling of doom in my heart and tightness in my stomach, I stared at the last text message I got from Harry: *Make sure you retain all the receipts. Maya will know what to do with them. H.*

Not sexy, but okay. We could change that.

Dear Harry, I typed.

I remembered that I wasn't writing a letter. Delete.

Hi there, did you know

Okay, no, awkward. Delete. Delete. Delete.

Hi there, Joe here.

Hi there, Joe here, Harry there, awkward here. Delete.

Hi, this is Joe, your

Christ, what was wrong with me?

Hi, this is Joseph. In the words of the immortal

I took a big swig of wine because there was a desperate lack of chill involved in what was meant to be first contact. Or was it? We'd done this before. This wouldn't be our first anything, surely.

I put the phone down and then, with a jump of my heart, I realised that I'd pressed Send! Fuck!

I stared at the text message for five minutes and, as no response came, wondered if, since I had no bathtub, I could drown myself in the shower instead.

And then, just as I was googling how to live off the grid as a hermit in a forest, my phone buzzed in my hand.

Hi :)

I stared at the word and the smiley and wondered if he'd mistaken me for somebody else.

It's Joe, I wrote.

Oh I know. Do you go by Joseph in the Words of the Immortal now or do I still get to call you Joe?

Joe for short is fine, I responded, slapping my forehead hard enough to smart five minutes later.

How are you? he wrote.

Well, at least he was still talking to me. Somehow, by some cosmic luck, I managed to text him like a normal human being hereafter, enough so, at least, to get him to invite me to a party he was hosting that weekend.

I'll send you the link, he wrote.

Moments later he sent the link to a website. While I imagined the party was something along the lines of the parties I usually hosted (namely, "everybody back to my place, bring your own drink"), it was, in fact, a large event at a hired venue for which one had to buy a ticket. It wasn't exactly what I was hoping for, but the tickets weren't expensive, and the money was going to a mental health charity of which he was one of the trustees.

A sensible man might have felt discouraged by an invitation so unlike an actual date. All I could think was, *I'm going to see Harry again*.

In a case like this, there was only one way to impress a man, and that was to bring friends. Dutifully, then, I gathered my friends, forced them to purchase a ticket, and promised them a good time in return.

This was the first time I met Gabriella. Since Frank had spoken of her so often and in tones of exalted horniness, the image I'd had of her in my mind was that of a blonde, skimpily dressed sex-vixen. So when the two of them arrived at my flat and she was standing, diffidently, at his side, I wasn't quite prepared for what I saw.

Gabriella looked . . . normal. She was in her midtwenties, a big girl, with a pretty, round face and dimples in her shiny cheeks when she smiled. She had small, twinkly dark eyes, a chestnut fringe to attractively frame her face, and she wore a flowery dress and black leggings. She greeted me with every sign of being overjoyed.

"Joe? Oh dear, Frank talks about you so much!" she said, beaming. She was much more the vicar's daughter than I'd imagined.

Chloe said, "Okay, so champagne-wise, how are we standing? Anybody? Joe, you have a cement mixer for a stomach, so you will be my test subject. Give me your glass."

"Oh shet," Frank said, when he realised what was happening, "are *you* going to be opening that bottle? Everybody hide!"

"What's that supposed to mean?"

"Last time you nearly had my eye out, woman. Give me that."

"Typical man," Chloe cried, pulling the bottle away from him, like it was her baby about to be confiscated by some evil military force.

"It's not a man thing," Frank said, irritably. "It's you who is cack-handed!"

On the quarrel went. Even after we did, safely, open the bottle and had some preparty drinks, they continued to bicker, and so in the cab I sat next to Gabriella, in an effort to get to know her better and, frankly, get my thoughts off Harry and the fact that I would be seeing him soon.

"Where'd you study?" I asked her.

"Sheffield," she said with a voice of ceremony, as if announcing something very special and important. "I read English literature and did some philosophy modules. I know what you're thinking: boring, right? But actually, I was really into it. Honestly, if you'd known me then, you'd have thought I was possessed or something!" She giggled.

"What did you study?" she asked then, staring right into my eyes, as if to say, *I want to know you, Joseph Kaminski. I want to* know *you.*

"Ah, I didn't."

I expected an awkward moment, but she didn't wait for it to even start.

"No? Well, too many people do, if you ask me." She changed the subject. "Frank showed me some of your work. It was breathtaking.

I mean it. I literally held my breath, and he had to tell me, he said, 'Gabriella, lass, breathe!'"

I liked her. She was bubbly and sweet, and much less scary than what Frank had, inadvertently, made her out to be.

Chatting to her took the edge off for me, because the nearer we got to the party, the tenser I felt. I hadn't seen Harry for two weeks. What if he'd stopped fancying me since then?

The venue appeared modest from the outside—a narrow Victorian building on Bateman Street. We stumbled out of the cab; Chloe and Frank argued about who'd pay, and Gabriella took my arm, gazed up at the sky, and said, "Isn't it romantic, Joe? The moon is like a pearl on a canvas of satin . . ."

I looked up, surprised to find that her description was accurate. The night did feel . . . momentous?

"That was beautiful," I said to her.

We rang the door and moments later were let inside by a smiling waitress whose crimson lipstick contrasted with the geisha-white of her foundation.

"Tickets please?" she said.

I showed her the tickets on my phone. She nodded and smiled and said, "Follow me."

Inside, the space was rather more up-market than the outside led us to believe, with pillars set in the walls and decorative mouldings. Chandeliers cast the rooms in a magnificent, flattering light. As everybody had taken Harry's order of "casual party" attire to mean "meeting the Queen," my friends and I were the only people there not dressed to the nines. Well, except for Chloe, who did, as usual, look like she'd escaped from the set of *Sunset Boulevard*.

We were first spotted by Maya, who was very chic in a frilly, floor-length dress of dark purple, with a black hijab. She beamed when she saw me.

"Joseph, you naughty boy," she said. "You're late, you missed the big speech!"

"Okay, I should have known better than to think Harry would ever have a simple party," I said. "What speech? Are we receiving the Pope? Why is everybody so formal?"

"Don't you know"—her eyes twinkled up at me—"we are in very exalted company."

"I knew it. He did invite the Pope."

She laughed. "Not quite. But you'll recognize a few faces for sure. Who'd you bring?"

I introduced my rather ramshackle entourage, but Maya didn't seem to notice anything amiss with them.

"Here, there's a waiter with a tray," she said, waving at a handsome young Spanish man who floated about the place gracefully, with long champagne glasses reflecting the tasteful lighting. We all received a glass, and Maya offered to introduce us to anybody we liked.

"Most of these are our clients, some are contacts Harry has in the mayor's office," she explained. Then, in a conspiratorial whisper, she added, "The strange ones are Malcolm's family. You be nice to them, you hear?"

"I'm always nice!"

"Oi, Joe." Frank elbowed me. "So, which one's your chap?"

"Over there," Chloe said, tipping the champagne glass up and downing it in one gulp. "Where's Enrique Iglesias? I'm out of tipple."

There was Harry. My heart lifted. He was standing slightly turned away from me, talking with great animation to a distinguished Indian couple. One of his colleagues saw me, stood in Harry's field of vision, gave him a sign that I was there, and he turned, eyebrows raised, eyes peeled. Chloe had coached me about how to play it cool when I saw him again. I wished this were a movie where everything suddenly goes into slow motion in moments like this. Instead, everything went too quickly. There I was, staring and grinning at him.

He smiled. It was the smile of long familiarity, a sort of *ah, there you are* smile.

Frank said something to me, but I didn't hear. Chloe was pulling on my sleeve, but it was like she was in another room. I just wanted to say something to Harry. I wanted to hear his voice.

But then his eyes didn't really meet mine. I only noticed it when the figure he had actually been waiting for moved past me and towards him. A large, suited figure. The figure of Kieran Jones.

It was like watching someone slip in front of a racing bus. Stunned, I could do nothing as the horror unfolded before me.

They greeted each other. Harry approached him like he wanted to hug, but seemed to instead stretch his hand out for a shake and then decide against it. Kieran patted his shoulder. *Nice one, Kieran,* I thought, bitterly. *Why not pat him on the head, while you're at it? Moron.*

I became suddenly aware of how far away Harry actually was from me—at the other end of a very crowded room. It felt like a greater distance than that. Like he was in another country. I swallowed something hard that had lodged in my throat.

"Joe?"

I stirred, at last, and blinked.

"Yeah?" I turned to Frank.

"I know the DJ," Frank said. "Want to see if we can get her to bring this zombie fest to life?"

I barely registered him, but yes, I did want to move away from where I was and do something, anything, other than stand here and watch Harry gaze at Kieran like that.

Maya and Gabriella were engaged deep in conversation, and Chloe had been recognized by one of her admirers and was allowing him to gush over how well she looked. Frank and I walked through a doorless opening to where the DJ stood on a little podium. Her name was Verena, and moments later Frank was kissing her cheeks and they were reminiscing about that time when they performed together at the Ultra Europe festival in Croatia. Frank's not musical in the slightest, but he'd been drunk at the time and somebody'd dared him, and he'd done much more for far less.

"That was the first time I crowd-surfed!" He laughed, while Verena brayed like a horse, crying, "Crowd-surfed? You were butt naked and they were carrying you away from security!"

Frank puffed out his chest.

"Would have got away, too, if they hadn't pulled my leg off."

"Stupid," Verena said, ruffling Frank's head.

I needed something to eat. Not really because I was hungry, but to get a moment away, to be by myself. A waitress in a Janelle Monáe suit floated past with canapés. I followed.

"Is that beef?" I asked, trying to discern something of the tiny little collections of crumbs on the tray.

"Joe?"

I looked up from the silver platter, astonished at this directness, and then recognized the waitress. The room suddenly felt very small, and the doors very far away. I forced my chest to expand to breathe.

"Amy."

Last time I'd seen her, my mum and I had just been D-ed, and she and her sister ignored my mum's "good morning" and crossed the street. My mum had looked as if she'd been slapped.

"Oh my God!" she said, feeling none of my reserve apparently. "You look amazing! How have you been?"

Fear hooked my stomach. An old feeling, like I'd just remembered an exam I hadn't prepared for. I found myself scanning the room for my other "brothers" and "sisters."

Amy seemed to be the only one, and she was smiling at me, waiting for a response.

"Good?" I ventured.

"Is it true what they say?" she said, leaning in, as if sharing a secret.

Considering the sort of stuff I'd heard my "brothers" and "sisters" say about those who'd become "worldly" I couldn't imagine what she meant, but it couldn't have been anything nice.

"That depends, I suppose."

She smiled conspiratorially. "They said you left to find your family in Africa and became a prince in Nigeria."

I bit my lip. She seemed absolutely serious, and I didn't want to guffaw in her face.

"No, I'm not a Nigerian prince," I said. "But thanks for checking."

She coloured, leaned back. "Oh, sorry. I thought— There was this woman who came by the Kingdom Hall once, looking for you. I thought—"

Someone waved for the canapés, and she reached for my arm, pressed it, and said, "Catch you later, yeah?"

What woman? Frowning, I watched her go.

"Pst."

Someone touched my elbow. Brown hair in a carefully crafted disorder, a crooked smile on his lips, and a glint of a dirty memory in his silver eyes. "Hey, stranger," Harry said. "Hiding, are we?"

"Hunting for food, actually."

I got to play it cool after all, even though all my senses were heightened and I really wanted to kiss the corner of his smirk.

"Ah, I've got something for you," he said with no small sense of satisfaction. He took my hand in a warm, firm clasp and throwing, "Come, let me show you," over his shoulder, he walked me through to the other end of the room. There was a door, painted the same fashionable dark grey as the wall, and he opened it only slightly to let us through. On the other side, there was nothing but a staircase in semidarkness. He closed the door behind us, making it darker still.

"What are we—" I began, but he reached for the front of my shirt and pulled me to him in one smooth move, placing a kiss on my lips. The kissing. It was like the sun came up again, bursting into the sky in shades of blood orange and gold.

I tugged on his belt.

"No, not here," he said, stopping me. "That's not what I wanted to show you. I just—I just haven't seen you in a while."

"Not my fault. I never went anywhere."

"Well, I missed—" He stopped, shook his head, and seemed to laugh at himself. "Never mind. Can I show it to you now?"

"You just said not here!"

"Not that, you perv. It's downstairs."

We went down two flights of stairs, to a cooler basement area, and through a big, heavy door into a professional kitchen.

"What's this?"

"I remembered how hungry you got, so I prepared," he said, grinning at me over his shoulder. "Wouldn't want to find you gnawing on my thigh later this evening."

"You sure about that?"

He chuckled, and then crossed the long silver cooking range to the oven and pulled out a foil-covered plate. He unwound it delicately, ceremoniously. A plate of fish and chips.

"I made it myself," he said, scratching the back of his head, a little redder about the cheeks. "It's a special recipe of mine."

"A special— Mate, this is—" I didn't know what to say. I looked about me—he'd clearly only cooked that one meal. There were potato peels on a small part of the surface, and bread crumbs, and he'd clearly used the deep fryer, because the basket had been washed and was lying, still dripping, upside down on a rack.

"Are you going to eat it?" he asked.

"Yes. Yes, of course." Right. Eating. I had to make my mouth stop smiling first. "Thank you."

We shared the chips, and I asked him how he'd found the time to cook.

"I was a little nervous before it started," he said with a humble shrug. "So I thought I'd do something with my hands. What do you think?"

They were the best fish and chips I'd ever eaten. They tasted of someone making a meal just for you. Sweet and warm and like home.

"Marry me," I said, putting my hand dramatically to my heart.

He shoved my shoulder, laughing. "Idiot. Eat your fish."

While I ate, he told me of his trip to Berlin. He'd gone there to meet a young Russian activist who'd been imprisoned and now, released, was publishing a sort of memoir or call to action.

"I really want it," he told me. "But she's justifiably scared of publicity."

"And publicity is what you do."

He nodded. "Hell yeah. I want that book in every house in the country. We are so bloody oblivious to the world around us and my job is so—" He sighed with frustration. "Well, there's something I *can* do, something we're good at, and I want to do it."

"What docs Malcolm say?"

"He thinks it's stupid. But if I host parties like these, and he can invite his aunts and uncles and have them meet the mayor or someone they've seen on TV, then I can keep him happy and go after my own things. Things that matter, you know?"

He was hot when he was righteous.

"I can help you," I said. "I can do book covers or posters, if you like."

"Thank you, but it will be a modest undertaking, if I get it at all—"

"I mean it," I said. "I'd be honoured to do something. You can pay me in shags. I warn you, though, I'm expensive."

Laughingly, he grabbed my collar again and kissed me.

He could not hide from his own party for long. I'd have stayed there with him all evening, and he seemed inclined to linger, but his phone was buzzing in his pocket, and we knew someone upstairs needed him.

I finished the whole plate and then washed it up, and then we went back upstairs together. Once back in the crowd, he had to attend his business, and I searched for my friends.

Frank had convinced Verena to play funk, and he and Gabriella were now leading the dance floor. Chloe was already tipsy. She was sitting on a tall barstool, and had acquired three more men in her entourage. She was entertaining them with stories of how she'd inspired Kurt Schwitters in the sixties, and how she'd hung out with Francis Bacon and David Hockney.

It was amusing to me how self-important she became when surrounded by those fawning idiots.

"She's like—like Jeanne Duval!" one of her acolytes told me, his ashen complexion positively shining in a blush of admiration.

"Didn't Duval give Baudelaire syphilis?" I asked.

"Kiki De Montparnasse!"

"Drugs and alcohol," I recollected. "Neal Cassady, perhaps?"

He shot me a poisonous glare, and I left, amused. The party seemed to be swinging now. Frank's music choices (or Verena's desire to impress him with hers) were waking these people up, and in the dancing room, the crowd was going steadily wilder.

In the first room, though, everything was still pretty staid and dignified. I went around, in search of Harry, to see if I could lend a hand with anything. As I moved across the room, I suddenly found myself almost at Kieran's elbow. *Shit. Better turn around.* He was engaged in a low-voiced conversation with a handsome old gentleman in a velvet suit jacket. I didn't want them to notice me, so I turned back, only to nearly trip into another man.

This one wore glasses, and his grey-brown hair was licked back from his forehead with something very flat.

"Oh! You're the gay, aren't you?" he said, very pleased to see me, apparently.

I stared at him. He was looking right at me, but I still hoped he might have meant someone else. He laughed. "I'm Paul! You work for my nephew Malcolm, don't you?"

"Ah, yes?"

I could feel Kieran turning beside me. The older gentleman he was with was observing me with stormy-grey eyes.

"No, no, don't worry," Paul said and then, winking, he added, "I'm awake, as you young people say. I know what's what, and all that, eh?"

Eh indeed, was my first thought. But having had experience with networking, I knew better than to say anything. What would Harry do in this situation? Probably smile and nod and find a way out with a smooth word.

"Sure," I said.

"Want one?" he asked, taking out a box of Marlboro Lights.

"I'm pretty sure we're not supposed to smoke in here."

"Let me ask you something," he said, sticking the cigarette behind his ear. "How difficult is it to be gay? I mean, on a scale of one to being married to a greedy arsehole, how terrible is it?"

I blinked, surprised. "Excuse me?"

"I was married, you know," he said. "Twenty years. Can you tell?"

He looked exactly like someone who'd been married twenty years, but trying to be polite I shook my head.

"She took me for everything. Just one day upped sticks and left, and took half my bank account with her. All the women I meet now, all they want to know is how much I earn and how big my house is. And when you tell them that you live with your mother and that you have the kids with you half the week, they lose interest at once. So, I've been thinking. I'd bloody love to have a boyfriend. Not the sex part, but all the rest. You could go out and see the footie together. He could pay the bloody bill once in a while. Nobody to nag at you. You could fart in front of each other. Heaven, if you ask me."

I rubbed the bridge of my nose. "Gosh, I don't know where to begin."

"How well would I do on your gay Tindr or Tumblr or what have you?" he asked, leaning back a little and presenting himself to me with his hand. His nose had the colour of smoked trout, his shirt stretched over the gut of a woman in her second trimester.

"I . . . I don't know what to say."

"Be honest. I'm okay with cuddling. And we could have an open sort of relationship, so he can go and get his rocks off with some other bloke and then come back to me. It's unusual, I grant you, but surely there must be somebody . . ."

"I—I really don't think a gay cuddler is what you want," I said, diplomatically. "Dating is hard for everybody, regardless. I'd say it's sort of harder for gay men, anyway."

"You're having me on!" he cried. "I thought you guys . . . you know . . . like rabbits!"

It's at this moment that Harry glided in, laughing nervously. "Mr. Peppard! How are you? I thought I missed you coming in. Has Maya shown you our canapés yet?"

He moved the old weirdo away from me and into Maya's direction. Kieran lifted his glass at me in a gesture of congratulations. "I think you've pulled, mate."

Harry turned to me with a surprised tilt to his head.

The old man, who'd been standing by watching the scene with a disgusted frown, sniffed.

"Malcolm had better keep his family under control," he grumbled. "One of his aunts arrived drunk and is sleeping under that table."

"Yes, thanks, Dad," Harry said. "You could give me a hand, you know."

"I am," the old man said. "I've stopped your mother from bringing her own canapés. Did you thank me? No."

Kieran repressed a laugh.

"Hardly a great accomplishment," Harry said. He was smiling, but I could see the strain in his eyes. "At least she offered to do something to help with the event."

"You've not seen what she was planning to bring," Mr. Byrne said. "If you had, you'd be publishing letters of thanks in the newspapers."

Harry rolled his eyes. "Yes, thanks, Dad."

Mr. Byrne, seeming to warm to the subject, waved his hand, as if presenting the headline: "Local fool thanks father. Poisoning of London averted."

He elbowed Kieran, who bit his lips, though his shoulders were shaking. Someone called Harry's name from the crowd, and he threw me an apologetic look and then rushed off to attend his guests. Kieran and Mr. Byrne returned to their conversation.

I watched as Harry hurried to greet some distinguished-looking new arrivals. From another part of the room, I caught Maya's eyes. She seemed a little forlorn, so I threaded my way to her side.

"What's the matter?"

"Oh, it's the usual." She sighed, chewing on her fingernail. "Everybody's happy to go to a charity ball, and to glam up and shake hands with people, but when it comes to loosening their purse strings..."

I hadn't considered. Glancing about me, at the smiling faces, hobnobbing for a tiny fee, I became resentful on Harry's behalf. How was the man to accomplish half of his noble goals if these rich bastards weren't willing to help?

"Leave it to me," I said, rolling up my sleeves.

Maya blinked up at me, wary. "Why? What are you going to do?"

"Nothing you won't have plausible deniability over, trust me," I said with a quick wink.

"Did you see that?"

Harry was drunk. His eyes were shiny, his cheeks flaring, and he was very loud.

"Ten thousand pounds!" he cried. He was sitting squarely on my lap, because we were stuffed into the back of the cab like a bunch of clowns.

"Not quite ten grand," Frank said. "Could've got more if Chloe'd agreed."

Chloe was napping in her corner of the cab, but I could respond for her. "She wouldn't get married for anything."

Harry hiccoughed.

"How'd you do it?" he said, stroking my face. I wasn't sure why he'd begun drinking so much, but when I found him at the end of the night, he could barely stand up straight.

"Oh, it was easy," Frank said. "We're artists—if we don't know how to get money out of people, trust me, we'd never get paid at all!"

Depressing but true.

"The trick is to be exuberant, energetic, and overbearing," Frank said.

"The mistake people make," I added, "is that they're afraid to ask. You and Maya were being very middle class about it. Frank and I went for the cowboy method."

Harry laughed and kissed me.

"Get a room!" Frank demanded. Gabriella giggled against his shoulder.

We spilled out of the cab together, Frank remembering to pay and tip the driver, and I had to half carry Harry up the stairs to the flat. I laid him down on the bed in the recovery position, a little worried about how much he'd had to drink.

His phone was vibrating, and fell out of his pocket as I placed him on the bed.

I didn't mean to look, but the messages kept flashing up on the screen as I picked it up to put it on the bedside table for him, and I worried it might be an emergency, considering how many messages were arriving all together.

02:49 Mum: *We are very concerned. K. says you have not been returning his calls, and that's hardly a mature way to behave. The woman I told you about is a relationship counsellor with a great deal of experience. I'll text you her number. Please give her a call.*

02:49 Kieran: *Had a nice time tonight. Sorry if it was awkward. Early start tomorrow, but I'll give you a ring when I get back from CD. Nice suit btw. Tyrwhitt?*

02:50 Kieran: *Ollie said he wanted to watch the rugby with me on Saturday. Maybe you can come with?*

02:50 Siobhan: *Do you want to have dinner with Ollie and Kieran on Saturday? Kieran's coming over to watch the game, so it could be like old times <3 <3 <3 Had a nice time tonight! Congratulations on the huge donations!!!*

Embarrassed, I put the phone away. I lay awake at Harry's side, listening to it buzz more, jabbed by irritation every time it did. It took much not to reply on Harry's behalf and tell them to get a life.

Early in the morning, I was woken up by Gabriella rushing out to make it to church on time. Harry and Frank were still asleep, so I helped her fix up and let her out.

"Tell him I'll text him later," she said, kissed my cheek, and then rushed out. I locked up after her.

I checked on Chloe, but she was right as rain, meditating in her room. She didn't acknowledge hangovers.

When I returned to my room after a lengthy shower, Harry was up. Bleary-eyed, he was checking his phone and rubbing his stubble. I remembered the messages I'd seen the night before and tried to see by his expression what he felt in response. But he only looked worn. That is, until he saw me, and his frown melted into a smile.

"Sorry," he said. "I don't really remember how I got here. Was I hard to handle last night?"

"You crashed immediately. Do you want Aspirin?"

He shook his head and stretched out his hand to me. It was a gesture of such easy familiarity, a tingle went down to my stomach. I sat astride his lap. The towel I had wound around my hips loosened, and he pulled it apart and threw it to the floor.

"How do you look this good after a night that long?" He laughed. "I feel like someone's dragged me out of the sewer."

He kissed my shoulder, then tilted his head sideways, examining my tattoo. "A hummingbird?" He let his finger trace its edges.

"Jamaican national bird. I designed it."

"Oh?"

"It symbolises peace and love."

"It's nice. Are you Jamaican?"

It was funny to me how we'd been so intimate before and knew so little about each other. He must have felt it too, because he smiled and said, "What?"

"I'm British," I said. "I was told my parents were Jamaican."

There was a question in his eyes, but clearly he didn't want to prod, so I volunteered, "I'm adopted. I don't know much about my birth parents."

"Oh, I'm sorry."

I shook my head. "Nothing to be sorry about. One day, when I've earned enough money, I'll go to Jamaica and find out more about them."

He caressed my shoulder again. "Can you not find out anything from here?"

"It's hard. My birth parents, whoever they are, didn't leave me much to go on, and they're no longer in Britain, which makes the process more complicated and far more expensive than I can afford. I'm working on it. Those drawers over there? All full of files and leads. One day, I'm going to find them."

"Why did they give you up?" he asked. Then, clearly catching himself, "Is that something I shouldn't be asking?"

I shook my head. "I don't really know. My mum says it's because they were very young, like teenagers. I'm not bothered about their reasons. My mum's a treasure, and I wouldn't give her up for the world. I'm so lucky she's the one who got me."

There was sympathy in his expression, so I smiled past it and said, "What about you? What would you tattoo on your chest, if you had to?"

He frowned in thought. "I don't know . . . a shamrock?"

I laughed. "Christ. Why?"

"Because I'm Irish," he said in an Irish accent he didn't usually have.

"You're Irish?" I said, imitating the accent.

"It's Irish not Oyrish."

It sounded the same to me.

"Say 'something Irish,'" he said in the accent.

"Sum-tin' Oyrish," I said, which made him crack up again.

"Here." He took my jaw in his hand lightly. "Soften that *t* sound you make there, and it's not an *oy*, more something between an *oy* and an *ay*."

I said it like he said it, mostly because he said it really close to my face, and then he kissed me. I said "Irish" again, and he kissed me again.

"Was this to shut me up or a reward for getting it right?"

"Neither." He winked at me.

"In that case . . ." I said, pressing his hand to my crotch.

"You have a very direct way of putting things," he murmured. "You should be a writer."

"Can you imagine the sort of things I would write?"

"I shudder to think." He kissed my jaw and curled his fingers around my cock.

"Probably porn," I said. "I wouldn't intend it to be porn, but it would turn into porn in the end. You know, like . . . 'Rory walked down the paddock to tell Brett about his uncle's secret plan to poison the king. Brett turned around. His lederhosen bulged invitingly.' It would go downhill from there."

At this Harry lost his composure and, shoulders shaking, let his forehead fall down on my chest.

"'Lederhosen'?" he said unsteadily.

"Oh yes, the whole kingdom is terribly fond of them. That and oil. And," I added in a moment of inspiration, "spanking!"

He turned his laughing face up to me and I kissed him.

"I like you," I said.

He stopped kissing me for a moment, surprised. "I like you too."

He wasn't as impatient as I was—he stroked and kissed me as though time didn't exist, and there was nothing but the two of us, a bed, and eternity. My hand wound into his hair and I closed my eyes. Why did this feel so much better than anything I'd ever experienced before? His lips, warm and soft, his tongue playful, everything felt so . . . *God, I love this . . . I love him.*

"What do you want to do?" he asked, when my lips were not on his, but pressing against the warm skin down his neck.

"Having you on your back is a start to what I want," I said, pushing him back against the pillow and kissing his collarbone, and then down to his nipple. Every part of him I felt on my tongue echoed warmth through my body to every nerve ending. A sweet sense of belonging, of wanting him close, closer, more than skin to skin . . . I sucked on his nipple, gently, and then he pulled my face up to his. His kisses were now full of tongue, as if he, too, wanted to taste me, as if there wasn't enough of me in him yet. We struggled to get my cover to stop dividing us, and then sighed with relief when we could touch more of each other. But it wasn't enough. I hooked his leg over my hip and he groaned, a sound I could feel on my skin, travelling with a shiver through me, inside of me. His cock was flat against my abdomen, warm and hard, a thin line of pre-come connecting his tip to my skin.

"Joe . . ."

I reached down to his thigh, holding him close to me, worrying I was holding him too hard, wanting to pull him to me harder. I was throbbing with desires I didn't want to speak out loud.

"God, you feel so . . ." I breathed.

"I know," he sighed. "Ah . . ."

"Fuck . . ."

I ran my hand up his side, and pulled him to me more sharply, letting him feel the edge of my lust, letting him know: *say something, do something, or I will.*

He sucked on my lower lip and thrust his hip up, suggesting, inviting.

"I want to fuck you," I blurted out.

"Oh God yes." He sighed, relieved, and then stuck his tongue into my mouth. My heart throbbed with painful anticipation. I'd never done that before, but now it would happen and with him . . .

I love you, I love you, I love you . . . my heartbeat sang painfully. I kissed down his chest, down his abdomen, wanting to make him feel this thing I was feeling.

"Ah, Christ," he hissed when I sucked him into my mouth as deeply as I could, my forehead resting against his abdomen. His hips rolled, his moans sounded strangled, his cock was hot and swollen in my mouth. Harry muttered, "Oh mother of— Ah!" He was sour and sweet on my tongue; when I came up again, every part of me tingled with love and anticipation, my muscles tense, my vision a little blurry with lust.

He'd pressed lube onto his hand and now turned himself over on all fours, or threes really, and backed towards me, massaging his dripping hand over his crack. At first I could only watch and then, dizzy and feeling my balls rise and tense, my cock twitch, I moved closer and touched him.

He paused, looked over his shoulder. "Fingers, yeah?"

I nodded and positioned myself over him, kissing his back, the muscles of his back and shoulders rippling as he shifted to fit under me. My one arm embraced him; with my other hand I pressed one finger into him. I could feel the intake of his breath against my chest. His skin hot on mine. His pulse fast against mine.

I kissed him, lovingly, and let my heart go.

"I love this," I said. "You're amazing. I love you."

"Oh Joe . . ." He pushed himself against me. "Oh God, I need you."

Two fingers, three. It was like an electrical charge between us. He looked over his shoulder again, then pulled away from me.

"I want to turn around," he said. He fell onto his back and raised his knees up. "Come to me," he said, extending his arms to me.

My heart was hammering against my chest, my blood on fire. *Heaven help me.* The pressure of him around me was almost too much. I tried to breathe, tried to somehow control my urge to drive into him, but my thoughts were being chased by instincts over which I had no control whatsoever. "Oh God . . . I think I'll come really fast."

"Slowly," he said. "Come deeper."

I pushed in all the way. I had to stop and close my eyes hard.

My arms stretched straight on either side of him; he caressed his hands up them, calm in contrast to the storm in my veins.

"How does it feel for you?" I asked, strained, watching him anxiously.

"So good." He glided his hands up my arms all the way to my neck and drew me down. "Come here, handsome. Kiss me."

I lowered onto him. My mouth descended onto his and I kissed him, deeply, and then began to grind. For a moment I could see and hear nothing, and everything inside me was liquid.

I pulled back a little and felt the tight clench of him, and the warmth of him, and the power of the friction, and I let out a groan deep from my throat.

"Oh God, Harry . . . This is . . ."

"So good," he said, again, like a sigh. His hands glided to my bottom and then he suddenly thrust up to me, hard. I gasped, surprised, since I was holding back from going really hard. But he clearly wanted it. His eyes met mine, a look so warm and longing it robbed me of my breath.

"Yeah?" I asked, returning the thrust of his hips.

"Oh yeah," he breathed, his eyes rolled up.

Once I began, I had no more control of it than I had of my heart beating. I was on my elbows now, covering almost the whole of him, my mouth open upon his, his arms around me, his knees high, holding me close, and his hips meeting mine in eager anticipation of each of my moves.

Whenever I came up for air and to make sure he was all right, he drew my head back towards him, kissing me deeply and winding his legs tighter around me, pushing against me, encouraging me to go on. So I did, holding nothing back, even though my bed was making unholy sounds and my bedposts were denting the wall. He came in hot jets against my chest, his moans stifled by my mouth.

It was for some moments that I lay heavily on top of him, having slipped out of him, my chest heaving and my heart trying to break loose. His arms were around me, his hand stroking my back. At some point, he drew the blanket over me, and then I fell asleep, holding him to me in a tight embrace, like I might drown if I let go. His heart thudded against mine. His sweat was my sweat.

"I do love you," I said, or perhaps dreamt.

Things to do when dating someone on the rebound:
1. Don't forget they're on the rebound.
2. See rule number one.
3. Tattoo rule number one on your forehead.
4. Hire an opera singer to sing rule number one to you in lieu of an alarm clock every morning.

Harry had told me that his sister was his twin, and that she would let me in if he ran late. Since the charity ball, he had popped by in the evenings, often tired from work and good for little more than a quick chat and some sleep. But this time we were going to go out, we'd agreed. I had news to share, and it was the sort of thing that called for a restaurant and drinks. I was to pick him up from his sister's flat, where he was still staying.

When I arrived, the door was opened by a tall, bearlike man with a beard, who let me in and introduced himself as Ollie. The Ollie, I presumed, who liked to watch rugby with Kieran.

Indeed, he didn't seem particularly pleased to meet me, even if he claimed the opposite as he shook my hand. His sister was worse. She held a mug in two hands and glared at me with suspicion and dislike from above its rim. This was Siobhan, then. The Siobhan who longed for the old times.

She said, "Harry's not come home yet. You'll have to wait for him."

We stood awkwardly in the kitchen until Ollie remembered that they had a sitting room and invited me to wait there. I thought that maybe they'd just leave me there, but no, they took seats opposite me on a red leather sofa, and I felt like I was at an audition.

"Do you want a drink, Joe?" Ollie asked in a way that made me think my choice of beverage would be used to form an opinion about me, all the options being unfavourable to my outcome.

"Er, no thanks."

We fell silent.

"So," Siobhan said, eyes still narrowed, "I understand that you're an artist? What does that mean?"

It sounded less like a conversation gambit and more like an exam question. My hands were sweaty. I shifted in my seat but attempted to smile.

"I did some art work for his agency."

"So you paint, yes?" Ollie asked. "Or sculpt? Or write? Poetry or something?"

"All sorts of things."

Ollie and Siobhan exchanged glances, as if to confirm to each other that I fell short of already low expectations.

My gaze travelled past them to the shelves on their TV unit. They held books and various decorative knick-knacks. Among them, unmistakably, framed pictures of Harry, Kieran, Siobhan, and Ollie together, their arms around one another on a windy beach, smiles on their faces. Of course.

I turned my attention to the other walls in the room.

"You have some nice prints," I said, nodding at the framed posters on the wall next to them. "What are these, old French advertising?"

Siobhan turned around, and softening a little, she said, "They're vintage French theatre posters. I collect them."

"Sweet. They're really cool. Do you like theatre?"

"I do."

"I sometimes work for theatres," I said. "Mostly staging and costume work. It's a lot of fun."

Something in her eyes came alive when I said this, but she held back.

"Once," I said, "I was helping with a production of *The Misanthrope*, and it was *such* a fiasco."

Her lips clenched. Ollie shifted in his seat, throwing warning looks her way.

"We had mice, for one," I continued. "Which meant that Arsinoé's costume had two enormous holes right here." I drew circles with my fingers around my nipples.

Siobhan tried to stifle a laugh. Ollie took the mug out of her hand.

"And then we forgot to ready Alceste's wig until the evening of the performance, so that when he put it on, it just looked like a grey afro."

"What did you do?" Siobhan asked, clearly unable to help herself.

"Okay, so there's a trick to wigs," I said. "Normally, you have to treat them with pomade, and comb through them, and that keeps them for some time. But this wig wasn't made out of human hair. In fact, the way it came out in the end, I'm not sure it wasn't made from some sort of martian rodent. Anyway, nobody used any pomade on it at all; they just let it stand, and so the hair stiffened and stood on all ends. But there's a way of getting around that— Here, let me show you."

When the door opened twenty minutes later, and Harry came in, rushed, Siobhan, Ollie, and I froze.

Siobhan was sitting in a chair with a full-on eighteenth-century à la candor hairstyle, which Ollie and I were in the middle of decorating with items from their Christmas decoration box. She looked magnificent. Harry's eyes widened. Siobhan's eyes widened. Ollie's smile checked, as if he'd been caught doing something illicit. Harry smiled.

"So, I see you met Joe."

Siobhan, back straight, said stiffly, "We were just keeping him company while he waited for you."

I could tell she was trying to sound like this had been a great imposition on her patience. Harry rolled his eyes slightly.

"Sure," he said, and then, turning to me, "Shall we?"

He didn't bother to change (and why would he, he was always very well put together), and so we left at once.

It was a cold evening, and we rushed from one indoor place to another, trying to avoid the mucky roads and the drizzle. Eventually, we found ourselves in a sushi restaurant.

We ordered two drinks, and Harry told me about Malcolm's latest idea: to bring his cousin onto the board of directors.

"He has no assets, education, contacts, or experience," Harry said, exasperated. "What could go wrong?"

"To be fair, Malcolm's a muppet," I said. "You could tell him you don't like his cousin's aura, and that'd probably sort it."

This startled a laugh out of Harry, and I was pleased with myself, because he seemed careworn. I ordered two more drinks. He drank them pretty quickly.

"Can I tell you my news now?" I said.

He smiled and nodded. "Shoot."

"Okay, do you remember how I wanted to find my birth parents and how I knew they'd left the country?"

"Yes?"

"Well, one of the waitresses at your party was from my old Kingdom Hall, and she told me someone came looking for me once. I got in touch with her afterwards, and now I've got a lead."

"A lead?"

"About my birth parents."

His eyebrows rose in surprise. "Oh! That's fantastic! Did you find them?"

I shook my head. "Just one woman. Her name is Yvonne Bailey. She'd given up a biracial boy around the time I was born. My father, according to her, was a Jamaican labourer who'd gone back before I was born. She lives in Madrid right now."

Harry reached across the table to squeeze my hand. "That's wonderful. Is she nice? What's she like?"

"We've only talked through Facebook. She's been tentative about contact. I think she's been trying for so long, she's a bit scared of being disappointed again. I can totally understand. Right now, I'm more parts scared than excited myself. But I'm trying to warm her up to the idea of maybe talking on Skype."

Harry thought this was reason to celebrate and I—though finding my birth mother brought up a whole mix of emotions—wanted to celebrate with him. He had put his phone on the table next to him. It kept buzzing. He ordered more drinks.

"Sorry," he said when the phone buzzed again. He put it in his pocket. At my questioning look he said, "Kieran."

Ah. Kieran. Yes.

Our food arrived. We didn't talk about it. His phone buzzed in his pocket, and because we weren't talking about it so hard, we could hear it, and know it was him, and it was like he was sitting right there between us, making annoying noises to interrupt any strand of conversation we wanted to start.

"Shit," Harry muttered and picked his phone out of his pocket and turned it off entirely. "Sorry."

He rubbed his face in a weary motion. I wondered what it was like going back to Siobhan's and seeing all those pictures of Kieran. I remembered his mother and her insistence on relationship counselling. How do you break up with someone if all your family was in denial?

"What's he want?" I asked, despite the nausea in my stomach at the thought of discussing Harry's ex.

He sighed, took a swig of beer, shrugged. "I don't know. He's the one who moved out. He's the one who'd decided he'd had it. I think he just doesn't like it that I might move on. Like it scares him that I'm not miserable over him."

I wanted to take the compliment, except it felt like he'd said this for my benefit.

"Do you want to get the tempura as well?" he asked, grabbing for the menu again.

"No, mate. I want to know what's bothering you," I said, taking the menu away from him. "You look like death. What's the matter?"

He maintained a mutinous, annoyed silence. I ordered two more drinks. Our food came. I waited for the third beer to hit him. Then it came pouring out.

"He keeps asking all these questions, and I don't know what else to tell him! I mean, yeah, I do miss him, of course I miss him, but it's not like I can text him that, even if he does ask, because we're not supposed to do that, right? When you're broken up? I mean, it's not rude to stop being all kissy-kissy, miss you, love you, and all that, right? Regardless of how you feel?"

An actual sensation of stabbing in my chest made me lift my hand up to rub it. "Sure."

"It's impossible to have a sensible conversation, of course, because nobody ever came to an agreement over text message, not in the history of the world they didn't! In fact, if you ask me, World War III will start over a text message. It'll be 'CU BRB xx' and then a mushroom cloud over London."

I made sympathetic sounds while trying to quickly think of something to say that was neutral and didn't sound like *He's an idiot and a bastard and you're well rid of him.*

"Kieran was the one who moved out," he repeated. "It was *his* idea. Not mine. *He* was the one with the 'It's not you, it's me' and the 'All we're doing is fighting.'"

He began to peel the labels off the beer bottles.

"And Siobhan . . . and my mum . . ." he muttered. "They don't know what it was like. He made them feel comfortable, because you couldn't tell we were together at all just looking at us when we were in company. He never called me any endearments. It was always 'Harry' in front of other people. He never held my hand. Never, *not once*, did he sit next to me at a family dinner or a party. As soon as we'd arrive somewhere, he'd split off to socialise by himself. Once, he shook my hand to congratulate me on a promotion when I found out in front of my parents. *Shook my bloody hand*! Like I was a colleague from work and not his bloody— I don't even know what! Because you know what? He never, *never* called me his boyfriend. Or partner. Not once."

Harry did make him sound like a tosser.

"Tosser," I said helpfully.

Two hours later, Harry was fully drunk and I had a clear picture of how selfish Kieran had been, how emotionally distant, how difficult. He once bought a car he liked, but which Harry didn't like, never asking Harry's opinion. And he'd once spent two Christmases in a row in Doncaster with his family because some uncle had made a suspicious comment about how much time Kieran was spending with "this Harry person." And he'd never book them into the same hotel room when they travelled together, lest someone in the hotel thought they were lovers.

Some of the things Harry told me didn't sound so very bad—like that time Kieran had gone out on a colleague's stag night and visited a strip club. I mean, sure, I could see why Harry wouldn't be thrilled about it, but all things considered it was a pretty standard thing to do. Other things he did, though, sounded awful, like that time Kieran's brother came to town, and Kieran was mean to Harry for three days straight, in case Kieran's brother suspected something.

A part of me felt almost sorry for Kieran. Both for the savage verbal beating he was getting from Harry, even if he couldn't hear it, and for how closeted he was and how that had ruined his relationship.

I know what it's like to be in an environment where you are perfectly aware that it's either your sexuality or everyone you love and care for. It's a choice nobody should have to make. And if Kieran did have to make it, I simply couldn't blame him for trying to juggle it as best he could, even if he bungled the thing terribly.

But whatever Harry was saying, all I could think was: *But you stayed with him. For seven years. And you wouldn't be so upset now if you hadn't felt something. If there hadn't been good, warm, affectionate moments. If you didn't feel something still . . .*

Eventually, when he was too drunk to walk straight, I got him into a cab and drove him to mine. I put him to bed, took off his shoes, covered him with my blanket, and then lay down beside him. It was a long time before I could get to sleep that night, waiting for the anxious buzzing in my head to quiet down.

"Joe?" Frank shouted. "Are ye there, pal?"

It was a bright Sunday morning a week later. Harry and I were in bed. He was reading the news on his phone, and I'd been drifting between a state of sleep and consciousness when Frank had rung.

"Yes, where are you? I can barely hear you," I said.

"I'm at the airport about to board my plane," he said. "I'm going to America. I was wondering . . . you wouldn't want to come over, would you?"

"What, to the airport?"

"No, not the airport, ye numpty," he said. "To America."

"What? What are you talking about?"

"Gabriella and I are going to Vegas! She wants to get hitched! Want to come along?"

"Christ, *now*?" I sprung up from bed, suddenly a hundred per cent awake.

"No, I'm over there for a conference, but afterwards. Say in a week or so. What do you say?"

"But— What— I mean— Are you *serious*?"

"It's going to be epic! Come on! Google yer ticket and come over, eh? I need a best man."

Having recently woken up, I wasn't sure I was hearing correctly. But I said, "Okay, sure. Give me a ring when you're over there, and I'll see about it."

"All right! Talk to ye later!" Frank laughed and rang off.

Seconds later my phone buzzed again. It was another message from Frank. This time it was a selfie of him and Gabriella in front of an aeroplane, smiles as bright as the sky behind them.

Harry looked up from his phone at me and smiled. I felt a little jump in my chest whenever he did that. Smiled at me, I mean.

"Do you fancy doing a trip to the States?" I asked. "I was just invited to be best man at Frank's wedding in Vegas."

"Really?"

"They're both ridiculous, but don't let that put you off."

"When is it?"

"Next week."

He stared at me. "Are you serious? I can't just go to the States at a moment's notice. I can't believe you'd consider going yourself."

"Why not?"

"Because!" he said. "Don't you have, I don't know... obligations?"

"Sure." I shrugged. "But he's my friend. And he's getting married. Besides, I've never been to Vegas before. Should be fun. Wanna go?"

He looked at me in a strange way. Like I'd just sprouted wings, except the wings were really beautiful.

"You actually mean it," he said.

"Of course."

"And you'd just take me with you. Like that. To your friend's wedding."

"Why not?" I leaned in and kissed him. "We could take a room in a tacky hotel," I said against his lips. "I'd feed you chocolate-covered strawberries. We could go to a burlesque! Oh my God, we could go and see those guys with the tigers!"

He laughed. "You mean Siegfried and Roy? I'm pretty sure they're retired."

"Damn it," I muttered. Recovering, though, I said, "We'll find something else. Cirque du Soleil! Blue Man Group! Come on, it's going to be amazing!"

He shook his head. Then, with a slowly spreading smile, he said, "I don't know. I'd have to check with work. I suppose I could swing it. Could be fun."

Excited, I climbed on top of him, just to make sure he remembered how much fun we could have, away from his "obligations." Away from his family and Kieran. The trip to Vegas, I thought, was bonkers. Not for me and Harry—that really did sound fun—but for Frank and Gabriella. I wished he'd confided in me earlier so we could have talked about it. He'd only just met Gabriella, and now he was suddenly going to marry her?

I thought, briefly, about hiring a detective to look into Gabriella, but a week wasn't really enough time to make this happen, and then Chloe pointed out that a) unless said detective worked for blowjobs (and was hot enough for either of us to want to give them to him) this was not a financial possibility; b) Frank was unlikely to listen to the findings of a detective, especially one who worked for blowjobs; and c) it was likely that as soon as Frank stood in front of an actual altar, the idea of marriage to a scatty vicar's daughter would strike him as laughable, and they'd give it up on their own.

Over the next few days, I emailed Harry my flight details once I booked, and focused on all the awesome stuff one could do in Vegas. There was a lot. Besides casinos, there were shows, the Grand Canyon, and amazing places to eat. I couldn't afford to stay for long, but I meant to get the most out of my three days. With Harry.

The idea of going away with Harry suddenly struck me as grand. Not having had any experiences with relationships, I never considered that going away together was something of a milestone. It didn't quite feel that way, but then how would I know what a milestone felt like? I had never experienced one before.

I saw a missed call from him when I came out of the Tube at Heathrow. Making my way along the enormous, bright corridors towards the main hall of the airport and dragging my bag behind me, I rang him back.

"Hey! I just arrived, where are you?" I looked around for him. People with massive luggage on trolleys hurried past me. One family with three very loud children was testing out the echo in the corridor, so I moved towards the wall to hear Harry better.

"Joe." His voice was low, heavy.

"Are you in Heathrow yet?"

"I'm really sorry, but I'm afraid I won't be able to come with you this weekend."

A moment of pregnant silence.

"Oh. Are you all right? Is it work? Is Malcolm being a little bitch again?"

"No, no, it's not Malcolm, it's—" he paused. "I wish we didn't have to talk about this over the phone. It's really not right. Listen, Kieran came over last evening..."

My heart plunged to the bottom of my stomach.

"Uh-huh?" I made myself say, because the expression on my face had made the cleaning lady, who'd just come out of the loos on the opposite side of me, frown in worry.

"He wants to give it another go," Harry said. There was a pause, during which a wave of nausea overcame me and made me dizzy. I put my hand over my mouth.

"We talked all night," he said, "and . . . I don't know, he wore me down. After all these years, I suppose I owe him another go. Owe *us* another go." I heard some noise on the other side, a rustling. Then his voice came back: "God, this is fucked up. I know you don't want to hear this right now. You want to go and enjoy your friend's wedding... I hope I didn't spoil it for you. Can we talk when you get back, maybe? I'm really sorry."

I wanted to say something, anything, but my jaw wouldn't open. Pain was shooting through my chest, my hand was clenched around the phone, and I knew I was hyperventilating when Harry asked, concerned, "Joe? Are you there?"

"Yes," I responded, more sharply than I'd intended. Like it was torn out of me. "Yeah, all right, well, I—I have to run now, so . . . say hi to Kieran, I suppose."

"I'm sorry, Joe. I really am. I can't express how—"

"Never mind now," I interrupted tersely. "Have a great weekend. Bye."

I hung up before he could say anything more. I wanted to throw my phone against the wall.

"Are you all right?" The cleaning lady, a broad cockney woman, with her hair pulled tightly back in a thin ponytail, examined me with concern. I'd gone down on my haunches and covered my face with my hands.

"Yeah, thanks," I choked out.

Harry and Kieran. Harry making fish and chips for him. Harry smiling up at Kieran from his phone. Harry falling asleep on him. Harry laughing at his jokes. Harry and Kieran moving back in together. *No. No. No. No. Oh God, oh God, oh God . . .*

The man in the booth checking the passports peered at me suspiciously.

"Are you all right, sir?"

"Yes, thank you."

I took my passport back and put it in my pocket.

In the bathrooms I checked myself in the mirror. I looked ill. Splashing water over my face didn't do anything, and I had to slap my cheeks to bring colour back into them.

Harry and Kieran. Harry and fucking Kieran.

Chapter Nine
THE BRACELETS

Six Months Before the Big Day

Harry and fucking Kieran . . . I can't believe it.

How I am progressing with my Plan so far:

1. Get Harry to come to Dublin with me under false pretences. ✓
2. Surprise him with sweet hotel room in fancy AF hotel I can't afford. ✓
3. Purchase suit that makes me look like James Bond. ✓
4. ~~Get fancy new haircut to impress Harry.~~ Make myself bald. ✓
5. ~~Make myself look sparkly and beautiful for Harry.~~ Iron shirt with cold iron and cover myself with mud-coloured goo. ✓
6. ~~Get restaurant reservation for the evening.~~ Piss off the one person in the world who could possibly get me restaurant reservation. ✓
7. ~~Seamlessly meet Harry after pretend exhibition and sweep him off his feet with elegant dinner at fancy restaurant, and late night stroll to Ha'penny Bridge.~~ Confront angry Harry while looking like a second-rate Jim Carrey impersonator and ruin both career and relationship in one swoop. ✓

Extra points:
1. Made Irish hairdresser cry.
2. Flashed Harry's cousins.
3. Have never been further from proposing to anyone in my life.

Also . . . Kieran is here.

I won't lie. Things aren't good.

I'm in the gallery staff bathroom, washing my face. I don't really care what I look like at this moment, but everybody was staring at me, so I thought best get rid of goo on face before asking Harry why his ex is in Dublin with us.

Harry comes in, but I don't turn to him. I'm worried I might scream. He takes a fistful of paper towels from the dispenser and hands them to me. His expression shows concern, mostly, which is rich, considering everything.

"Are you all right?" he asks.

"Oh yes, dandy. You?" My high-pitched voice betrays me.

"I don't even know where to start," he says. His phone buzzes. He glances at it and then puts it away. I toss the paper towels scrunched to a ball into the wastebasket.

"So," he says, "do you know why my cousins are making lewd jokes about the size of your, er, equipment?"

I shrug. "They're all in the closet?"

"Joe," he says, his eyebrows raised, the corner of his mouth twitching in amusement, "did you expose yourself to my cousins?"

"What I may or may not have done in a moment of confusion is beside the point," I say, defensively. "You have brought Kieran! On our anniversary!"

He becomes more serious at once.

"Right. That. I *haven't* brought him. In fact, I didn't know he was in town. We ran into him by accident."

I narrow my eyes because he can sell those fairy tales to some other chump.

"Where is your exhibition?" he asks. "They say it's in three weeks' time, just as previously planned. They claim they never rung Chloe or anybody to change the date."

This is why I don't plan. Harry would have had contingency plans attached to the main thing, whereas I find myself without answers. Luckily, Harry gets distracted.

"What is that thing you put on your face?" he asks, frowning.

"A facial."

"What was in it?"

"I don't know. Mud?"

He touches my cheek, carefully, and then turns it so I face my reflection in the mirror. My skin has erupted in angry red blotches, on my forehead and cheeks mostly. It's like I'm having an allergic reaction to something.

"I probably left it on for too long," I say.

"Why were you wearing a face mask?" he asks. "Why didn't you tell me—"

We're interrupted by the door opening again. It's Kieran.

"Oh," he says, startling. "There you are. The curator lady wants to know if you mean to sue her, after all. She's on the phone with her lawyer right now."

"Ah." Harry's hand drops from my cheek. "Er, tell her I overreacted. I'll apologise in a minute."

"Okay," Kieran says, his eyes swivelling from me to Harry. "Everything all right?"

"We're fine," I say, pushing him out and closing the door. Nosy bastard.

Harry eyes me with apprehension. For a moment it feels like he wants to embrace me, but then his frame relaxes. "We can talk about everything later. This isn't the place. Come on."

Hoping that this could buy me time, I follow him back out into the gallery. We find Kieran leaning against the reception desk, charming Orla into a smile. She spots us, and her smile falls, especially when she glares at Harry.

"I take it that my little 'thieving enterprise' is safe for now?" she asks Harry, with a healthy dose of bite. Harry nods.

"Yes, sorry, there was a misunderstanding," he says. Chastened, he apologises again and then looks to me. I'm pretty sure my chances for work in this gallery have now dwindled to nothing, and that my actual, real exhibition next month will probably be cancelled, and I suggest we go now. Orla takes this news with no hint of regret, and so Harry, Kieran, and I leave.

Outside, it has begun to rain. I want to go to the hotel, but Kieran is still with us, and I have no intention of inviting him up there. What the hell is he doing here, anyway?

"I don't suppose I could tempt you to dine with me?" he says to Harry, before belatedly glancing at me, by way of extending the invitation. *No*, I want to say. *No, you cannot tempt us, Kieran.* The nerve of that guy.

"As a matter of fact," I say, "we have plans. We were going to go to the Restaurant Patrick Guilbaud tonight."

Harry startles. "*Really?* The Patrick Guilbaud? I've been dying to go there."

"It's an excellent restaurant," Kieran confirms. "What time's your table?"

Well, that's just grand. I only said it to get rid of Kieran. Now I am forced to say, "I—I haven't been able to get one. Yet."

"For tonight?" Kieran says, surprised. "Mate, you won't get a reservation on the same day, unless you're the Taoiseach."

I stop myself from sticking my tongue out at him.

"Wait, let me see if I can help you out." He puts his iPhone to his ear. Well, isn't this just the cherry on the top of a pile of shit. Harry watches Kieran, as he says, in that arrogant, self-important way of his, "Dylan! How'ya doin' you old tit, eh?" And then, moments later, "Nah, mate, it's just a friend of mine . . . Yeah, a table would be great . . . Nah, nah, don't worry about it . . . Yeah, that's great, mate. Sure thing. Thanks again. Bye."

He puts his phone away, smiles at Harry—I hope his teeth rot—and says, "They'll let you in at six. It'll have to be through the back door. I'll have to escort you, but it won't be a problem. Want to get a drink beforehand?"

I don't want to drink with Kieran. In fact, I would be very glad if he just walked away. And he must know this. He must know he's the last person I want to see. If I were him, I'd just bow out at this point, but of course, he is a cunning bastard, so instead he made it impossible to refuse his presence. Either he comes with us, or we don't eat at the bloody restaurant.

Harry looks to me, wavering. I do want him to eat at the restaurant he's been dying to go to. I throw my hands out in frustration and say, "Do you know of a good place?"

Kieran beams.

We head out along the river. As we do, Kieran spots the Ha'penny Bridge, and says, "Oh have you been on it yet? It's gorgeous. Come, you've got to see this."

He reaches his hand out to Harry, but then only pats his shoulder. I might have to kill him tonight.

"I really don't think—" I start, but he's crossed the street already, and Harry takes my hand and we are forced to follow. The sky is grey, so the lamps, which stick up from decorative, white-painted cast-iron arches, illuminate our way, and even in the drizzle it is powerfully romantic. Or would have been if Kieran hadn't ruined it.

He tells the story of the bridge: how it was erected in the nineteenth century to replace the decrepit ferries that used to get people from one side of the river to the other, and tells us about how the name has changed. Harry listens to him and I put my hood up, put my hands in my pockets, and wonder whether, if presented with all the evidence, any jury would really convict me for pushing the bastard into the river and watching him drown.

He then leads us across to the other side, and into the Grand Social, a bar in a black-bricked building, with enormous posters announcing the various acts that perform there live, later in the evening. Kieran says it's his favourite hang out in Dublin. I dislike it intensely already.

He orders our drinks for us, knows the staff by name, and we're informed the drinks are on the house. Then he takes his jacket off, to reveal that he's been spending the past four years in a gym, apparently. He was always big, but previously he used to be wide and stocky, with a small potbelly. Now all his weight has been transformed into muscle. His stomach, waist, and hips are flat and narrow, while his upper chest is built up and broad. If anybody asks me, he looks like Johnny Bravo's mean older brother.

Harry says, "Been working out, have you?"

"Oh, you know." Kieran shrugs modestly. "I've a bit more time on my hands now."

"Why?" I ask. I don't know much about Kieran, but I do know he used to work a lot.

"I quit my job," he says. "Starting my own security agency. Been a dream of mine for some time. You know how it is—on your deathbed you don't regret not having spent enough time in the office. I want to spend more time doing *meaningful* things."

I would find this more interesting to listen to if he wasn't patently addressing all this to Harry.

"Well," Harry says, "it's amazing that you finally had the courage to do it. I've been telling you for years . . ."

"Yeah, yeah." Kieran laughs. "I should've listened to you from the start, I know. I wish I had! I wouldn't have wasted all these years on butting horns with everyone at work . . . all this time I could have been, er—" he coughs "—doing other things. You know."

There's a jar of olives in the middle of the table, and I'm sorely tempted to flick one at him. Harry smiles, apparently charmed by this very obvious hint that Kieran wishes he could have spent more time with him.

"So," I say, interrupting this little interlude, "you seeing anyone, Kieran?"

"Who? Me? Oh no." He shakes his head, colouring. "Let me tell you, Harry's a tough act to follow!"

Harry rolls his eyes self-consciously and hides his smile by taking a drink. At this stage, I'd need a little cannon to shoot the olives at Kieran to do justice to my feelings.

Harry can see that I'm unhappy and, probably imagining it would shorten my suffering, suggests we just eat here.

But Kieran extolls the wonders of Restaurant Patrick Guilbaud. It's got two Michelin stars, he tells us. It's incomparable. My own appetite, in all honesty, is completely gone. But Harry, despite pretending he doesn't mind where we eat, is clearly very interested in the restaurant, and so we set off for it half an hour ahead of time to make sure we get our table.

Kieran dines with us. I don't want him to, but by the time he knocks on the back door of the restaurant, which is situated in the ground floor of the Merrion Hotel, and his friend lets us in, it becomes increasingly inevitable that he must be invited to sit down with us. He demurs at first. Then he agrees to stay for the starter. And then he stays for the main, because Harry is intrigued by the eight-course degustation menu, so Kieran's assistance is obviously needed.

"I eat for two," he says, patting his flat stomach. I wonder if flinging my spoon at him would really be such a crime against good manners.

He and Harry talk extensively of the food and how it compares to that time a friend of Harry's invited them to eat at Noma, which at the time had been named the best restaurant in the world. That was in Denmark, and apparently the whole menu's theme, when Harry and Kieran visited, was onions, which to my mind sounds gross, but apparently it was incredible. They both stumble over each other as they try to explain to me how great it was.

"Oh God, there was a special onion tea!" Harry says.

"Yeah, I *so* didn't want to try that, but Mr. Bossy Pants made me," Kieran says.

"You said you liked it!"

"I said a lot of things." Kieran winks.

Harry laughs, but then stops in the middle when he sees my expression. He immediately grows sober.

"This is amazing, Joe," he says, pointing at his plate. "I can't believe we get to eat here."

This wasn't my doing. It was Kieran's. We all know it. We go silent and it's awkward. By the end of the evening, having performed my part of slighted lover admirably, I feel like a complete arsehole. But it's too late now to be a good sport about it, and so when Kieran says goodbye (at last!) Harry and I walk back to our hotel in silence. We have to cross the Ha'penny Bridge again, but by now, even if I remembered to bring the bracelets, which I didn't, it doesn't seem the right time to talk about marriage anyway.

Our hotel room is a right mess. I forget that I left it with my clothes, underwear, the packaging from the suit I bought, and the packets of beauty products lying everywhere. The ironing board and iron take up the middle of the room. The bathroom looks like I've bathed baby elephants in it. Harry stares bewildered.

"Did a bomb go off in here?"

"I—I was in a hurry."

"Okay," Harry says slowly, before turning to me. "Do you want to tell me what you've been up to all day?"

I don't. I don't want to tell him. This is not how any of this was supposed to happen. I don't know what to tell him; I don't know how to explain. It seems too fantastic, really, to be believed, anyway. I drop onto the bed and shrug.

"So . . ." Harry says. "No exhibition today?"

I nod. "I just wanted us to come to Dublin for the anniversary."

"Okay," Harry says, again very slowly. "So . . . why didn't you tell me?"

"I wanted to surprise you."

"Well, mission accomplished." He looks around. "I'm still reeling. What the hell happened to your hair?"

"I had it cut."

"Why?"

"Don't you like it?"

When I look up at his face, I can see he's keeping himself from laughing, with difficulty.

"It's—it's different," he says, at last. "It'll take some getting used to."

"You don't like it." I sink my face into my hands. "You hate it."

"I don't hate it," he says, laughing. "It's just hair. What made you do it? I mean, the whole of it! You *love* your hair!"

I do. I do love my hair. And now it's all gone, scooped up and binned. Nothing left.

"The girl sneezed," I say miserably.

Harry barks a laugh. "Oh God, are you joking?"

"No! She sneezed and she made me bald up on top and that's how— Stop laughing, it's not funny!"

"Oh Joe . . ." His voice is quivering.

"What?"

He shakes his head. "You're one in a million," he says. "Come on, lie back."

I fall back onto the pillows, tired and defeated. Has anybody ever botched anything so badly? I doubt it. All this energy, all this effort, and nothing to show for it. I look around and see that Harry is rifling through his luggage in search of something. He withdraws a white tube of some sort of salve.

"Put your head on the pillow," he instructs. "This should soothe your rash."

Sitting at the side of the bed, he places the cool gel with the tip of his finger over my cheeks, my chin, my forehead, and then over the bridge of my nose. He spreads it out delicately. My skin does feel soothed, although I'd say it's more his ministering to it than the ointment.

"How is that?" he asks softly.

"Better."

He continues to smooth the salve over my face. Then he spots something, undoes the buttons of my shirt, and says, "Okay, I think maybe it wasn't the facial that caused the reaction. Did you use anything else?"

I point to the pile of beauty products on the table.

"Oh Joe." He stares at it in disbelief. "Why?"

"I wanted to look nice."

"You look like you've been out in the sun too long. Your chest, your belly—" he strips me of my shirt "—and your arms, all red. Take off your trousers."

I take off the remainder of my clothes. It's far more comfortable, anyway. The rash is unevenly spread in blotchy patches across my body. It's worse on my face than anywhere else, prompting Harry to conclude that the mask must have aggravated the problem. He massages the whole tube of salve into my skin. I'm not complaining. I like the feel of his hands on me.

By the end of it, I'm a glistening mummy, and I have to lie very still to let my skin absorb the healing properties of the medicine.

"So all this," he says, screwing the lid back on to the now-empty tube, "for our anniversary?"

"I wanted it to be nice. It didn't quite come off as I'd planned it."

He smiles. "No, I suppose it hasn't."

"Why did you have to invite Kieran?" I ask. "It's our anniversary. Why didn't you tell him?"

Harry sighs. "I did tell him. Before you arrived and when I'd first bumped into him, I told him I was here for our anniversary. And your job."

"Why didn't you tell him to bugger off, then?" I demand.

"That would have been mean."

"No, it wouldn't! If you didn't want to say it, I'd have done it for you! Gladly!"

He tilts his head a little, like he wants to say, *You do astonish me.*

"Can't you understand why I would feel a little awkward about it?" he asks. "We agreed to be friends, after . . . you know what. And I wanted to be true to my word. Besides, it wasn't so bad, was it?"

"It was horrible. He flirted with you the entire time!"

Harry raises his eyebrows in surprise. "So what? Don't you trust me?"

I grumble something indistinct, and he shakes his head again.

"Come on, let's not talk about him anymore. You're right, it's our anniversary and he shouldn't be a part of it. Can I give you my present now?"

"Oh!" In all the chaos of planning, I didn't even consider that Harry had to get me something as well. "Yes, please!"

He laughs at how easily distracted I am, then reaches for his bag again and withdraws an envelope. It has a heart drawn on it. I tear it open and inside I find two plane tickets. To Jamaica.

"Woah!" I cry. "Are you joking? When?"

"That's the bad news," he says apologetically. "They're for September. I can't take too much time off until then because of the merger."

Harry's agency has recently been absorbed by a bigger agency because of a fuckup by Malcolm, who managed to drop a really big client. The downside of all this was that Harry was no longer top dog, but only one of many team leaders in a much larger corporation, and thus couldn't decide his own workload or schedule anymore.

I stare at the tickets hungrily. It's my dream to go. Of course, being mostly broke, as I usually am, this was never anything I thought I would do until much later in life.

"This is— It's amazing! Thank you!"

I want to hug him, but I'm conscious of my slippery state, and so only kiss his lips.

"Hand me my bag," I say.

He reaches down under the table, where I'd tossed my rucksack.

"Open the back pocket."

He reaches inside, as instructed, and withdraws the two decorative boxes Freya made for the bracelets. They're grey cardboard paper and are tied together with a blue and white ribbon.

"What's this?" he asks.

"Open them."

He opens one, then the other. The bracelets, each in its own box, look shiny and new, and somehow more precious now that Harry is holding them.

"I designed them," I say. "And then had them made for us."

"They're lovely, thank you," he says, trying his on. "Oh, those are our initials, aren't they?" He examines the clasp.

"Yes."

"Thank you," he says again.

I feel suddenly sad. When I asked him to reach for them, I wanted to give him a present because he gave me one, but seeing the bracelet on his wrist now, I remember what they signified when I designed them. These aren't just any bracelets. I'd never give something like it to anybody else.

"Bollocks," I say, crossing my arms.

"Hm?" Harry looks up from examining his bracelet. "What did you say?"

I shake my head.

"Are you upset?" he asks, worried. "I really love it. Who made them?"

"Freya Nancarrow."

"She's very good. I'll remember to thank her."

"It was supposed to be different," I say. "It—it wasn't supposed to happen like this."

"What wasn't?"

I point at myself—my naked body all shiny and streaky from the cream he's rubbed into me—and the room in such a mess.

"I was going to take you to that restaurant myself. And then I was going to make us go on the Ha'penny Bridge, only of course Kieran had to ruin it."

He frowns. "What are you talking about?"

"The bracelets!"

"Well, what does it matter about the restaurant and the bridge?" he says. "We're here now, aren't we? And we did go to the restaurant, and we went to see the bridge."

"Yeah, we did," I say, petulantly. "We saw the bloody bridge, and it looked amazing, and I was going to ask you then, but Kieran had to shoot his stupid mouth off . . . Not that I'd have done it with him looking on, anyway. Stupid oaf. Don't they have a law on how big a guy can grow? He shouldn't be allowed on bridges, if you ask me. He's a hazard to people's safety, that's what he is."

"What?" Harry's shoulders are shaking. "What on earth are you saying? Ask me what?"

I can't look at him. Lying back, I grab a pillow and put it over my face.

"Joe, what are you doing?" he asks, in a mixture of exasperation and amusement. "Joe?"

The pillow absorbs the sounds when I say the words: "I want to marry you."

It's out. In the worst possible way, it's out now. I breathe in through the pillow and hope to suffocate and die.

Then the pillow is torn away from me, and Harry, serious, wide-eyed, looks down at me.

"*What* did you say?"

"Nothing."

"Don't toy with me," he demands, suddenly urgent. "What did you say?"

I can't meet his eyes. "I said, 'I want to marry you.'"

For a moment he just stares at me. I'm lying flat on my back, fully naked, and it's the weirdest proposal ever, officially. If it even is a proposal. I didn't ask a question, after all.

"The bracelets," I say, because Harry is speechless, "they were supposed to be an engagement gift. On Ha'penny Bridge. After dinner. It was supposed to be romantic. Even Chloe said it would be. And Siobhan cried like a baby when I told her. I was going to look fit, in a suit and with a new haircut. It was going to be epic, I promise. And if you like it, we could do it again. Maybe Paris this time. I'll find out where Kieran is going to be and we'll go in the opposite direction to that. My hair could grow back a little. I'll book everything in advance. It's my first time planning anything ever, so you have to cut me some—" I don't finish, because Harry grabs my face and kisses me, hard. When he stops, abruptly, he turns away, stands, and rushes to the bathroom. I rise up onto my elbows and feel a little bereft. Isn't he going to say anything? I mean, it'll break my heart if he says we're not there yet, or that he doesn't see himself married to me, but that would still be better than if he just pretends I never said it.

"Harry?" I ask meekly.

I hear him blow his nose. When he comes back, his eyes are red rimmed. He clears his throat and returns to the side of the bed as before.

"I'm fine," he says, taking a steadying breath. "Sorry, I didn't expect that. I—I didn't know."

"Oh, okay. Well, I didn't say it to upset you."

"No, of course not." He laughs, his voice trembling.

"You don't have to say anything," I rush to add. "I mean, I know I didn't ask properly, but I won't if you don't want me to. Honest, I'll never say another—"

"Joe."

"Yes?"

"I love you," he says. "And I want to marry you too."

"Oh." I smile. "Oh, okay then. God, that's a relief."

I fall back on my pillow, laughing. He's laughing too. It doesn't feel quite real yet. But the relief does.

Harry leans down towards me.

"Careful: the salve, your nice shirt!" I say.

"Fuck the shirt," he mutters, before descending on me.

It was the first time I'd ever planned anything in my life, and it's the best, most successful plan, I think, anybody's ever had.

Chapter Ten

FRANK'S WEDDING

Five Years Before the Big Day

I didn't particularly want to board the plane to Las Vegas. But what could I possibly achieve by not going?

Thoughts of Harry and Kieran together, sitting far away from each other at family dinners, ignoring each other at parties, calling each other "compadre" raced through my brain. The lady sitting next to me on the plane watched me warily, because I sat, staring blindly at the movie playing in front of me, tapping the table with a pen.

I imagined what might have happened the evening before. Kieran arriving at Siobhan and Ollie's was scene one. Those two would not have turned him away. If Harry had wanted to send him off, they'd have encouraged him to stay. Yes, it was their fault. I hated them both with a passion.

What next? Well, that overbearing giant would have forced Harry to sit there, guilted and harassed him into compliance. He'd have been all like, "Seven years!" and "Down the drain!" and "Your mother and your sister and everybody who knows me!" and "Seven years!"

I imagined Harry standing up to him, righteously indignant, crying, "I love Joe!"

The scene in my head turned into a cartoon. If Harry loved me, that scene would not have ended with the two of them agreeing to try again.

Jesus. It came to me now, like someone shutting the car door on your fingers, except it shot all through me. This was what Harry *wanted*.

If I featured in this scenario at all, it was likely more in the tones of "But what do I tell Joe?": a complication and a nuisance; a bump in the road of Harry and Kieran's grand romance.

As soon as I picked up my luggage in the airport in Las Vegas, drowsy from a nervous nap I fell into during the last hour of the flight, I was faced with another problem. I had a hotel room booked, but it was booked under Harry's name, since I was going to share it with him. The thought of hearing his voice again made everything inside of me clench. I rang Frank instead. This was about him, after all, and I needed to, for a couple of seconds, think about something else.

He picked up but whispered, "I'm in a meeting right now. What's up?"

"I just wanted to tell you I've landed."

"Grand!" he said. "Gabriella is going to pick you up." He turned away from the phone and spoke to someone in the background, and then quickly returned to me, "Okay, Joe, I've got to run. You have a good time. I'll see you tonight."

Gabriella was waiting for me at the gate, just as he said. She looked bigger and bouncier than ever, like a ray of flowery sunshine which, frankly, I was in no mood for. She saw me approach, her smile turning into a worried frown.

"Are you all right?"

"Bumpy flight," I said, to ward off any questions.

I wanted to be alone. She'd hired a car and after locating it and driving into the busy Vegas traffic, she asked me where I was staying.

"Er, that's . . . that's still up for debate," I said. "I was going to bring someone. He had the hotel reservations."

"Oh," she said, a little surprised. "Well, you can stay with Frank and me, if you like. Our suite is enormous. I mean, honestly, it's like a little flat, anyway. There's a sofa. Or you can take the bed and Frank and I—"

"No, no, that's all right," I said, hastily. I had not listened to Frank's excessively blunt accounts of their sex escapades not to know what went on in any room those two were let loose in.

"It's the Palazzo," I told her. "If you can drop me off there, I'll figure out the rest."

"You sure?" she asked, concerned. "I can help you find another room."

"No, that's all right, thanks."

She suggested taking me to lunch, but I pleaded a headache and jet lag, and so, reluctantly, she left me in the enormous lobby of the Palazzo, giving me her number and insisting I ring her when I was ready. Before going, she looked me in the eyes and said reverently, "I'm so happy!"

With that, she swept away, and I had to determine whether nights in the desert were warm enough to sleep rough on a bench somewhere, or whether it was the sort of thing the good people of Las Vegas would frown upon.

In the centre of the opulent, golden-coloured hotel lobby, there was the centrepiece—a marble statue of antique-looking figures, which changed colour every couple of minutes, surrounded by flowers and plants and further encircled by four purple columns. It was like good taste just sort of fell asleep on that one. I took a seat on the edging of the weird little garden and considered my options.

There was a room in this very hotel booked for me. If Harry hadn't cancelled it (if it wasn't too late to cancel) he was going to get charged for it. Harry would probably refuse to pay for it, and so the whole cost of it would fall on me. I'd already spent all of my money on the flight here. It would be stupid, surely, not to at least sleep in the room I was going to pay for and couldn't afford?

On the off chance that it might work, I approached reception and asked whether they had a booking for Harry Byrne. They did. But then they wanted to see the credit card with which the booking was made, and I had to ask them to excuse me.

Fuck.

My options unfolded before me: sleep rough in a city I'd never been to before. Sleep in a room with my horny best friend and his sex-fiendish vicar's daughter. Ring Harry. I took out my phone and stared at his number. Then I put my phone away and sunk my face into my hands.

My phone rang. It nearly fell out of my pocket when I tried to reach it.

It was Harry.

"Yes?" I sounded too eager. Inside, my stomach was flipping over.

"Joe?" Harry was keeping his voice down, as if not to be overheard.

"Yes."

It wasn't fair. It wasn't fair that his voice immediately made me think of the way his body felt underneath those white crisp shirts he wore. Hard and warm. It wasn't fair that it made me want to touch him again.

"I just remembered . . . I've got your room reservation. Or did you get another room?"

I don't know what I was expecting. Something less like *This horrible thing I told you before is still on, I'm just checking we can all move on from there in a peaceful and civil manner.*

A childish part of me wanted to dramatically declare that he shouldn't worry about it, and in a tone that would give him every reason to be worried. But I didn't have the energy for that.

"I didn't," I said.

"Can I email it to you?"

"Er, no, they're asking for your credit card. Can you just tell me the number? I'll . . . I'll write it on my arm or something. The battery on my phone is pretty low."

He huffed a little laugh. "Of course it is. Are you familiar with chargers? You know what they do?"

I didn't make a noise, and he must have caught on that this wasn't an *oh that Joe* moment for me.

"Tell you what," he said. "I'll take care of it. You just wait five minutes, and then go to reception, all right?"

"Okay."

There was a pause. He asked, quietly, "Are you all right? Was your flight okay?"

"Sure, fine, thanks."

"Er, is the hotel nice?"

"Don't you have stuff to get back to?" I asked. I didn't want to sound as tetchy as I was, but seriously? What the hell did he think we were going to chat about? He'd just dumped me for that caveman who was going to make him miserable again and— I stopped myself from reeling down that way.

A moment's pause. A sigh. "Of course," he said. "I'll take care of it. Give me five minutes."

I hung up.

An enormous man in a baseball cap pushed past me with his equally barrel-shaped family, and I returned to reality. I was in Vegas. On my own. About to witness the union of two zanies. I was ravenous and tired, and I desperately needed a room. Figuring that enough time had passed for Harry to do whatever he meant to do, I proceeded to the reception. Whatever Harry had told them seemed to have done the trick: they gave me a key, a floor and room number, and asked me to enjoy my stay.

When I reached my room, all I could do was close the door behind me, take off all my clothes, and throw myself onto the bed. My head was spinning.

I had to call him. I had to apologise for being a dick, for everything, beg him to reconsider, beg him to take me back. I threw myself across my bed, hunted for my phone and . . . it was off. Battery had died. Of course.

I took a shower. A cold, sobering shower would sort me out.

The sickening thought of Kieran walking into a shower cubicle with Harry came to me. I banged my head against the shower door. It was like they were right there, arms around each other.

I'd been a side character in their love story. A thing they had to overcome to find each other again. The truth of it seared. He'd told me I was a rebound. I remembered it now as distinctly as if it had been yesterday. He'd told me, and I hadn't listened.

I showered, patted myself dry, and returned to bed.

Staring at the ceiling, I thought about how fucking stupid I was.

There was a knock on my door. I wrapped the top cover of the bed around me like a cape and padded over to the door.

A uniformed young man greeted me with a bright, "Hello! Is everything to your liking, sir?"

No. Nothing is to my liking and everything is awful. What do you want?

"Yes, thank you."

"We just want to make sure you have everything you need."

"I suppose I do."

"Would you like to have your lunch now, sir?"

I didn't stay in fancy hotels a great deal, but even I knew this was an odd thing for them to ask. Usually one arranged one's own lunch, didn't one? Then it occurred to me that this had been organised by Harry, and it would've been entirely his style to have thought of us being too tired to go out for lunch and instead eating in.

"What sort of—" I began, and he swung forward a trolley with a silver cover over a plate. He lifted the cover with panache to reveal steak and chips, and I stared. There was a little paper flag stuck onto a toothpick, stuck into the top of chip-mountain. It had writing on it, so I plucked it out and read:

Joe, this is to let you know I paid for the room, meals included. Please accept this for an apology. I'm really sorry I can't be there. I hope you have a great weekend. Please give my best to the bride and groom. Harry.

"Sir?"

I realised I hadn't moved or said anything for at least a full minute. I put the flag down and said, "Thank you." I tipped him, rolled the trolley into the room myself, and closed the door.

It was the most confusing steak I'd ever eaten. It tasted of nothing. I kept staring at the little flag and thinking, *What the . . .*

The hotel phone rang. It startled me out of my thoughts. It was Frank.

"Joe?" he cried, excited. "Is that you?"

"I'm in my room. Eating lunch. Everything okay?"

"Perfect! Gabriella just rang to tell me she's picked you up. She said you were tired. Will ye be okay for a piss up tonight?"

Yes. Alcohol. *Yes*, my heart cried.

"I'll be sure to take a nap to be ready for it."

"Fantastic! Tomorrow's the day! I'll ring you later. Bye!"

I remembered now that perhaps I should have a conversation with him about this whole wedding business. Gabriella was a charming character, but this marriage was, surely, rushed. Not that I'd know anything about it, since I wasn't likely now to ever find myself in a situation to get married. Perhaps Gabriella was pregnant. They'd had enough sex to produce a small army of children, after all. My thoughts immediately travelled to being a godfather. Would they ask me? Would I say yes? I would probably say yes. And then what if something happened to Frank and Gabriella? I'd be stuck with a child.

Courage flooded my wounded breast. I imagined myself heroically stepping up to the task. Single-parenting the shit out of that child. Of course, the poor thing would have to live in the death trap that was Chloe's and my flat, surrounded by statuettes of butts and my naked self-portraits . . . No, that wouldn't do.

Eventually, I fell asleep, having, in my imagination, grown into a respectable King of Suburbia, polo neck sweater and pipe in mouth and all. Harry would see me and collapse in jealousy and regret and then I would take him back, magnanimously . . .

When I awoke from my nap, the night lights of Vegas created a surreal cityscape out of my room's window. It took me half an hour to quite believe I was really here. It was a moment before I remembered the rest. I was here alone. The big bed I was in would continue feeling big and Harry-less. As would the rest of my life.

A massive empty hole opened in my gut. It was a pull of longing so sharp, it suddenly brought tears to my eyes.

"Shit," I muttered, and tore out of bed.

Finally finding a charger, I plugged my phone in and then took another shower. There were several messages from Frank on there, about how he and Gabriella would be waiting for me in the lobby.

When Frank spotted me, downstairs, he stretched his arms wide, and gave me the biggest smile imaginable. I ran into his arms and he squeezed, hard.

"Okay, you sorry bastard!" he cried. "We're going to party like the world's ending. Are you ready?"

"Like you wouldn't believe."

"That's what I like to hear! Gabriella! Gabriella, darling, light of my life, are you ready?"

Gabriella, beaming happily at me, nodded.

"And this"—here Frank, with his arm around my shoulders, presented another woman—"is Gabriella's friend, Rachel. She arrived two days ago. Isn't that sweet? Warms a fellow's heart right up, it does.

Rache, this is my best mate, my best man, *the* best man, Joe. And I know what you're thinking: he's a looker. But he's also never swung your way in his life, have you?" He shook me. I could tell he was overexcited by the amount of bollocks he spoke. Rachel, a dark-haired beauty with too much makeup on, raised an eyebrow at me, but didn't seem the least bit embarrassed.

"You're the gay, then?" she said, in the worldly tones of a brothel madam. "I prefer partying with gays. You guys are more fun, anyway."

I wasn't quite sure what to do with that "compliment," so I just let it hang. Frank turned us around and cried, "To the bars!"

Apparently Napoleon, when he met opposing French forces in the field, had such great power of personality that men from the opposing camp would just drop their weapons and join him. It sounds improbable until you meet a man like Frank Brodie.

As the four of us left the hotel together, I knew what Frank wanted. In my frame of mind, I was in just the right mood to help him do it. He wanted to loudly and exuberantly celebrate his approaching nuptials. I wanted to drown out thoughts of Harry. The recipe for both contained two vital ingredients: loud music and masses of alcohol.

Five hours later, we came out of a bar drunk and in the company of ten other people who decided to join our group and demanded to be part of the wedding. Frank became "Frankie Boy"; two men attempted to carry Gabriella upon their shoulders like an Egyptian queen; and one very well-groomed, very WASP-y young man elaborated extensively on the subject of how "adorable" my accent was.

When we woke up in the morning, it was in Frank and Gabriella's room. The scent of chlorine in my hair informed me I'd gone swimming at some point. There were sixteen of us, and besides Frank, Gabriella, and Rachel, the rest of the cast didn't look familiar to me at all.

With heavy heads, we went down to have our breakfast. Rachel looked like death. Gabriella blinked hard and tried to smile at Frank, who was still bursting with energy and seemed to feel extra charged by the success of the night. Of the four of us, he was the only one who didn't appear worn by the long night—normally with his sand-coloured goatee and his enormous smile, he bore a strong resemblance to Robin Hood; now he managed to somehow look like Robin Hood after a successful robbery.

"It's the sort of thing," he said, enthusiastically, "you'll tell your grandchildren about! That night Grampa set Vegas on fire! Ha! Coffee anyone?"

After breakfast, Gabriella had to go and buy something to wear for her wedding, so she took off with Rachel and I was left alone with Frank.

It was, I reckoned, the only opportunity I would get to talk to him about this venture. Not being the sort of guy who ever talked people into or out of anything, I wasn't entirely sure how to broach the subject, but Frank neatly brought me there himself, when he asked, "So! Out with it! What do you think? Isn't she the sweetest thing you ever saw?"

I wondered how he could sound so certain, so absolutely delighted with another person, without a hint of doubt or fear. Was it because he'd not faced as much abandonment as I had? Was it like a self-fulfilling prophecy, whereby he was certain of love and acceptance, and consequently got it? Was it because he was white and straight?

I couldn't understand it. A pang of jealousy hit me, and I had to turn away and mutter, "She's lovely, of course."

"Eh?" he said, laughing. "What's with you? You know she won't replace you in my heart! Nothing ever could!"

Idiot. I had to smile though.

"I know," I said, rolling my eyes. "You've known each other less than two months, Frank. What's with the rush?"

"Oh, Joe!" He beamed at me. "I cannae tell you! I just want . . ." He seemed like he would burst searching for the right word. "I just *want*, you know? I could die in a plane crash on the way back to England. We could both drown in our bathtubs tomorrow! I could fall into a manhole! I could be bitten by an exotic spider smuggled into the country in a crate full of durian! Who knows how long I have left? I want to do everything I want to do, before I die."

How does one argue with that?

"Now," he said. "Let's go and look at some of those shows we talked about. I'm thinking Le Rêve. You?"

I'd heard it said that Frank became this way after he lost his leg, but in fact I'd known him before the accident and after, and there was little difference. Even at the beginning, with the shock of the lost limb, and the getting used to a new way of moving, the prosthetic hardly slowed him down at all.

Around noon, Frank and Gabriella went off to make last arrangements (or so they claimed), and so Rachel and I got lunch together at the Grand Lux Café. With nothing else to talk about, I asked her about Gabriella.

Rachel was picking on a tiny salad, while I tried to get my hands around an enormous burger. I was feeling a little sorry for her, so I moved the plate with my chips closer to the middle of the table.

"Gabriella's such a meek little thing," she told me. "I never thought she'd end up married to that Scottish weirdo. Or any Scottish weirdo, for that matter."

From all Frank had told me about her, she seemed anything but meek to me.

"Is this out of character for her, then?"

"Out of character!" Rachel threw back her head and laughed. "Oh God, if you only knew! She teaches in Sunday school. She volunteers in a woman's shelter. Before she met McPreposterous, she used to dress like a Puritan. I was the one who dressed her up to go out with him. She was shaking like a leaf. Her parents disapproved of course, but I couldn't look on while they sent her on dates with all these wankers who kept telling her how biblically speaking her role in life was to give birth to their children. So I thought I'd encourage her to try something new. We signed her up to this website, and I picked him out for her. I thought I'd mix it up a bit for her. You know? Give her a bit of a taste for the wilder life? Little did I know!"

I was so astonished by what she said that for a moment I could do nothing but stare at her. "Are you serious?"

"Oh yes." She stuffed her mouth with a bunch of chips. "Oh!" she said, noticing what she'd just done. "Oh, don't let me have any more of those. I'm not supposed to eat carbs!"

I pulled the plate with the chips back to me.

"So," I said, "this is unusual for her?"

"Unusual! It's like she's possessed! Her parents are going to kill them both for this. But then, you know, she's had such a dull life so far, and there are such things as divorces, nowadays, right? Who can it harm? Let her go a bit wild. She's had no youth to speak of. Might as well do it now, while she's still reasonably young. Plus, while I do think McChaos is certifiable, he is sort of fun to be around, isn't he? Not to marry, of course, but for a proper night out."

I tried to get my head around this. All I could think was: this was a catastrophe waiting to happen. It must be stopped. I know they say opposites attract, but within reason, surely. Maybe Gabriella thought that he wasn't like this all the time, that he'd calm down eventually. But he *was* like this. *All the time*. She needed to know. Someone needed to tell her. I imagined three months from now, some bloke named, I don't know, Joshua, whom she'd known at Bible camp and whom her parents loved, coming in and then Frank getting a phone call like I had at Heathrow, all about how *They wore me down* and *I owe it a go*. Fuck this.

Determined to have a talk with her, come what may, I left Rachel, excusing myself with the lie that I needed to make an urgent phone call. Then I ran out to Gabriella and Frank's hotel. Gabriella was in her dressing gown, with her hair standing on ends, when she opened the door to their room.

"Is Frank here?" I asked.

She was pink to the roots of her hair. "He's gone out to fetch, er . . . I was . . . napping. Before the wedding, you know?"

He was obviously on a condom run. "Mind if I come in?"

She opened the door wider. It was as though a hurricane had swept through the place. Pillows, duvets, chairs, tables, all strewn around the enormous suite in mad disarray. I could hear water running in the bathroom. She excused herself and rushed to turn it off.

"Frank's going to rent us a limousine," she said with a small giggle when she came back and saw me pick up a brochure off the table. "I told him I've never been in one, and so he decided that I must."

Well, that sounded about right. I put a chair back on its legs and offered it to her. I paced to the window and then back. With all the hurry, I didn't have time to think of the words to say or how to say them. She seemed so innocent and happy, it made me sick to my stomach to ruin this day for her. But people should be honest about their expectations, because (as I'd just learned) sometimes they are way too keen to fool themselves into thinking they're all on the same page.

"So, how is it going? Have you got a dress yet?" I asked.

Gabriella was not the sort of woman who understood awkward conversations. Whatever gambit you threw at her, she was ready to smilingly pick it up and continue on your chosen path. So, though we knew each other barely at all, she said, "No! Do you want to help me pick one? I've been with Rachel, and there's so many lovely plus-sized options here, you know? But I haven't yet seen The One, if you know what I mean. What are you wearing?"

I hadn't thought about it. Before the trip, Harry had raised the question of suits, but I'd never gone so far as to think of acquiring one.

Harry would have been prepared. He'd have had a suit for me too, knowing him.

I had a sudden flash in my mind of him and Kieran, suited and handsome, side by side, in a church. I grabbed the back of a nearby chair, hard.

"Oh, sorry!" she said, hastily. "I didn't mean to— Oh, are you all right?"

I turned away, cleared my throat, and said, "Yeah. Fine. Sorry."

She watched me, concerned. "Can I get you anything?"

"Jet lag," I said, waving my hand. "It'll pass."

"Oh. Okay."

She waited for me to say something more. I remembered why I was here. I cleared my throat again.

"Ah, I just— I thought I'd check in with you. Sometimes Frank can be, er, a little reckless, I suppose. I thought I'd check that you're really okay with getting married so suddenly."

"'Reckless'?" she said, with a laugh. "Have you ever met Frank? Of course it's reckless. It's how he does everything. Like the world's on fire and he only has a few seconds to get things done."

She knew her Frank Brodie well.

"Okay," I said. "That's—that's true."

"He's so enthusiastic about things," she continued, enamoured. "So full of vivacity and life. I feel so blessed to have met him."

"I spoke to Rachel, though, and she told me that this wasn't like you. I just think that sometimes it's very easy to get swept up in one of Frank's schemes, and that this one is maybe a little too wild, if you see what I mean. I wanted to check in case you've changed your mind or . . . or thought the better of it."

"Isn't that sweet of you!" she said, with a giggle. "I mean," she sobered up a little, "it's not that I'm taking marriage lightly, you know. I'm not. And yes, sometimes it *is* difficult to keep up with him. But . . ." here she leaned in forward, as if confiding a secret, "he chose *me*!"

For a moment I wasn't sure what she meant, but she went on, "Only think of all the girls he could have picked, and he picked *me*! He's so . . . so *exciting* and full of life and I'm this . . . this *nobody*. Nobody has ever looked at me the way he looks at me. Like I'm special and precious and—and worth doing all this for!"

I shouldn't have come. This was none of my business.

"So if he wants to marry me," she continued, "I'm not going to stop him. Unless . . ." she paused and her eyes widened, "unless he sent you here to talk to me? Did he want you to talk me out of it, to save face?"

"What? No!" I said, panicked. "Good God, no! I haven't seen him since you two left to—" I looked her up and down, involuntarily "—to, er, make arrangements. Listen, no, he wants to marry you today. I mean, he's going to marry you, unless you stop him. He's extremely determined, trust me. I was just worried that perhaps the whole thing's a bit hasty."

"Ah." She seemed relieved. "Well, yes, it is. It is hasty."

She raised her shoulders, as though an excited thrill had passed through her.

Perhaps some people simply belonged together, and were impossible to tear apart. Like Gabriella and Frank. Or Harry and Kieran.

I turned to her and smiled as best I could. "It's going to be epic."

She beamed back at me. "I know."

If you'd asked me, when I first met Frank, what his wedding would be like, I'd have described pretty much the scene that ensued. A bride he barely knew but who was enchanted by his weird, frantic energy. She, dressed in a glittery silver dress, he in a purple suit for some reason. A chapel in Vegas. An Elvis impersonator chaplain—Frank insisted he had to have one and in fact had to buy the costume and dress a poor but very game chaplain in it to make this particular dream come true—and afterwards a piss up to end all piss ups.

At dawn he had arranged for a helicopter flight over the Grand Canyon—a wedding gift for his bride—and by that time none of us had slept a wink, and we were all of us plastered.

The helicopter pilot was telling us about the sights below through the heavy headset, but we were all so tired and drunk and giggly that I don't think we heard a word the poor chap was saying.

Frank had his arm around Gabriella, who looked like she'd gone to heaven and from now on there'd be nothing but bliss for the end of her days. Rachel fell asleep on my shoulder. I watched the red, orange, and deep brown of the canyon below, stretching as far as the eye could see.

I thought of Harry.

Chapter Eleven
OLD MAN BYRNE

Five Months Before the Big Day

"Are you sure this is big enough?" I ask, dryly.

I'm still half-asleep, but Harry's already up and about. I can smell the coffee from the kitchen; the shirt he's wearing is ironed, but as yet unbuttoned; and he's hanging up an enormous five-month calendar on the wall opposite our bed. Unlike ordinary calendars, this one ends on August the twenty-eighth. Or, as he calls it, the Big Day. Where he managed to find a printer desperate enough to produce this calendar, I don't know. But each day is filled with a multitude of tasks, with a little tick box next to each task, and the whole thing is framed with pictures of us from the past four years. I admit, it's adorable.

"Looks good, doesn't it?" he asks, as he steps back from it. "Five months isn't a lot of time to plan a wedding. We have to be strict with ourselves."

"You're the one who set the date," I say, stretching. He wants us to use the Jamaica tickets for a honeymoon. "Come back to bed."

"Can't. I only have two hours before work, and I've got to narrow down the caterers to three options so we can taste-test them. Siobhan insists on importing the champagne from France, and I'm not sure she realises that this isn't like Aunt Wendy's sixtieth, where she can just forget the champagne in her old mate's garage in Canterbury, and we all go down the pub instead."

He's cute when he's all severe and responsible. I crawl to the foot of the bed and tug on his hand to get him closer.

"I know what would relax you," I say with a smile. "And it's got nothing to do with Aunt Wendy's sixtieth."

"Joe, we really don't have the time," he says, as I draw his shirt down his arms. "You could help me out, actually, and research bands. I've contacted three, but at such short notice, they're all booked up. I thought you might know someone."

"Sure," I say, kissing his chest, up to his collarbone, and then up his neck.

"Joe . . ."

Fortunately, it turns out that there's a way to get Harry instantly horny.

"Yes, future husband?"

I can feel the shift immediately. His hands come up around me, and I reach his mouth at last.

"That's not fair," he complains between kisses. "You've weaponised our engagement."

I grin.

"Turn around," I tell him.

It works like a charm. I don't know what it is about the word *husband*. To him, it's like an aphrodisiac. It started in Dublin, where he ravished me right after the proposal, and so far it continues to hold up its power. If I knew he was going to like it so much, I'd have done this ages ago.

His mouth is on mine, his arms are around me, and I know him so well, it's like playing a favourite instrument. I know the weight of him, I know his strength. Over the years, I have lifted him and squeezed him, I have spread him and enfolded him, so that now every move of mine has a corresponding move from him and I can tell what he wants me to do by how he twists and pulls, or pushes and wriggles into place.

"Husband," I whisper against the warm skin of his neck, and I can feel the gentle shiver, the little buzz of electricity at the word. It's a power I have. He's embarrassed about his own reaction—there's a flush in his cheeks—but I love it. I love that I can do this now.

It's like a best-of album, a compilation of all we like, compact, efficient, quick, and delectable. The sheets brush, the bed creaks, he's in my arms, my very own, mine, and he presses me to him with the same strength, kissing me with the same meaning. *Mine, mine, mine*, his kisses are saying.

"I love you," he says, pressing lube into my hands. He squirms when I reach down and behind him, and I feel a thrill when I prepare him, a rush of blood, a pounding in my chest. It's not the same *I love you* that he says when he leaves for work, or the *I love you*s we exchange before going to sleep. Or the *love you* with which we say goodbye over the phone. It's the *I love you* that means *look what you're doing to me, you sexy bastard*, and it makes me grin.

Afterwards, when he wraps me in his arms, heat beating off his skin, our pulses still racing, he mutters, "Don't let me fall asleep."

"Mhfhrhg," I mutter, contentedly, against his nipple.

His phone rings half an hour later and startles us both into consciousness. He falls out of bed and picks it up, while I blink against the brightness in the room and then drop back on my pillow and marvel that the day has only just begun and I achieved so much already. I made Harry Byrne come. That's got to count for something.

Harry doesn't sound so happy. Whoever's on the phone with him has said something annoying, because his hand is in his hair and he's pacing.

"Yes? Well, that's impossible," Harry says. I lift up onto my elbows and watch him. He throws me a worried glance and then retreats into the other room, closing the door behind him. Weird.

I can hear his muffled voice. "What kind of incompetent . . . No, I'll take care of it. Yes, I said I would, and I will."

I try to guess who it might be. He's only got one client he doesn't like talking about, who calls at all hours of the day and night. Like last night. He's never worked with anybody that persistently annoying. I'm including Malcolm in this.

"Okay. I'll speak to you later. Bye," Harry says.

When he returns, I ask, "Work?"

He looks up, as if barely registering that I said anything. He's got frown lines on his forehead, and his hair is standing up from where he tugged at it earlier.

"I've got to shower and go," he says, reaching for his shirt. I was careful—when I stripped him of it, I left it hanging neatly off the side of a chair. I fall back on the pillows and throw my arm over my face to shield myself from the brightness of the day. The bathroom door closes behind him.

Harry comes back from the bathroom fifteen minutes later, smelling of shower gel and cologne. "By the way, I thought we could have dinner with my parents this Saturday. Are you free?"

My brain is too slow. I'm still distracted by the phone call. I can't think of an excuse.

"It's time we tell them," Harry says, buttoning up.

"They'll find out eventually," I mumble.

"They have to find out from us."

"They will, when we say 'I do' in front of a registrar. Really, you're obsessing over technicalities here."

He smiles and shakes his head at me.

"Saturday," he says. "Make sure you're free."

His phone rings, and he looks at the screen, sees who it is, and shuts it off.

"Who was that?"

"Nobody." He puts the phone away.

I can't help it: I watch him across the room, study his expression. It's not merely these phone calls (which seem to have become more frequent). He's stopped opening his bank statements in front of me. Whenever the post arrives, he takes his letters into his office and locks them in a drawer. Once, when he forgot to log out of his email inbox on the laptop and it appeared when I moved the mouse, he jumped so quickly to close it down, he tripped and bashed himself in the shin. He had a stonking bruise afterwards, but when I asked him what was the matter, he evaded my question.

Now, too, he changes the subject.

"I think I left it at work," he mutters. "Do you know if Maya sent me the quote from the chair people? I thought I pinned it to the wall."

Fuck it. I'm asking him.

"It's not Kieran who's calling, is it?"

This makes him freeze mid-move. He's just been bending over to check under his desk while buttoning his shirt, but now he lifts up, slowly, to look at me. "What?"

The longer he's not speaking, the longer I have to imagine him going, *I suppose we should talk . . .*

I have a gnawing feeling, like a prickle up my spine.

"No," he says. "No, it's not Kieran."

He takes his phone out of his pocket and shows me his last calls. It's a long number.

"Where is this from?" I ask.

"It's a lady in Australia. She has no idea about time zones, apparently. Remember? I told you about her before?"

Maybe I'm being ridiculous. "Sorry."

He takes my face in his hand and kisses me.

But why does this client have his private mobile number? And why does he hide his bank statements? And his emails?

It's nothing. I know it's nothing. It can't be anything, because why would it be? I mean, what earthly reason would he have to marry me, of all people, if he really was in fact trying to get back together with Kieran? I'm being ridiculous.

Kieran has been travelling a lot, lately, though.

I'm being paranoid.

I watch Harry, frowningly, as he begins to rush again.

"Oh," he says, when he puts his engagement bracelet on, "remember about the bands. And are you sure you still want to design the invitations yourself?"

"Yes," I say. "Leave it to me."

In Harry's world, that means *Help me*. "I've sent you some ideas," he says. "Check your email. And don't forget." Like he'd let me. Like he won't text me at some point today to remind me. He throws his tie around his collar and allows me to tie it for him while he puts his cuff links in.

"If I get in early, I might get the caterers done before my meeting," he says. "Thank God for Maya. Yesterday, she printed out all the forms for me, put them in a folder and cross-referenced them. Harriet saw it and made a huge deal out of it. I'm pretty sure she's going to try and poach Maya from under me."

"The girl's going to have to move on eventually."

"I know," he sighs. "Just not now."

I finish with his tie, and he checks himself out in the mirror. He looks like one of the characters on *Mad Men*. I want to undress him again.

"Okay, love, I'll see you later." He turns, kisses me, and reaches for his suit coat. "Be back by six."

I don't like preparing the wedding. Of course, getting married itself is fine, but the preparations are a nightmare.

Harry and Maya have always been close, but now that they have a wedding to plan, they're texting each other constantly. One time, he texted her while we were having sex. He denied it afterwards, and I know he's embarrassed about it, but it happened. To be fair, we were at it for a long time, but still—he reached over to his nightstand and texted her an idea for table names.

Knowing that he's so into this stuff, I make an effort. I offered to design the invitations because he is very particular that our wedding reflects "us." And now that he suggested I take care of the music, I wait until he leaves the flat, and then look up Frank's friend and DJ, Verena, to tell her that I need a band.

Verena's astonished to hear from me. "You're getting married? *You*?"

"Yes," I patiently reply. "Harry's very traditional, and he wants a good reception, so I mean to make that happen. Anything you can swing for me?"

"It's a bit short notice," she says. "But I'll think of something."

She promises to get back to me on this. I make a tick on the giant calendar on our wall. Harry will be ecstatic about it.

I have my own secrets from Harry. For example, my nearly daily trips to the gym. Frank signed up on recommendation from his therapist, who thinks it's a good way to manage his postdivorce depression. Harry's fed up with Frank's constant negativity about marriage, so I don't tell him that I see Frank this often—but I reckon my going to the gym with him is a good way to a) encourage Frank to go, and b) get fit before my wedding night.

Besides the exercise alone, I cheer Frank up by letting him think he can lift more than me. It's also fairly easy to play on his vanity and raise his gloomy mood that way. I comment on how toned his abs look now, and he's mildly mollified.

"Are you checking me out, perv?" he says, colouring a little, evidently pleased.

"Sure," I say, generously. "I'd hit that if I weren't already taken."

It makes him smile.

Afterwards, we're cooling off in the car. It's a pleasant late-spring day—the sort of day you wish you could spend in front of a lake, or lying in a meadow with a good book. Not in a gym car park, in front of a bunch of warehouses, the sun beating down on your bonnet, the wind sweeping the earthy scent of the pet store across the road at you.

The exercise does calm Frank down a little. It punctures through his energy, and he talks about Gabriella almost without his usual heat.

"She's not even bothering to show up at the meetings. It's just her lawyer," he says. "I mean, what's she afraid of? What does she think I'll do to her?"

"Does she want anything? Money?"

"All she wants, apparently, is to be rid of me as soon as possible."

I don't know what to say. It's all the more awkward because he's my best man. But when I suggested that perhaps I'd go without a best man, he flipped out and demanded to know what that was supposed to mean. So I offered him the job, and he angrily accepted, warning me that all marriages end in either divorce or death.

The horrible thing is that I don't know what went wrong between them. Their marriage was impetuous, sure, but they seemed to get on so well, for a time. And then she announced she wanted a divorce— according to Frank, entirely out of the blue.

I'd warned her. In Vegas, I had that talk with her, and I did suggest it had all been too rapid. But she'd been determined to go through with it at the time, and I certainly never saw a flicker of wavering in her then.

I consider briefly what to do about it, but then remind myself that it's not my place to do anything. As much as it pains me to see him like this, all I can realistically accomplish is sit there and listen to him pour out his sorrow.

"How about a drive?" I say, turning the key in the ignition.

He moves his seat back a little to stretch. "Let's go."

On Saturday, Harry and I drive up to Harpenden to dine with his parents and tell them about the engagement.

"Stop fidgeting," he says, as we leave the comfort of our street, for the heavy Saturday-morning traffic.

"Why don't we put it in a letter?" I ask. "That way they can deal with it in their own time, and we can go and see them afterwards, when they've rehearsed a response."

"You're being silly," he says. "Siobhan already knows, and she's thrilled. Ollie is on our side. My mum loves you and she loves weddings. I don't know what you're worried about."

"Yeah, you do, or else you would have mentioned *him*."

"My dad will be fine. Come on—" he puts a hand on my knee "—relax. Do you remember what he said the other day? He said your work was impressive."

"No, he didn't."

"Yes, he did."

"No, he said he was impressed anybody would buy my doodles," I say. "Like I'm a crook who gets by by selling people snake oil."

Harry laughs.

"And then he asked me if I ever intended to get a real job," I continue. "Which is probably why he thought that my spending two months designing that escutcheon that hangs over the front door at his club was just a hobby for me. You do know people charge a lot of money for that sort of work, right?"

Harry's amused. "He received a lot of compliments for that thing, and you know he's the worst for expressing his feelings."

I don't think Harry appreciates the gravity of this situation. But there's no turning back. When we arrive at his house, his mother Bonnie embraces him and then me and immediately starts telling us all about every single member of Harry's enormous family. His cousins are breeding like rabbits, so there's a lot to go through, and then there are the various medical procedures the elder generation of Byrnes and Linfords have lined up, which we must hear about.

I like Bonnie.

She, like all of Harry's friends and family, was a devout Kieran fan and staunchly anti-Joe when Harry and I first got together, but she was my first convert.

Mr. Byrne, in fact, is the only Kieran-fan who continues to persist in his belief that either Kieran and Harry will reunite or else Harry might change his mind about homosexuality altogether. This last remains his favoured option.

As we enter the sitting room, the old man gets up from his armchair with a heavy sigh. He hugs Harry and then reluctantly shakes my hand.

"So," he says to Harry, "which way did you come, then?"

In a tradition as old as time, the two then go over the various roads that we could have taken but didn't, Harry's reasons for choosing the roads he did, and his dad's opinion about why Harry's choices were all catastrophically wrong. You'd think we didn't just arrive safely, soundly, and on time. Meanwhile, Bonnie looks up at me and asks, "What happened to all your lovely hair, dear?"

Without thinking I say, "Oh, it's a funny story!" but then I catch Harry's eye, and realise that they don't know about Dublin yet, and so I say, "I cut it off."

She blinks at me. Ollie and Siobhan, who already know the story, smile.

"That's—that's very funny, dear," Bonnie says, patting my arm consolingly. "Would you like a drink?"

I accept a drink and then let her take me off to her atelier—their refurbished attic, really—where she keeps her latest work (in fact, I'm the one who taught her how to paint). In all, it's like any other visit with Harry's parents.

We sit down to dinner quite amiably.

Three years ago, Siobhan and Ollie told us that they were trying to conceive, and as nothing came of that, they are now trying different fertility treatments, which is the primary subject of conversation at the table. They're matter-of-fact about it, and Bonnie is full of good advice, which is not at all awkward. She says things like: "Remember to do it in the mornings" and "You have to lift your legs right up after he, you know, deposits himself inside of you" and all this while ladling spoonfuls of something that resembles soup and is made up of hot cream, oysters, mushrooms, carrots, and pineapple onto our plates. Bonnie is "creative" with her cooking.

If anybody asked me, this doesn't seem the appropriate time to mention the engagement, but Harry is absolutely bursting with the news. So, when there's a lull in the conversation (right after Ollie, with a perfectly straight face, accepts old Mr. Byrne's stricture to do "it" often and to do it properly), Harry takes my hand, under the table, and says, "Actually, Joe and I have some news of our own."

Siobhan and Ollie look at us from the other side of the table, eyes wide. I share their apprehension, but Harry apparently notices nothing.

"What is it?" Bonnie asks, and a plump, moist mushroom falls back into the soup from her spoon, splashing droplets of it on her hand.

"As a matter of fact," Harry says, "Joe and I are getting married."

My heart breaks a little. His face is so hopeful, and he is so geared up and excited, and the reaction around the table is as though someone had frozen time. Ollie and Siobhan wait for the outburst. Bonnie is speechless. Mr. Byrne's jaw clenches and then he exhales a deep, shuddering breath.

"Oh!" Bonnie says, after what seems like a decade. "Oh! Why that's— How lovely! How fabulous . . . Is . . . is that legal?"

"Yes," I say, quickly. "It's legal, and it's going to be a lot of fun. We're going to have a reception, and I was looking into bands, and it's going to be a brilliant party, with all our friends, and . . ." I try to talk so that Harry doesn't hear how heavily his father is breathing. I do hope he's not going to have a heart attack.

But Harry notices nothing. He interrupts me, "And it's in five months. For our anniversary I gave Joe a trip to Jamaica, and he gave me this." He shows off the bracelet. "He designed it himself. Isn't it nice? It's to celebrate the engagement."

Bonnie blinks at the bracelet.

"Oh yes, that is pretty!" she says, smiling, then asks me, "How did you do that?"

I tell her, and then Harry says, "We thought it would be sweet if we got married before the trip, so that we could make it into our honeymoon. Joe's always wanted to go to Jamaica to learn more about his background. The trip's in September, and they're supposed to have good weather there all year around, from what I'm told."

Bonnie, I notice, starts blinking more rapidly. Oh no. I thought she of all people wouldn't take it badly. Siobhan stands up and gets a box of tissues. Ollie now chimes in.

"Beautiful place. I went there for a diving holiday in my gap year."

"Not the time to brag," I tease him, and he laughs. Bonnie dabs at her eyes.

"Oh," she says, "well that's a— It's such a surprise! I don't even know what to say! What does one say? Oh!" Suddenly she bounces up. "A cake! I'm going to make a cake!"

"What, *now*?" Siobhan startles.

"No, silly! For the wedding!" her mother chides.

Oh God.

Harry turns to his father, who's conspicuously quiet.

"Dad?" Harry says. "Are you all right?"

Mr. Byrne eyes him reproachfully, and then me.

"And which one of you is wearing the white dress? Him?" Here he tosses his head at me. I have a sinking feeling in my stomach.

Harry laughs. "Neither of us is wearing a dress. You know that."

"Well?" the old man says. "Do I? Which one of you is the wife, then? That's what marriage does, doesn't it? It makes two people"—here he points at Ollie and Siobhan—"husband and wife. At least tell me you're the husband."

Harry's laugh turns uneasy. He's taken aback. "We're both going to be husbands."

Silence falls. I wish I were Aladdin and could lift us out of the room on a magic carpet, and then maybe hypnotise Harry so he remembers none of this. Instead, I'm powerless and have to wait for this to develop. But it doesn't. Mr. Byrne just snorts, shakes his head, and says, "Dinner's getting cold."

Bonnie licks her lips, her eyes darting around the room, before saying, "So, er, when's the date? You picked one already have you?"

"Twenty-eighth of August," I say. "We picked a hotel in Chelsea; it's licensed for weddings, so we can have the ceremony right there. It's really nice; you'll love it."

"That sounds charming. Do they have a planner to help you out?"

"They do," I say. "But we're doing most of the planning ourselves."

The conversation descends into the nitty-gritty of wedding planning, which is the subject I'm hoping will hold Harry's attention. But he's quiet now, as is his father.

I have tolerated Harry's dad for years now: his little digs at my expense, his glares, his demands that I lack a "sense of humour." For the most part, I tried to remember he's from a different generation and his ideas are, well, old-fashioned.

But now Harry is sitting, extinguished, at my side, and his happy glow of the past month is put out. And now I hate his father.

After dinner, Bonnie wants to show us her wedding album, and Siobhan does her best to cheer up Harry by repeating anecdotes about her own wedding, during which almost everything went tits up.

"The bus with the guests went to a different St. Mary's Church—" she says, and Ollie interrupts (always in the same place): "And who gave the bus company the address?"

"I did." Siobhan rolls her eyes good-humouredly. "And so the guests were at one church and I was at a different church . . . and then of course the veil got stuck in the door of the car and got completely muddied—"

"The weather was atrocious!" Ollie says.

"—and so I had to take it off. Seven hundred quid it cost me, and I wore it for a car ride!"

"And then little Molly cried the whole time . . . couldn't hear a word. And poor Aunt Louisa . . . Do you know, her funeral was a better-run affair than our wedding, wasn't it, Ollie? What? I'm just saying!"

I don't listen to any of it. Mr. Byrne is sitting in his armchair, glaring at the carpet, and I'm sitting in the sofa, next to Harry, glaring at the old man. Then Mr. Byrne rises abruptly and leaves the room, and Siobhan determinedly continues as though nothing happened. Harry listens to her politely, but I know his thoughts are with his dad. Bonnie laughs more than is necessary at Siobhan's anecdotes, which everybody in the room has already heard and witnessed firsthand anyway.

I excuse myself. The corridor next to the stairs leads into the kitchen, and from there to a utility room, which has a door that opens up onto the garden. I can see the stubborn old git standing out there, lighting a cigarette with his thick-fingered hands.

Trying to control my temper, I open the door and step outside. A brisk wind glides over my short-cropped head. I pull the sleeves of my sweater down over my hands—a sweater Harry had picked because he wanted to make a good impression on this old bastard, I remember.

"Hey," I say. It doesn't come out friendly.

Mr. Byrne lifts his head and looks at me. He doesn't pretend to be welcoming. "I'll be right in."

"No, I wanted to talk to you outside."

"Not in the mood for conversation," he mumbles.

"Good, so you can keep your mouth shut and listen to me."

He raises his gaze from the flicking of his lighter, surprise and anger mingling in his hard, worn face. Harry will kill me for this. Well, fuck it.

"I don't know how people reacted when you told them you were getting married," I say, "but if they were half as mean, petty, and stupid as you were being back there, I sincerely pity you. Harry's been looking forward to telling you all month. And you couldn't even get yourself to say a measly 'congratulations'?"

"What did you just say?" He steps closer menacingly.

"Yeah, come at me, man," I say, pushing up my sleeves. I can hear the blood roaring in my ears, and I know I shouldn't, but just the memory of Harry's expression, the way his smile fell and that light went out of his eyes when he saw this old prick's reaction pushes me over the edge. I speak through my teeth, "I haven't bare-knuckle boxed in years, but I think I remember how I won light heavyweight champion."

He pulls his chin back and frowns in surprise.

"Easy," he says, though the dry amusement in his voice makes him sound more like Harry and thus makes me want to hit him less. Not that I really intended to hit him. I didn't. I lower my shoulders.

"Look"—I try for a more measured tone—"you don't have to like me or the fact that your son is getting married to me. But Harry is really excited about this." I take a deep breath to steady my outrage. "You and I want the same thing—for Harry to be happy. Well, at the moment I'm doing my job, but you're being a failure at yours."

He watches me the way a dog watches a cat he's about to bare his teeth at. But he doesn't say anything.

Well, fuck him too, then. I turn around and go back into the house.

Chapter Twelve

THE BROKEN HEARTS CLUB

Five Years Before the Big Day

The rules of the Broken Hearts Club:
1. Don't make fun of the club's name.
2. You are allowed to be miserable. No, you don't have to get over it. You can be unhappy to the fullest extent of your abilities. Moaning and whining is encouraged.
3. Insert inevitable Fight Club joke.

I returned from Vegas a changed man.

Throughout my visit there, I kept myself sane with the help of continuous drunkenness and junk food, but on the plane trip back, which I spent mostly being sick in the tiny, cramped toilet cabin, I decided that this was not a sustainable method of dealing with reality.

Harry was with Kieran. For reasons beyond my control, this was the state of affairs now.

My parents left me for adoption.

My mother's husband left me for his religion.

The love of my life left me for his.

I dragged myself through Heathrow, via Tube and bus, back to my flat with Chloe, and then locked myself in my room. Chloe asked if I was all right, and I said, "Raging hangover."

She chuckled. "Without one, any marriage of Frank's would've been annulled, no?"

I laughed mechanically and waited for her to walk away from my door. Collecting my thoughts required space and silence. I couldn't ever really think unless I was making something with my hands.

I took out a pad and began to sketch. Everything went quiet in my head when I sketched. At first I continued an old drawing I'd started for a friend who wanted something for a fantasy novel she'd written, but then I couldn't focus on that and started something new. At first it was a salamander, then it turned into a jungle with flowers and parrots, and then it appeared, as if by itself: a hummingbird.

Then I drew a spider—it let itself down by a long, thin thread, and had a mischievous face. I'd read a lot about Anansi when I was younger. A trickster god in Jamaican mythology. Then my hand flowed freely and with more determination.

I was exhausted, but I couldn't sleep. The night felt long and heavy, and the day that followed felt like an unwanted obligation.

As I lay awake the following night, thinking of all the nights that would come—long, empty nights—I thought again about Amy and about the woman who had come looking for me once.

Our conversations had petered out over the past couple of weeks. Her reluctance to let herself hope again had won over my desire to at least talk. But now I thought of her again. Now that Harry was gone, and I was adrift once more, that pulling sensation in my chest was near unbearable, but thoughts of Yvonne, of the possibility, sparked and glowed somewhere tender inside me.

I sent her a picture of my drawing.

Okay, I think we can talk. I'm sorry if I'm being a pain. I didn't think I'd ever hear from you. A lot of feelings.

These were Yvonne's words after she saw my drawing. We'd been writing ever since, and, at last, we agreed a time and date. It felt like an exam. At first I was equal parts nervous and excited. Then I was just nervous. Even the prospect of hearing her voice made my heart race. Would I feel a connection? I felt plenty of connection with my mum, but I wondered if there was going to be something else with Yvonne—something deep and primal, something nobody could deny me, take away from me.

Something nobody could choose or reject.

When the day arrived, I bathed and combed my hair and dressed in a shirt I bought, with a collar and everything. Chloe even helped me tidy my room.

"You look great, honestly," she said, trying to sound light.

"Thank you."

We set my laptop up on my desk, and then Chloe left me, closing the door behind herself very quietly. She left the flat shortly after.

I paced my room. My hands were clammy, and even though I opened a window, the room felt small and too warm.

A blip informed me there was a message. My heart in my throat, I approached the laptop. It wasn't her. It was an email. At first I thought it was spam, because I never get contacted by serious journalists, but this was a journalist from *The Guardian*, and he asked if I was free to talk about my recent work with P&B Designs. Duncan Webb. I recognized the name, but couldn't immediately place it.

Why was the name making the little hairs at the back of my neck stand up?

I put it down to my appointment to speak with Yvonne, and closed the email.

She rang first. The sound of the Skype ringtone made my pulse jump, and I had to undo my collar button. It was difficult to breathe.

I sat down. Pressed the little green button. The image popped up after one second's delay. I forced a smile and possibly I waved—later I couldn't really recall; it was like it all happened through a haze—and I saw her smile as well, a fond smile.

"How are you, Joe?" she said.

I could tell. It wasn't her voice or her face, and yet it was both. She wasn't my mother. I could tell she knew it too, almost at once.

"I'm good. How's Spain?"

"Oh lovely. Very hot today."

She sniffed. I wrinkled my nose. Fuck.

She put her hand to her cheek, wiped away a tear, and then started laughing.

"Oh, this is ridiculous," she said. "I'm sorry. What do you want to talk about?"

I didn't want to talk about anything. She was obviously upset. We were staring at each other, both wanting the same thing, and unable to offer each other squat.

The call only lasted fifteen minutes in the end, both of us too polite to quit it too abruptly. Afterwards, I couldn't sit in one place. I texted Chloe and she came home, saw my face, and then stretched out her arms. She is not a natural hugger. Chloe hugs are rare.

"It's all right," she said, rubbing my back. "It's a journey, that's all. You're not at your destination yet."

Oddly comforted, I let her make me tea while she told me about a new project she was interested in. I wasn't really listening, and she wasn't really trying to get through to me, only to fill the air with words, to lift the silence.

At some point, as she poured the hot, bubbling water into my mug, she said, "Amazing how one job put you in touch with people from so many different circles."

Something about her words struck a chord. It connected something in my brain: the name Duncan Webb, and where I'd heard it before. I'd been stupid to not see it at once. Maya mentioned his name to Harry once.

My heart bumped. I pulled my shoulders together and sunk deeper into my chair. Chloe continued to talk.

". . . he's thirteenth in line to the throne or something like that, and I'd told him no once, twenty years ago, so I'm not sure why he thinks I'd say yes now and— Joe? Christ, what the—"

She came rushing from the kitchen. I'd sunk my face into my hands, and I suppose that was the first time she'd ever seen me cry.

"Well and what's this!" Frank cried, when he returned from his honeymoon in Mongolia. He was tanned and somehow bigger looking. Marriage became him.

I, on the other hand, had lost weight and felt faint from not eating. My appetite had deserted me completely, and I had trouble sleeping. I asked him about Mongolia, but Frank said, "Oh bugger Mongolia, pal, you look like death! What the devil is the matter with you?"

Of course, since he'd been busy with the wedding, I hadn't told him about Harry and Kieran, or even about Yvonne, and when I told him now he just gaped at me in surprise.

"Bloody hell!" he said. "I'm sorry, mate. This calls for drinks. Come, it's on me."

I didn't feel like drinking, but equally I had no strength to resist him, and so out we went, and I hoped that perhaps it might help a little. Frank, convinced that all I needed was a good time, swept Chloe and Gabriella along, rallying us to be cheerful. He was good at that sort of thing.

All the parts of a good night out with my friends were there: as usual, Frank attracted a random collection of hangers-on; as usual, Chloe regaled us with anecdotes of her past encounters with surprising people and being a total legend. There was an additional surprise of hearing Gabriella kill it at karaoke.

But the yawning emptiness inside me could not be drowned out by their laughter, their good time, the loud music, or the endless martinis they kept buying me. In fact, their laughter was jarring, the loud music oppressive, the alcohol nauseating. It accumulated with every minute that passed until I needed to get outside, into the night, where it was quiet and not so crowded. Frank and Gabriella must have seen me try to slink out unnoticed, because moments later they followed me. Gabriella was in her flimsy dress and clearly cold, and Frank was flushed and drunk.

"Where are you going?" He laughed. "You should see how young the bloke who just hit on Chloe is. She's a minx, for a sixty-year-old."

I tried for a smile. "That's all right. I think I'll head home now."

Frank's eyebrows rose. I had never been one to leave a party early. "Are ye serious?"

It had been raining earlier, but now it was drizzling. Cabs splashed through the streets, the beat of music came through faintly from the inside of the club. I stuck my hands in my pockets, lifted my shoulders, looked at my feet. "Yeah, sorry."

Frank rolled his eyes up to the heavens, impatiently. "Mate, he was one guy. There'll be others. I'll find you a cuter one if you just come back inside. Won't we, love?" Here he turned to Gabriella, who smiled pityingly.

"You wouldn't understand," I said, shaking my head. "I should go."

"Come on!" Frank cried. "Forget him, and come with us. I swear, I'll make it better if you try a little harder and play along."

"No, thanks," I said, trying to turn around.

He grabbed my arm. "Come on, ye ninny, forget him and—"

"I can't forget him!" I snapped. "It's impossible. He was the one." Tears gathered in my eyes. This was highly embarrassing, and I was grateful for the drizzle.

Frank scoffed. "Bollocks to that. No such thing."

"What about Gabriella?" I said, waving at her dramatically. "She's your one, isn't she?"

Frank laughed. "If you mean she's the only woman who'd ever put up with me, you're right."

Gabriella folded her arms around herself and he, noticing, asked if she wanted to go back inside. She shook her head.

I rolled my eyes. "Well, whatever. He was it. And I had a window of opportunity and now he'll marry Kieran and be with him forever, and I—" I clamped my mouth shut, since my voice had begun to crack.

Gabriella, seeming touched by this, sighed. "Joe . . ."

"He was the one, I know he was," I said, staring down at my shoes. They could take everything from me. Fuck it, let them. But they couldn't take that. I knew what I knew.

Frank tried to sound lighthearted. "You don't know your arse from your elbow, and you're supposed to know *that*? Come on, mate."

I don't know why I expected Frank to understand such a thing. Of course he would try to laugh it off.

"It's a gut thing, all right?" I said. "Like, I knew Yvonne wasn't the woman I was looking for. And I know Harry is the One."

"Wasn't he all high-strung and sarcastic?" Frank demanded. "And wasn't he constantly pining after—what did you call him?—his troglodyte ex?"

I bit my lip. "He and I . . ." I began and then broke off. How could I explain it to him? This wasn't a thing words could do. Songs could do it and colour and shape and texture, wild bursts of light and shade could do it. Not words.

"What do you want with that bloke anyway?" he asked. "You were too different; it was never going to work out! You're not a conventional sort of man and he—"

"He made me feel calm inside," I interrupted, mostly because I wanted him to stop talking. This did the trick, though. He shut up at last.

In the darkness of the night and the drizzle, with the streetlamp behind him, I could not make him out that well. He turned to Gabriella, who was faithfully standing by his side and, as if remembering what he'd said to me about her, his whole persona seemed to soften.

"Go inside, lass," he said. "You'll get drenched. I'll grab us a cab."

She looked to me, wavered, then gave me a quick squeeze and ran off back into the club. Frank and I stood in silence for a moment after she left.

"I know I'll get over it eventually," I continued. "He's in love with Kieran—was from the beginning—and I suppose it's precisely because I love him that I have to be happy that he finally gets what he always wanted. And I am. Or I will be. But I get to be a little miserable at the same time, don't I?"

I expected Frank to laugh at me, but he was quiet, and then hung his head and said, "Yeah."

"Or a lot miserable," I said, my voice quivering.

He put his hand on my shoulder, pressed, and then let it slide down my arm. He took hold of my hand. After a moment, he said, "I'm sorry."

"Not your fault."

"No, I'm sorry I tried to stop you being miserable. Mate, you've the right to be as miserable as you want. I mean truly bloody shoddy."

I let go of his hand and threw my arms around him, and he, being Frank and not doing anything by half measures, hugged me tightly to him. We stood in this wet embrace for a while, until Gabriella and Chloe came out together, having got impatient with us.

We returned to Chloe's and my flat soaked, since we hadn't been able to find a cab and had instead rushed off for the Tube and got splashed by a passing car. So, cold and wet, we gathered in the kitchen, with towels around our shoulders (Frank and Gabriella together under my large bath towel) and our hands around mugs of hot cocoa, which Chloe had made.

That was when Gabriella officially declared the opening of the Broken Hearts Club.

For the record, we didn't arrive by that name at once.

Gabriella said, "We should start a club. An—an association of the lonely and depressed?"

"Hand me the sleeping pills now, will you?" I muttered.

"The Lovers Of Never Ending Recovery Society," Chloe said with a mischievous twinkle in her eye.

"The L.O.N.E.R.S.?" Gabriella frowned, working it out.

"Really, Chloe? Really?" I demanded.

"If I'm going to be part of a club," Frank said, "it's going to be called the Cobras. End of."

"Are we forming a crime-fighting ninja clan?" I asked. "Besides, what's the point of forming a club of broken hearts—"

"The Broken Hearts Club!" Gabriella cried, and Frank high-fived her.

"—when I'm the only one with a broken heart?" I finished.

"It's so we have a space where we can complain about the things everybody else wants us to shut up about," Frank said. "Like . . . I hate that I lost my leg. It's fucking wank. I cannae tell you how I'm reminded of it almost every bloody day."

I blinked, surprised. Gabriella kissed his cheek.

"Well," Chloe said, "now I can't say my thing, since that's nothing to losing a leg."

"It's not a competition," Gabriella said. "Say your thing."

Chloe rolled her eyes. "I suppose I never got over Carrie Fisher dying. She was a hero of mine and consequently ought to have been immortal."

"I get that," I said. "I hate that Terry Pratchett died."

Frank raised his hand. "Freddie Mercury."

He turned to Gabriella to ask for her pick, and she looked around as though tempted to say something, but then suddenly blushed and, shyly, shook her head. It made the loose, wet strands of her head fling back from her face and spray Frank who, in return, bear-hugged her. Chloe rolled her eyes and turned to me.

"What?" I said.

"It's your turn now," she said. "Spill it."

"Spill it?" I laughed. "I already told you . . ."

"Bloody tell us again," Frank said, with his arm still around his wife. "Anything you want."

My heart felt heavy in my chest, and all I could think to say was, "He won't call or text me. But he keeps doing these things for me . . . I don't know what to make of it."

"What things?" Gabriella asked.

"I mean, I don't *know* it's all him, but it can't be anybody else," I said. "I keep getting phone calls with job offers, and phone calls from journalists wanting to talk about my 'process,' and last week I got an email inviting me to join one of those snobby London clubs people go to to hobnob with other people who think they still live in the nineteenth century."

They all looked at me, surprised.

"Considering what my usual work calls look like, it must be him. I can't think who else. I want to call him and ask what this is supposed to mean, but I'm afraid he'd tell me."

"What are you afraid he'll tell you?" Gabriella asked, quietly.

I shrugged. "Maybe I'm afraid he won't pick up. Or that he's doing all this because he's sorry for me."

I sniffed and rubbed my nose with my sleeve.

"Maybe," I said, after a pause, "it's none of those things. Maybe it's worse than that and he's just a decent bloke who wants to do something nice for me. And that's . . ."

"Way worse," Chloe said. "That's brutal." She shook her head, sighed, and then said, "Okay . . . I wasn't going to say this because I thought it wisest not to mention him at all, but . . . I saw him the other day."

My heart throbbed painfully. "What? Who? Harry?"

"He was coming out of a coffee shop with some moustachioed bloke, and I'd just found the cutest lamp in this antique shop next door. I was going to walk straight past him, you know, out of solidarity, but he was so excited to see me, you'd think I was his long-lost sister or something."

"What—what did he say?"

She shrugged. "He wanted to know how you were, and if you were all right, and whether you were doing okay and . . . yeah, there was no getting away from him. Luckily, Mr. Moustache got impatient and dragged him away or else I'd still be standing there, repeating that you're fine and I'm fine and everything's fine . . ."

My heart lurched. "Did he say anything about wanting to talk to me?"

Chloe glanced at Frank, who looked away and rubbed Gabriella's arm.

"Well, Mr. Moustache was right there," Chloe said. "It's not like Harry could tell me anything in private. And, you know, I'm not his biggest fan. I might have been staring hatefully at him the whole time; who's to say?"

He could have asked. I blinked at her, barely able to breathe past the lump in my throat. The journalists, the invitations, the offers . . . they were just that. If he'd really wanted to see me, he could have asked Chloe or, in fact, asked me.

He could have asked, and he hadn't.

Chapter Thirteen
FINAL PREPARATIONS

A Week Before the Big Day

It is one week to the wedding. The calendar on our wall is full of ticks.

Harry made baked pasta—at least that's what we call it, since it has no name, because Harry came up with it by himself one day, freestyling with leftovers. He plies me with wine, and I hope for news à la "let's drop all this wedding preparation crap and elope." I can see that he wants to tell me something by the intent look in his eyes as he pours the wine.

At last, when he puts the bottle down, he starts twisting the bracelet around his wrist in a nervous gesture, lost in thought.

I watch him, surprised, and then lift my glass and say, "Cheers?"

He looks up at me, blinks at last, and softens into a slight, crooked smile.

"Ah. Yes."

We clink glasses, though his sloshes and nearly spills. He's usually very graceful. I frown as he settles the glass back down.

"You all right?"

He lifts his eyes to meet mine. He clears his throat. "Don't be cross."

"If you want to cancel the elaborate wedding and do this my way, I'm not cross, I'm ecstatic!" I say.

He laughs nervously.

"No, it's not that. We're still doing this the hard way. But I have to go away for a couple of days."

"What? Where? Why?"

He puts his hand on mine.

"It's just for a couple of days. I have to meet a client; she lives in Malmö."

"What?"

"It's just for a couple of days, so I can sort her out, and that way I won't have to think of work until we get back from Jamaica," he tries to placate me.

"What about all the preparations?"

Despite his planning, the wedding still has lots of loose ends. Decisions have to be made. Emails need to be sent.

"You can deal with them, can't you?" He smiles. "You're such a great planner and executor of plans."

"Well, now I know you're taking the piss. Who knows what I might do if you leave this to me. I might shave my eyebrows or flash your grandparents this time!"

His smile broadens. "I'm certain you won't. And if you do, it's just part and parcel of being with you. I've learned to live with it."

"When will you be back?"

"Before the wedding." At my shocked expression he adds, "Well before the wedding. I promise. It's an emergency, and if it weren't important, you know I wouldn't go. I'd have sent Maya or someone."

There's nothing I can say. I gulp my wine instead.

It's not that I'm unwilling to help—it's that Harry has managed everything so far and he's the best person to tie up the loose ends.

Siobhan is in France, officially in search of the best champagne for our wedding. Unofficially, she's on a piss-up tour of French vineries after the latest round of IVF treatments failed. I don't know how to handle her in the state she's in.

Harry's mum has promised to make a cake for the wedding, and Harry's the only one who can dissuade her from making it with shrimp or peppers or boiled turkey.

And then there's the wedding planner. Her name is Arabella, and while I'm sure she's a perfectly sweet person in her private life, in her professional life she's the snootiest, haughtiest woman I've ever dealt with. Which is why I never deal with her—Harry does. Because Harry knows how to deal with pricks, since he does it all the time at work.

Hell, he managed to survive ten years cooperating with Malcolm I-Thrive-On-Sun-Energy-Like-A-Fucking-Carnation Peppard!

Harry has to go, and I have to let him. I watch him pack, and listen to his many instructions, and try to stay calm.

"I put everything in an email for you," he says, "and I updated your Google calendar, so you'll get automatic reminders about deadlines. You'll be fine."

I nod, too quickly.

"Honey," he says, putting a hand on my arm. "You'll be fine."

"Yes, of course. Pf, child's play, this."

The cab he ordered is already waiting for him downstairs. I offered to drive him to the airport, but he refused.

"Just try and relax," he says, "and don't do anything needlessly elaborate. Okay?"

I give him a thumbs-up. This is making me uneasy. Despite his outward appearance, I know this wedding has been wearing on him. He's been sleeping less and losing his patience with people on the phone more.

Now, too, he's got rings under his eyes because he didn't sleep almost at all last night, and I know his phone rang at least twice between 11p.m. and 5 a.m., by which time he was already showered and dressed. Obviously this Malmö client of his is a stressful case. Not that I ever heard of this Malmö client before, but whatever. I mean, the company he works for is a much larger enterprise than what it used to be, and it sort of makes sense he's suddenly so sought after internationally. Right?

What's the use wondering why he is suddenly so popular, at all times of the night, with mysterious foreign clients?

I'm not suspicious. This is perfectly normal. Unprecedented, sure, but I trust Harry. He's got to do what he's got to do.

Like leaving the country a few days before the wedding.

Normal.

Totally unremarkable.

Totally cool.

I'm sure it's only my paranoia, anyway. He's been nervy and jumpy lately, but so have I. A wedding is serious, expensive business, after all.

Anybody would feel the pressure. And Harry in particular because of his need to be in control of everything.

He kisses me goodbye, somewhat absentmindedly, and then rushes off, forgetting his bag. I have to run after him to give it to him before he drives off without it.

Should he have packed that heavily for a couple of days in Malmö?

"Okay," Bonnie tells me, showing me the drawing of the planned wedding cake. "This . . . is it. What do you think?"

It's heart-burstingly horrible. It looks like a three-tier strawberry, but, she tells me, "the green is made up of salad-leafs and the red of ketchup. The pips are caviar! Isn't that sweet?"

"That," I say, "is very . . . c-courageous."

Harry and I have quarrelled three times over the wedding cake. Mostly because I'd like to have an edible one, and because Harry thinks a cake isn't as important as having our families actively involved in the wedding.

"Isn't it though?" she says, sounding excited. "I mean, you don't want to go all trivial, with chocolate or fruit cake or something like that, do you? We want to be original and bold!"

"Oh yes, bold," I say, smiling. "That's what you want from a wedding cake. Boldness. By the way, what's underneath the, er, ketchup?"

"Oh, I'm glad you asked." She turns a page over in her notebook. You can't fault her for lack of enthusiasm. "Okay, so the bottom tier is coffee ice cream. I know what you're thinking: won't it melt? Well, yes, but I think we should present the cake on a bed of ice cubes, and possibly put a bowl underneath that so that when it melts it can drop into the bowl and we could put cones on the side and kids can just reach in and dip them in the ice cream!"

"Yes," I say. "That sounds fantastic."

"The second tier," she continues, "will be strawberry jelly. You know, because strawberries, duh!"

"Duh!" I confirm.

"And then the third tier"—here she reaches out to touch my arm to ask me to brace myself, as though that's necessary—"will be fruit. Nothing but fruit. I'll shape them in the freezer. Of course when they melt they'll fall down into the ice cream soup in the bowl, so it will be a sort of healthy, delicious ice-cream-fruit soup! With jelly! What do you think?"

"Oh, so many things," I say. "What do you call this abomi— I mean, this delicacy?"

"It doesn't have a name, silly." She giggles. "I came up with it by myself. It took me ages, but I think the end result will be worth it. The sweetness of the ketchup really blends well with the sharpness of the fruit."

I look at her carefully. She's too old to be pregnant, surely. But at least she's nice about this. Her husband, when I finally force myself to ask him about the cars, tells me to stop bothering him.

"If you're going to be a nagging little housewife, Harry did right to leave," he says, not even looking up from his newspaper.

"Okay, thank you," I say.

I ask Bonnie if she heard anything from Siobhan.

"No," she says, sadly. "Gosh, it's been a while, hasn't it? I don't think she's taking it so well."

It's possible that a few weeks after she got the period she was hoping not to get wasn't the best time to send her out to look for the tastiest alcoholic beverage in France. To be fair, at the time she seemed in need of a distraction, and I thought she might like being away from everyone's pitying stares and, what was worse, her best friends' yummy-mummy get-togethers. Harry was dubious, but I championed the idea, thinking a trip was what Siobhan needed. Perhaps I underestimated just how much she needed it.

The flower lady keeps ringing me to ask about delivery times and places and to give me updates. I know nothing about the flowers because Harry managed that. Harry managed everything.

Meanwhile, in the last few days we'd only actually spoken twice: once, a day or so after he landed, he rang me up to check how everything was going. He sounded exhausted, though, so the conversation was short. Yesterday, after I texted him a bunch of times, he rang me back, claiming to be very busy, and apologising for the lack of contact.

Something isn't right. I can feel it in my bones. On the phone with him now, he sounds tense and tired, like he wishes I'd stop calling. It's unlike him. But I don't get to ask him what's going on because, after checking in on me, he immediately says he has some urgent business and then rings off before I have the chance.

Arabella rings up.

"Hiyah!" she chirps. "How are you holding up, daah-ling? Okay? I was just checking if you told the registrar what time you wanted your ceremony."

"Hasn't Harry told him?"

"No, he hasn't. He said he was going to get back on this and then never did. Well? What time do you want to start?"

I don't know. I don't know when weddings start. Besides, it feels ridiculous to be deciding this now, so close to the Big Day. In movies I know it's always in daylight, but who knows what Harry wants?

"Er, six?" I venture a guess.

There's a silence on the other side. Then she says, dryly, "Want to take another shot at it, daah-ling?"

She makes me feel like that time when Harry asked me to get us a charcuterie platter and when I asked for it in the fancy boutique butcher's shop Harry likes, they looked me up and down and asked if I meant charcoal and if I was, in fact, trying to put together a barbeque. Like I'm an uncultured lout or something.

"What's wrong with six o'clock?"

"Well, honey, I presume you don't mean in the morning, so we're talking 6 p.m., yah?"

"Yah," I mimic her because she's already annoying me.

"Well, you wrote on your invitations that you want the guests to arrive at noon. You haven't got anything planned for them for the following six hours. Unless there's something I don't know about?"

"Oh, yes, of course." I remember now. "Then twelve thirty should be all right, right?"

"Are you sure?" she says, in the wheedling voice, like I'm a child who declared that two plus two equals pi.

"Why? What's the matter with twelve thirty?"

"Well, it doesn't allow much leeway for latecomers, daah-ling, that's all."

"Okay, what time do you think it should be?"

"How about 1 p.m.? How does that sound?"

I feel like screaming at her: *Then why the fuck didn't you just say so at the beginning you bloody . . .* but I don't. Because I'm zen.

"That sounds fab," I say. "You're the best."

"Thank you, daah-ling. I'll be in touch. Mwa!"

I punch a sofa cushion.

The flower lady drives me nuts. I enlist Chloe to help me with her. She doesn't know any more than I do, but she's got cold common sense to guide her, and if it goes wrong, she says I can blame it on her.

Harry's dad won't get back to me about the cars, which, frankly, works out just fine, because as I'm reviewing the situation, I can't figure out why we need cars anyway. The ceremony is at the same place as the reception. I can't reach Harry to ask him about this, and now I'm really freaking out. His phone is off. His phone is *never* off.

No news from Siobhan. So, we will have a dry wedding.

Haven't had a proper night's sleep ever since Harry left. It's like going to sleep with the front door open. It's not right, and I can't seem to get calm without him in bed next to me. Why is his fucking phone off?

The wedding is in two days.

I'm not in a good place right now. Everything in the flat is making me nervous, so I go out a lot and try to keep myself busy. I texted Harry three times today and got no response. He's not back, and I don't know what time he's coming back. Something tells me that's not normal.

It's as I'm sitting in a coffee shop, doodling and trying to keep my nerves at bay, that I realise I've just drawn a familiar profile. Frowning,

I look up from my notepad and scan the coffee shop more consciously. Then I jump up, shocked. It's Gabriella!

This is the woman who has taken down Frank bloody Brodie. I should do something. Say something. But what?

She sees me. For a moment we stare at each other. Then she waves, shyly.

She rises from her seat, excusing herself to the person she's with—a man! A bloody man! Frank is going to kill himself if he ever finds out—and walks over to my table.

"Hey," she says. With all the anti-Gabriella propaganda that Frank and I have been indulging in, I forgot how nice she is. Somehow, this makes me more resentful of her. I mutter an unintelligible response, meant to indicate that I have nothing to say to her, out of solidarity with Frank.

"How have you been?" she asks.

"Fine."

"Oh, okay." She nods, waits for me to say something, but as I don't, she says, "Okay," again, and prepares to turn around.

"Wait," I say, quickly. "Wait. I want to talk to you."

I don't want to talk to her at all. I don't know what I'm saying. She's surprised too, but pulls a chair forward and sits down. She's dowdier than I remember her from her time with Frank. In fact, she doesn't look well at all. She's all pale and pasty-skinned. She's not wearing any makeup.

"How have you been?" I ask her, suspiciously glancing back at her table.

"Oh, well, you know . . ." she says. I've never seen her this serious before. Her smile seems so forced, it's like a grimace.

"Frank's miserable," I say. Probably this is not something I should be telling her, but I can't help it. I want her to know. It's not right for one person to cause another this much pain and not even know about it. "He's the worst I've ever seen him."

She's surprised. "Really?"

"What do you think? He doesn't sleep, he doesn't eat. All he does is swear and drink. He doesn't know what happened. You don't go to the meetings with the lawyers. He never sees you. Why would you do this to him? What's the matter with you? How could you?"

I didn't intend to start harassing her, but it comes bursting out of me.

Her skin loses more colour with every accusation I throw at her.

"Gosh," she says, folding her hands nervously. "I—I didn't know. I didn't think it would be this bad . . ."

I clench my jaw. What's wrong with people? How can she not know it would be this bad? What did she think? That it was going to be *good*? If you're going to leave someone, at least have the bloody balls or ovaries or whatever to tell them to their face!

I think of Harry. But no, Harry isn't leaving me. He's just on a work trip to Sweden two days before our wedding and keeping a very romantic and completely appropriate radio silence.

This is about Gabriella and Frank.

"What happened?" I ask. "Was he mean to you? Abusive? Neglectful? Did you fall out of love? Is there somebody else?" I turn my attention, again, to the bloke at her table.

"No," she says, horrified at the suggestion. "No, of course not. I love him so much, but . . . but I can't go on pretending. You wouldn't understand. You don't know how frightening, how tiring it is . . ."

She bites her lip.

"You wouldn't understand," she says, rising to her feet. "Look, if you see him, tell him . . ." She stops again. "I'm really sorry. I'm sorry he's sad and unhappy, but I hope it will get better. And if it helps, I'm not happy either, and I don't think I'll ever be again."

I stare up at her, completely speechless. I mean, what the fuck does that mean?

"I'm going away," she says. "I'm going to teach with the Bible Institute in Chapada, Brazil. So, if he complains about my not being there, at the meetings, that's why. You can tell him. It might help."

Then she turns, dramatically, and walks out of the coffee shop. Her companion rises and follows her out. I send him evil stares, but I don't think he notices.

Bonnie is the one who drops the bombshell.

We're going through the order of service—not a thing I expected to have to deal with, since we're not doing a church wedding—when

I mention to her, half-jokingly, that perhaps there should be a point in there about Kieran bursting in, crying out Harry's name like in *The Graduate*.

Bonnie says, "Oh, you don't have to worry about him. He's in Sweden at the moment."

I go entirely rigid. Something inside me catches, my heart stutters.

"Sweden?" My mouth feels dry and my tongue unwieldy. "N-now?"

"Oh yes. I have him on Facebook, you know? Very handy to keep track of people. He's been there for the past two weeks, I think. Extended holiday. So you don't have to worry about him bursting in on you or anything. He's safely away."

She gives me a reassuring smile. At least I think she does, because I see spots in front of my eyes.

I tell myself that it's nothing. A coincidence. It happens. Like when Kieran was in Ireland just when Harry and I were in Ireland. A coincidence. A damn inconvenient, infuriating coincidence.

I ring up Maya.

"Hey!" I say, sounding positively chipper. "I've been trying to reach Harry, but am having a hard time. Is he in touch with you?"

"Harry?" She seems surprised. "No, why should he be? He's taken time off for the wedding. I haven't heard from him since last Friday."

"He's supposed to be meeting a client in Malmö. I thought maybe he was in touch."

"Malmö?" She says it like she's never heard of the place. "We don't have any clients in Malmö. What did he say the client's name was?"

He didn't give a name.

"Must have been a misunderstanding," I say, though by now my voice is trembling.

You know how they say that before you die, you see your entire life flash before your eyes? Well, now I'm seeing my entire relationship with Harry flash before mine.

What if it isn't a coincidence?

I ring his number, but it goes straight to voice mail. I leave a message.

"Harry? It's me, Joe. Er, I don't know how to put this, but, er, I know that Kieran is in Sweden right now, and you're there, and you're not picking up your phone, and it's starting to freak me out. The wedding's in two days. If you don't ring me, then . . . then maybe there is no wedding. I don't know. I don't know what to think of this. I just—" I take a deep breath. "Just give me a ring, okay? At least to say you're all right. Anything else we can discuss when you get back."

He'll come back. Definitely.

Chapter Fourteen
GABRIELLA

Four and a Half Years Before the Big Day

It had been six months since Harry chose Kieran.

My date's name was Ralph, and he was ten years my senior and worked as a business analyst for a financial consulting company. He was handsome, in a Gary Cooper-ish sort of way, and charming. The entire date, he tried to convince me to go to Cornwall with him. He had a summer house there and he said it would be a nice break from the city.

"I'd teach you to fish," he said. "Even if you don't like fishing, just the views alone are worth the early rise."

He smiled suggestively. I remembered to smile back.

"Do you surf?" he asked.

"No, I never tried."

"I can teach you. It'll change your life, trust me. Do you want more wine?"

I did, but I shook my head. The way he was undressing me with his eyes made me wonder. I *could* sleep with him. I didn't want to, but that was part and parcel of my being hung up over Harry. And Harry was having sex. Lots of sex with his boyfriend. He probably wasn't sitting there looking at a complete snack in front of him, offering him wine, Cornish surfing, and a boisterous shag, thinking about me.

My phone rang.

"Excuse me," I said to Ralph and hurried away from our table to pick up. It was Gabriella. She sounded out of breath.

"Oh Joe, oh please, please help me!"

"What is it? What's the matter?"

"It's Frank's birthday. I've no idea what to do! First I thought concert tickets, then I thought a trip to somewhere . . . but I don't have any money, and I've no idea how he usually pays for all the things he does, and last year he wrestled on TV on his birthday and how am I supposed to compete with that?"

"He won't care about that. Just invite us to the pub, that'll do."

"That won't do at all!" she insisted, sounding genuinely panicked. "Please tell me what I should get! And for the love of all that is holy, don't tell him I asked you!"

I told her I'd come around to her place later that day to discuss Frank's birthday. It was only after I hung up that I realised I'd cockblocked myself.

Ralph's smile faded when I told him I had to go.

"Call me when you're done?" he said in his deep, raspy voice.

"Sure, I'll try." I knew I should, but as I was leaving the place, I felt no regrets. In fact, relief made my steps lighter and quicker.

Gabriella was in a worse shape than even her panicked phone call had suggested. She'd researched Frank's past birthdays and decided that nothing she could ever plan would live up to any of them.

"I mean, for Christ's sake, three years ago he adopted a cheetah!" she cried. "How does he even come up with this stuff?"

I laughed, remembering the morning he found out about the cheetah.

"We were drunk and we thought it would be funny," I said. "Look, he doesn't want you to remake that *Hangover* movie for him. He just wants to spend time with you."

She shook her head. "No, I need you to give me ideas. I know. I'll . . . I'll give him a horse!"

"What?"

"No, you're absolutely right, horses are expensive. There's stabling, insurance, vet fees . . . Oh gosh, I—I don't know! I don't know!" She shook me by my shoulders. "A dolphin?"

"Why does it have to be an animal?" I asked, bewildered.

"I don't know!"

I made her chamomile tea and forced her to take a seat, and then we talked through sensible options.

"Ballooning? Clown school? A parade?" She showed me the list of ideas she'd prepared.

"Crikey," I said, leafing through them. "You do know it's his birthday, right? He's not being crowned King of Thailand."

She stared at me desperately.

"Okay, okay, deep breaths," I said. "Some of these aren't as, er, silly as the others. Hot-air ballooning for example. That could be done, and I'm pretty sure Frank's never been."

She let out a shaky breath. "Really?"

We looked up prices and booked us in for a consultation.

I thought this would chill Gabriella down, but when she lifted her mug of tea up to her lips, her hand was a little shaky.

Frank came home from work just as I was leaving. I was near the door, putting on my coat, checking the messages that had come in from Ralph while I was helping Gabriella out, when the door opened and Frank's grin came in, followed by the rest of him.

"Joe!" he cried, overjoyed to see me.

We hugged and I explained I was on my way out.

"Nonsense! Have ye eaten? I can see ya haven't. Stay. Chloe said we needed to feed you better. Gabriella? Light of my life?"

Gabriella came bouncing from the sitting room. I startled a little, because the transformation was so remarkable. There were the shiny cheeks, the dimples, the twinkling eyes again. Only a moment before she was chewing on her nails and her foot wouldn't stop tapping. She hugged and kissed him in greeting and then Frank patted his stomach and declared he could consume a walrus.

"Actually," I said, waving Ralph's text messages in front of him, "I've got a date."

"Oh!" Frank's eyes went wide. "A date, eh? What's his name? What's he like?"

Ralph was easy to talk about, I realised, because he might as well be made up, that's how little I felt about him.

"Tall, dark, and handsome," I said. "Wish me luck."

I was getting much better at pretending to be fine. Outside, I texted Ralph to inform him I was having dinner with friends. Thus escaping the clutches of both a happily married couple and a man who wanted to tackle me and drag me to his house in Cornwall, I went to a pub, found the darkest corner, and nursed a pint of ale on my own.

It wasn't the same pub where Harry and I'd first hooked up, but it did make me think of him. Why lie, everything made me think of him. Every blue shirt with rolled-up sleeves, every crooked smile, every kebab, every time I had to shower, he was there, poking me in the chest.

I rubbed the place that ached and leaned back in my chair. This was what forever was going to feel like.

Chapter Fifteen
THE BIG DAY

Over the past four years, I have periodically had this nightmare in which Harry suddenly doesn't love me. Each time it plays out differently, but each time there's this empty feeling I get, like my heart's been ripped out of my chest because he's looking at me but he isn't smiling. He's completely indifferent, cold. His gaze, when it is fixed on me, is emotionless, blank. As though he were looking at a stranger. Sometimes he goes away with someone else. Sometimes he just completely ignores me. Each time, I wake up feeling like the world's ended.

It's the same feeling I had when my family was D-ed by the Jehovah's Witnesses. We'd sit in the Kingdom Hall at the very back, my mother, my father, and I, and all our friends would sit with their backs turned to us. They'd cross the street when they saw us in town. They'd blank us when we reflexively greeted them, as though they didn't know us.

Throughout this time, my father would do the very same thing in a private capacity, only to me, at home. He wouldn't look at me, pretended he didn't hear when I spoke. And when my mother left him, he, too, would cross the street when he saw me coming.

I can't describe how absolutely terrifying it is to be treated as though you're nothing.

I wake up on my wedding day, drenched in cold, prickly sweat. Perhaps I should have cancelled it, considering that I haven't heard from Harry and he isn't back. But, paralysed by fear, I did absolutely nothing.

The last thing he said to me was yesterday morning. He sent a text message saying: *I messed up, Joe. I'm sorry.*

When I responded asking what he meant, he didn't get back to me. I rang, I texted. Nothing.

Now, with the sun invading our bedroom, with the sheets still retaining some of his scent, I try to gather my energy to start the day.

In my head, I decide how to feel. My fiancé has left. A week before the wedding, he took off on a mysterious journey, lying to me about its purpose, and refusing to talk to me. His ex, the man who he would be married to if that man weren't an idiot, is on that journey with him.

I feel like I may have been a little naïve for thinking that there was any normal explanation for this.

The late-night phone calls, the emails, the bank statements.

I reach for my phone. I wish, I *hope* to see a little red dot with a *1* over the text message icon, or a tab saying I have missed calls from Harry. But when I look at my phone, there's nothing. I ring him, even though now I don't expect an answer. It goes straight to voice mail.

"Hi, Harry." I sound dejected, but what would you sound like in these circumstances? "So today is the Big Day. If you're freaking out right now, I get it. I'm freaking out right now too. We don't have to get married today. Or ever. It was probably a stupid idea to begin with . . ."

I press my fingers into my tear ducts and try to choke my tears down.

"Mate," I say, "just fucking *talk* to me. At least once. I mean . . . *Fuck*."

I ring off.

Kieran's in Sweden. Harry's in Sweden. And yet, I don't believe it. And even if it's true, which I don't buy, I'm not letting it happen.

I call again.

"Okay, level with me here," I say to the voice mail. "What is it? I thought you *wanted* to get married. I mean, I wouldn't have asked if it wasn't something I thought you wanted. Or did I get the wrong signal? Was it about Kieran all along? Is that what it is? Did my proposing to you finally open his eyes? Is that what you're doing in Sweden? Fuck, Harry, honestly?"

I hang up, because I start crying and I don't want him to hear me cry. Then I get pissed off. I ring him again. Voice mail again.

"Listen," I say, "Kieran isn't the guy for you. He never was. *I'm* the guy for you. Okay? I am. I can prove it to you. Just bloody come back, and we can talk, and I'll show you. He's just a fucking poser who never knew what he had until he lost it, and the moment he has you again, he'll go back to behaving like a fucking bellend. And even if he doesn't, even if he's all changed and promises you the world, well . . . well, I'll give you more than the world. I'd do anything for you. Just come back. Okay? I promise I won't be cross or anything. I love you. I love you more than Kieran ever did or could." I take a deep breath. "Just send me a text or something. Anything. Talk to me."

There's a knock on my door.

"Listen," I say to Harry's voice mail, "I'm going to be there today. At our wedding. And I hope to see you there too."

Chloe and Frank come in. They're both already dressed for the wedding. Frank has shaved even, which, in his frame of mind, is a small miracle. Chloe looks pretty in an emerald-green dress, her grey hair pinned up. Like an old Hollywood star, I tell her.

"Any news?" she asks.

I shake my head. Frank gazes at me with wonder in his eyes.

"Man," he says, "it's like looking in the mirror. Fucking scary. What are you going to do now?"

"I'm getting dressed," I say. "And then I'm going to check in to the hotel. And then I'm going to shower and get dressed for the ceremony."

Frank and Chloe stare at me like I've lost my mind.

"Oh, Joe," Chloe says. "Oh, I don't know . . ."

"What, are you fuckin' nuts, pal?" Frank goes down the less delicate route. "Face it, the man's bolted. Like a fuckin' . . . like a fuckin' bolter. It's like I'm telling you all this time! Marriage is—"

"Enough," I say, and it actually works. Frank shuts up. "I know what you think. I know what you both think. But maybe he will come back. You don't know that he won't. Well, I'm going to be ready for him if he does. Now, before I lose it, will you help me pack?"

Frank mutters under his breath that I'm a lost cause and the only kind thing to do now would be to send me to a good shrink. Chloe says nothing, but she eyes me apprehensively, even as she picks up the wedding suits from the wardrobe, both of them still in their plastic covers. I have the shoes, two boxes, and Frank grabs the two overnight bags. I packed them the night before. They're for our wedding night at the hotel.

We were going to spend last night doing a stag do, but with one of the stags missing, I wasn't really in the mood for partying.

The three of us move solemnly down the stairs in a procession and then load it all into Frank's car. We don't speak on our way to Chelsea. I do, however, receive phone calls, one from my mother, the other from Harry's mother, each asking me how I am. They ask about Harry too, and when I say that I haven't seen him, there's the same little silent pause that I expect to hear all day.

A normal person, I reckon, would turn back right now, and ask his friends to call it all off. And perhaps this is me living in denial, but I can't believe Harry would do this to me. No, it's not that I can't believe it. It's that I *know* he won't. Determined, therefore, to see this through, I set my jaw and ignore the ominous silence from Frank and Chloe.

Arabella rings just as we're arriving in front of the hotel.

"Daah-ling! Been trying to reach you all morning! Can't get hold of your groom. Where is he? Late night last night?"

"Er, no," I say. "He's not come back yet."

The fucking pause again.

"Ah," she says. "Well. That's . . . unfortunate. Okay, then. Are we . . . Oh, I see you're here now."

She hangs up and then comes over to the car, in her enormous heels and power pantsuit, and air-kisses both my cheeks.

"You look . . . nice," she lies unconvincingly, and then shakes hands with Frank and Chloe. "So let's get you up to your room. I've got some foundation on me that might help."

I smile wryly, though I don't feel like smiling. "Somehow I don't think your shade would suit me."

"Oh that." She waves her hand dismissively. "I have every shade. This is not my first rodeo." She winks at me, and I'm actually a little grateful for the pretence.

I iron my suit pants in silence. Frank is sitting in the armchair, readjusting his leg. Chloe is telling me that my mother has brought all her poodles after all. I told her not to. The hotel has a no-dog policy.

"Go and ask Arabella," I tell Chloe. "She can maybe find somewhere to put them."

Just as Chloe is about to do so, Siobhan enters the room, screaming.

"There you are! Can I use your loo?"

"There's a loo for guests downstairs," I say, but she's already locked herself in mine.

"Okay, then," I mutter, returning to my bloody suit trousers. I just want to give them a quick swipe with a not-too-hot iron. Harry taught me how after the disaster in Dublin. When I say *he taught me*, I mean that he stood behind me, with his chin on my shoulder and guided my hands, teasing me gently as we ironed one of his shirts together, and all I took from that lesson was that sex on the floor isn't comfortable. My heart pinches at the memory.

He's going to come back, though. I know he will.

I check my phone, again, but there's nothing. Probably because he's too busy getting to me. It's fine, I tell myself. I'll be ready for him. I read the text message again. *I messed up.*

Siobhan makes a weird squealing noise in the loo.

"Siobhan?" I ask.

There's no response.

I look at Frank, who shrugs. So I head for the bathroom door, when several things happen at once. The door to my room opens and Arabella, Chloe, my mother, and my mother's four poodles all burst in, at the exact same moment as Siobhan rushes out of the bathroom, falling into me and spilling the warm contents of a small glass on me.

I cry out. "Fuck! What is that?"

It stinks like . . .

"Oh God, it's my wee!"

Siobhan has her hand on her mouth. Arabella and my mother gape. Chloe and Frank gape.

"Tell me that's not your—" Arabella starts.

"Dress shirt. It is," I say. Siobhan breaks out in tears. My mother hands Arabella the reins of the poodles.

"I'll go out and get a new one," she says. "Never fear, dear, you'll be right as rain in no time."

She leaves. Arabella looks at the leads in her hand, then at the bathroom.

"Okay, I've too much to do. They'll be all right in there, won't they?"

And without waiting for a reply, she tosses the leads in there and closes the door on the dogs, and then quickly leaves. The dogs start barking. Siobhan throws herself into the armchair, crying. I feel at the end of my tether here.

"If anybody has a reason to cry right now, it's me," I say. "Come on, it's not that bad. I'm going to get a new shirt."

She looks up at me, her face blotchy, her eyes swollen and red with tears. She says something in a voice so high-pitched I can't hear her. There is the vague smell of something burning in the air, but I'm trying to hear Siobhan.

"I'm pregnant," she says at last between sobs. "*Pregnant!*"

"Oh my God!" I say. Chloe shakes her head in commiseration. There isn't space enough here to go into detail about her views on pregnancy.

"Yer with child?" Frank cries, trying to cheer her up. "That's bloody fantastic!"

Siobhan can't stop crying, though.

"I spent the last two weeks getting drunk," she says. "My baby will be an al-al-alkie . . . I didn't know! We weren't even trying! I shouldn't be ah-ah-allowed to care for a baby . . . Look at the sta-a-ate of me . . ."

Someone find Ollie . . . I'm about to say, but as I turn, I see that my trousers, which I left on the ironing board with the iron, are on fire.

Suddenly everybody is in my room. Ollie and Siobhan are sobbing together in the corner. Someone let the poodles out, so they are milling in between the legs of the hotel staff, Arabella, my mother, Harry's parents, Frank (with his leg now attached so he can yell at people better), and Chloe, with her dress covered in patches of extinguisher foam. It's not a big enough room to hold everybody comfortably, but there's a silence that falls over us all when the manager, a Mr. Alan Yates, tells me that it's time for me and my party to vacate the premises.

So this is how it ends. I know now that I won't get married today. I should have known days ago, but I kept on hoping. And now it's official.

I want to protest, but I'm speechless. Out of hope, and out of words.

"Well," I say, lifting my chin at Alan Yates, who has been so pleasant when Harry was negotiating our stay here with him. Now he looks pissed off and implacably so. "I suppose I'll have to go downstairs to tell my guests."

Frank puts his hand on my shoulder.

"I'll go and tell them."

"No, I'll do it," says Chloe. "You take Joe home."

"Okay," Frank says.

The crowd starts discussing who is taking whose car to go where, but an angry roar of "Hey!" makes them all go silent once more.

It's Mr. Byrne.

"What is this?" he demands, outraged. "Where are you all going?"

"Sir . . ." Mr. Yates clears his throat.

"Don't *sir* me," Harry's dad says. "We're sorry about the curtain getting burned, but there's no need for you to just kick us out like that. It was an accident. Accidents happen."

"And the dogs, sir . . ." Mr. Yates says.

Mr. Byrne shrugs. "What about them? They're gone. They were just here for a quick visit, they didn't destroy anything, and they're out the door now, see?"

When Mr. Yates turns his head, my mum is disappearing out of the door with her dogs in tow.

"Harry isn't here," I say, miserably. "There can't be any wedding if he's not—"

"Nonsense!" the old man says. "He'll be here. Harry's a gentleman, that's how I raised him. If he made a commitment, he'll stick to it. You don't lose faith in him now, son."

I stare at him wide-eyed. He stares back. I'm pretty sure he didn't mean to say it, but then he decides to ride it out, even though the colour in his cheeks is slightly heightened.

"So," he says, clearing his throat. "Let's go downstairs and see how we can entertain the company in your fine hotel while we are waiting for the, er, final touches to be done."

He puts his arm around Mr. Yates and turns him out towards the door. Bonnie follows, saying, "I do think your reception room looks so sweet. You have done *such* a good job . . ."

Their voices disappear as they go down the corridor.

Siobhan, Ollie, Chloe, Frank, and Arabella now all look at me. As though I hold any answers. I don't.

"Well," I say, a little bitterly. "At least this is precisely what a wedding organised by me would look like. True to form, that's what this is."

Arabella takes out her phone. "Would you like me to call the police? Maybe they could track Harry down?"

"What? No," Siobhan says, wiping her nose with her sleeve. "Maybe try calling him again?"

"It goes straight to voice mail," I say.

"Okay, radical idea," Ollie says putting his hands up, "but have you tried ringing Kieran?"

Chloe hisses like a cat. Siobhan punches him reproachfully in the arm. Frank frowns.

"Not really keen to hear from him right this minute," I say.

"Okay, but he was in Sweden when Harry was there," Ollie says. "Maybe he knows something."

I meet his eyes. He knows it and I know it. If we're calling Kieran, it's only to find out if he and Harry are making another go of it. Even at this stage, with all evidence pointing to it, I can't believe it. In fact, the more the evidence points to it, the less I believe it.

However, I have about fifty people downstairs, waiting for a wedding that probably won't happen. If nothing else, I owe them an explanation.

"I don't have his number," I say. My heart feels heavy and numb now. Frank goes over to the hotel fridge and takes out all the liquors.

Ollie takes out his phone, shoots me an apologetic look, and then presses the Call button. I don't think I can bear this. Siobhan puts her arm around me, then remembers her urine on my shirt, and whispers, "Maybe we should take this off?"

"I don't have another one," I say, and then we both hear Ollie say: "Hello?"

I freeze. Kieran picked up.

"Hi, Kieran," Ollie says, looking at me, wide-eyed, like he doesn't know what to do—as though he expected, just like I did, not to be able to reach Kieran. I stretch out my hand for his phone and he hands it over. Kieran is mid-speech when I put Ollie's mobile to my ear.

". . . so weird to hear from you," he's saying.

"Hey, Kieran," I say. "It's Joe Kaminski here."

"Oh!" Kieran sounds surprised. I'm not sure why he should be.

"Quick question, any idea where my fiancé is right now?"

"Your— You mean Harry?" Now he sounds amazed. "I don't know. Why? What happened to him?"

"You haven't heard from him?"

I can feel a collective sigh of relief escape everyone in the room at once.

"No, mate, I haven't heard from him in months," Kieran says. "Why? What's the matter? Did something happen to him?"

"Er, no. He was in Sweden these past few days, I thought maybe you bumped into him."

"No, I never knew he was here. Sorry, mate. Did he go missing? You want me to contact the police here?"

Now I feel like a complete idiot. What if something *has* happened to Harry? Oh my God, what if he was kidnapped, or killed, or in an accident? *I messed up, Joe. I'm sorry* suddenly has a terribly sinister ring to it. And all he has on his phone are my stupid messages full of jealousy and rage . . . Now I feel sick to my stomach. I lower myself slowly to my chair.

"Oh God, I don't know," I say. I rub my eyes. When I move my hand away from my face, it's wet with tears. "I don't know, mate. I don't know what to do! I hardly heard from him since he left. It was really weird. Has he ever done something like this with you? Do you think I should call Interpol? *What do I do?*"

I can hear Kieran's breathing on the other side. "Relax. I'll look into it. I know people. I will find out. Send me his flight details."

"I don't have them! He never gave them to me!"

"That's all right, it's all right, honestly, calm down," he says, and in a weird way his self-assured way of speaking does comfort me on some level, even though my hands are shaking and I feel like I'm on the brink of a nervous breakdown. "We can do this together, all right?" he says. "We'll get to the bottom of this. I'll call the local police, and they'll instruct me how to proceed. Meanwhile, how about you talk to his parents, and get them to talk to the police in England."

"Yes, yes," I say, although half the things he just said went in and out of my head without attaching to any meaning.

"What I need you to do now . . ." He keeps talking, but I notice something is different. The room has gone strangely quiet. Everybody is staring at the door. I look up.

"Listen to me, Joe," Kieran says. "Joe?"

Right there, in my hotel room door, stands Harry. Siobhan gasps. Frank's eyes are so wide, you'd think he's seeing a ghost. Chloe looks to me.

At first I think it's my imagination, because by now I have pictures of him floating dead in a Scandinavian river, with one of those alcoholic Scandi-noir detectives down on her haunches examining him with a mixture of pity and cold disdain. But he's here. His shirt is crumpled, his jeans are stained, he has sweat stains under both armpits, his hair is a mess, and he's pale and bleary-eyed, but he's alive and well, and right here on our wedding day. I throw off the phone and run at him until he's in my arms. I'm hugging him so hard he laughs.

"I can't breathe," he says, though his arms are around me as well.

In the background, I hear Ollie telling Kieran that Harry is found. Siobhan and Chloe demand to know where he was. Frank says he's opening the whisky.

I don't care what they say or do.

Harry came back to me.

Chloe herds everybody out of the room under protest. When Harry and I are alone, he takes the room in, with the curtain blackened on the floor, the trousers singed to the ironing board, the empty alcohol bottles on the table, the vague scent of dog.

"Was there a fire in here?" he asks.

"Oh yes," I say. I stare at him. It's really him. He's here. "Where have you been? Why didn't you call me? Did you get my messages?"

"Yes," he says, smiling apologetically. "I got them all at once, during a layover at Doha."

"Doha!" I cry. "What— Where— *Why*?"

There's a knock on the door.

Arabella shouts, "The registrar is readying to leave, boys."

"Just—just hold on to him for another five minutes, okay?" Harry shouts back. He turns to me again. "Okay, promise not to be cross."

I remember his message again. *I messed up,* it said. *I'm sorry.* A thousand thoughts tumble through my head. What could he have possibly done to merit such a message?

"What did you do?"

"Okay, okay . . ." He keeps saying that word, like he's buying himself time to think of the right way to frame his news. I know he hasn't gone back to Kieran, so what else could he have possibly done? Maybe he met another guy altogether? That seems far-fetched even to my tired, paranoid mind.

"Okay," he says at last. "Do you remember how you wanted to propose to me, and you went to such lengths to plan the perfect proposal because you knew I would appreciate all the planning and preparation that you went through?"

"Yes."

"Right," he says. "So . . . so here's the funny thing . . . before you proposed to me, I had a similar idea."

My heart jumps. "You—you wanted to propose to me?"

"I wanted to do something special, you know, to show you . . ." He takes in a shaky breath, tugs at his hair. "Well, anyway, I thought to myself that you would like it if I did something wild and spontaneous."

I laugh. "What do you mean? What did you do?"

"Right . . ." he says. "Er, would you like to go down and get married first, real quick? And then I tell you everything?"

"No, you bastard, tell me now!" I say, though I can't help laughing. "What happened?"

Visibly nervous, he paces the room.

"Okay," he says, rubbing his mouth. "I don't know how to say this without you punching me right in the face."

"Did you sleep with someone?"

"God, no!" He looks outraged. "No. It's not that. It's . . ." He swallows. "I tracked down your birth parents."

My mouth falls open. For a moment, his words don't make any sense. I think of my Jehovah's Witness father, and I think, *What did you do that for?* but then the word *parents* connects with *birth* and I have another, quite different feeling rising up.

"You—you what?"

"I know," he says, anxiously. "I know it was a terrible idea, but it just came to me one day. You were writing a Christmas card to that Yvonne woman, and you looked so— And I remembered all the false starts and—and then I thought, 'Hey, here's a crazy, spontaneous thing I could do for Joe' . . . and then I did it. I hired a private detective and I found them."

I stare at him.

"They live in Australia. I was going to leave it at that, and just let you know that they're there, in case you wanted to get in touch. And that's what I should have done," he says. "But you know me. I can never leave well enough alone. So I contacted them. Just to say hi, you know? To check them out and see if they're all right. I didn't want you to get in touch with them and find out they're horrible people. Which is when things started going horribly wrong."

"The phone calls," I say in a sudden light bulb moment. "The phone calls in the middle of the night from Australia! Your emails! Your bank statements! How jumpy and nervous you were these past few months. Was that *them*?"

"Er, yes," he says, chagrined. "Them and their lawyers."

"What?"

"Well, it turned out, after I got in touch with them, they were in legal trouble. I—I might have helped them out a bit."

"What sort of trouble?"

"Drugs. No, they're not junkies or anything like that. They live in a sort of bohemian commune, and they were arrested on charges of drug dealing. They were entirely innocent," he rushes to add, at my horrified expression, "it was all a misunderstanding, but they couldn't afford a good lawyer, and so I hired them one. And you know me, once I'm involved in something, I *involve* myself in it. So this past week they had their hearing, and I thought I'd just fly out there and make sure it went okay. It was a tense week, but we managed to get them out of it. It didn't feel like the sort of thing to tell you over the phone. I was going to be back yesterday, and then I was going to tell you everything, but my flight got delayed."

He sighs. I don't know what to say.

"At my layover in Qatar, I got all your messages," he says. "I felt horrible and was going to ring you right back, but then we were herded onto our plane, and I thought it's probably more important I make it here on time than call you back right away. So I'm here now."

Seeing my speechless face, he exhales deeply. "I don't know how you do it. I don't know how you just throw yourself at these schemes without a moment's thought! I promise, I will never do anything spontaneous ever again."

Arabella interrupts him with another knock on the door. "Boys, the registrar is packing up. What do you want to do?"

My head's spinning. It's all too much. I want to ask him a million questions. *My birth parents.* I couldn't believe that he'd seen them. Talked to them.

"I know this was way, way over the line," Harry says, looking absolutely crestfallen. I realise that he thinks I'm wavering about the ceremony. "I'm so, so sorry . . ."

"Boys?" Arabella says.

"I'll tell her to let him go, shall I? You'll need time to process this and—" Harry begins, quietly.

"No," I say, snapping back to the moment. "I want to marry you. Today."

He looks surprised. "Y-you do?"

"Above everything." I take his hand.

"Thank God," he says, laughing with relief.

Chapter Sixteen

HARRY

Four and a Half Years Before the Big Day

I was on the bus home from Frank and Gabriella's place when Ralph rung again, offering to take me out to dinner. He was being persistent. For the past two weeks, he'd been ringing nearly every day.

"I'm very busy at the moment," I lied. Then, knowing that it was what I was supposed to do, I added, "Tomorrow, maybe?"

"It's a date," he said, sounding like he was smiling. Oh God.

I rung Chloe to see what she was doing for dinner.

"Stuck at work until late, I'm afraid," she said. "You can have some of my leftovers. In fact, I insist. Your mother looks at me like I'm never feeding you. How are the lovebirds?"

Gabriella was still in bed with the cold she caught while trying out hot-air ballooning for Frank's birthday. It meant they had to spend Frank's birthday at home, with her in bed.

"Disgusting, as you can imagine."

"I can't imagine Frank being a particularly good nurse."

"Actually, it was sort of sweet. Their internet went down so he ended up re-creating the last ten minutes of *A New Hope* for her. He kicked one of her plants across the room."

Chloe laughed. "I'm sure that helped with her headache."

"It was a distraction, at least."

I got off the bus and jumped over a puddle. The bus stop wasn't far from my building, and I was still on the phone with Chloe when I went up the stairs, skipping steps. She was telling me what I could have to eat for dinner, when I nearly tripped.

"Wah!" I cried.

"Joe?"

Chloe said my name at the same time as the man sitting in front of my door. It was dingy in there, but my heart stuttered when I heard the voice.

"Harry?"

"Harry!" Chloe cried on the other side.

Harry got to his feet. I stared at him like he was a famous person. Like I couldn't believe I was actually looking at Harry Byrne. I hadn't seen him in months, and my first thought was how fucking hot he was, before I realised that he wasn't looking very well at all.

"Hey," he said.

"Give him to me!" Chloe cried over my mobile. "I'll give him a piece of my—"

I hung up on her.

"What happened to you?" I asked. He was unshaven, which was unusual for him, and he had lines on his face, as if he'd not slept.

He scratched the back of his neck.

"Nothing," he said. "Just—just thought I'd come by and say hello."

I stared at him. "What?"

Thoughts tumbled in my head: *Does Kieran know you're here? Come by and say hello? After six months? Are you high?*

I didn't say any of that. I merely stared. He cleared his throat.

"Can I come in?"

I remembered the door and the key in my hand. Wordlessly, I opened it and let him pass through. Then I meticulously locked the door behind me. Buying time.

The flat was an absolute tip, as usual. There was a painting I'd started a few weeks ago standing in the middle of what normal people would call a sitting room, and consequently the floor was covered in a paint-bespattered tarp, and the sink was black with paint.

Harry briefly scanned the painting, smiled slightly. "That's nice."

"Thank you."

He ran his hand through his hair, ruffling it in a way I used to find adorable, and so I looked away and waited, staring at the window.

"How have you been?" he asked, at last.

"Good, thanks. You?"

He mumbled something about feeling fine. It occurred to me now that perhaps he'd come to tell me he and Kieran were getting married.

Perhaps he was worried about me finding out some other way, and so he, considerate as he thought he was, decided to travel all this way, to break it to me gently.

It came upon me like a massive wave: I would not be able to handle that. The last thing I wanted was to break down in front of him, but that was precisely what would happen. It would break me.

I could see no way of escape. He was standing there, his eyes begging me to understand, and I knew he would subject me to this, he *would* do this, in the name of what he imagined to be decency.

He opened his mouth, but I stopped him before he could say a word. "Don't tell me. Honestly, do me a favour and just—just don't tell me. I don't want to know."

He closed his mouth again. The pink around his eyes was more pronounced by how ashen his complexion was. A vein stood up on his forehead.

"If you ask me," I said, "this is a huge mistake. I mean, massive. I mean, it's one of those things where you can see the train wreck from a mile away, but you're supposed to be gracious about it and not say anything. So I'm not going to say anything. I'm just going to leave it at that."

He stared at me, his grey eyes wide. "Uhm. What?"

I exhaled, impatient. "You and Ötzi."

Harry bit his lip.

I continued, "So if you came here to warn me or to give me a heads-up, please don't. I don't want to know. I'd rather live in a world where I never know."

As I spoke, I knew I was lying to myself. I did want to know. I just didn't want it to be true. Frustrated, I turned away and paced over to the kitchen.

"Do you want tea or something?" I said tersely over my shoulder.

"No, thank you."

I put the kettle on anyway and started to rummage through the cupboards in search of tea. Or coffee. Or, really, nothing at all. The clutter in our cupboards was wonderful, because it gave me an excuse to busy myself with searching through every jar and rattling every half-empty box.

"I'm not with Kieran anymore."

I froze.

"We broke up. A month ago."

I turned, slowly. "What?"

He shrugged. "It wasn't working. From the start it was wrong. That thing that was broken before we split up that first time . . . it was way more broken than I think either of us realised. I just never noticed, wouldn't have known, if I hadn't—" he paused, looked up to meet my eyes and then, gulping, gave me one of his crooked smiles "—if it hadn't been for you."

Who knew knees could actually go weak? I turned away. I'd let this happen before. I wasn't going to let him just burst into my life, explode into my heart, wreak havoc indiscriminately until he made up his mind what he wanted.

"So, what? Kieran disappointed you again, so you came here to shag yourself happy again?"

His smile fell. "No . . ."

I scoffed.

"You have every right to be angry," he said. "I was stupid. It was a stupid, stupid thing to do and I regretted it pretty much as soon as I had a good night's sleep over it."

At my uncomprehending stare, he said, "He'd come over in the evening . . ."

"I don't want to know." Panic swept over me. I'd imagined the evening of Kieran returning over and over again, until it made the edges of my sanity as solid as wet paper towels.

"Please, let me explain . . ." He took a step towards me, but I took a step back. No way could I cope with him touching me on top of everything else. My composure hung at the end of a very thin and worn thread.

"He'd come in the evening," he continued, determinedly, "and we talked, and he told me how much he'd hated being in the closet, how he hated having to lie and hide all the time, and what a toll it took on him. He told me how he hated how he'd treated me, and how ashamed he was of everything he'd said and done. He'd started counselling, had made progress telling his family and colleagues at work . . ."

All I could think of was my oblivious, goofy-arse self packing for the trip at that very same time, thinking about how much fun I'd be having with him in Vegas. I'd imagined flying together, sex in the hotel room, sightseeing. I remembered Harry's phone call.

"While he was doing all of that stuff for me," he continued, "I had cheerfully moved on! I'd met you, and was having—" He paused, threw up his hands. "I was having a great time with you." He laughed, like he was being ridiculous. "The wonderful thing is, I think at the time you seemed like a great hookup precisely because you were the last man I thought I'd ever—"

A prick of fear. *Say it,* I thought. *I was the type to play with and leave, wasn't I? I'd always been that. Say it, I dare you.*

"I honestly thought," he said, putting his hand in his hair and pulling in frustration, "that I'd been in love with Kieran. At least at the beginning. I had no idea that I hadn't been, ever, until I met you and fell so much harder than I ever thought was possible. And it happened so fucking quickly too. I mean, Jesus, Joe, it made no sense! I'd known you a few days and I couldn't sleep without thinking about you. You, with your card tricks and your infectious laugh and your ready response to absolutely anything somebody might say to you. You drove me wild. And him? I'd known him for years. We'd travelled. We'd lived together! We knew each other inside and out. I'd been the one who demanded more commitment, who accused him of not loving me enough. Then you came along and suddenly— I felt so guilty and ashamed, like I'd cheated or—or gaslighted him, or something."

I held on to the kitchen counter. Dizzyingly, his words hit me.

"We spoke all night," he continued, "and I was tired, and I didn't trust myself. I didn't think that what I was feeling with you was . . . permanent. I thought perhaps this was the sort of thing you did all the time. Perhaps this was only exciting and intense for me because I'm boring and I—I just haven't experienced that much before. What Kieran was saying made sense, even if I wasn't feeling what I should have been feeling. God, I hated calling you the next day. You have no idea."

"Getting that call was no picnic," I muttered.

"I'm sorry."

He looked so worn and defeated; his handsome face was like an aged, deflated version of his normal self.

"I was trying to be fair," he said. "And somehow, in the process, I hurt everybody. I'm an idiot, and—and if I'm too late and you're seeing somebody else or—or you've moved on and don't want to bother with me anymore, I understand. I just needed to tell you."

My knuckles showed white as I held the kitchen counter.

"I love you," he said.

He didn't look like a man in the mood for foolishness or comforting lies. I let go of the counter. Something that had been sitting on my chest for the past six months rose up with a skip. It was like I could breathe again.

"I don't think I'll ever stop," Harry said. "I tried. It would have made my life so much easier if I could have just, for one goddamn minute, stopped thinking about how much better every single thing was when you were there."

He cleared his throat, his voice growing thick over the tears. "I was the happiest I've ever been. With you. What happened that night had nothing to do with you or how I feel about you. It was all me. It was me trying to be rational and logical, and to do what I thought was the right and responsible thing to do. And I fucked up spectacularly." He threw his hands out and then put them on his hips. "D'you know what the funny thing is, Joe? All the reasons why I couldn't be with Kieran—the fact that he wouldn't commit, that he didn't want to buy a house together or get married—I wouldn't give a damn if you didn't want those things. I'd take you any way you'd want. I'd take you for a week or a fucking lifetime. I'd be the best bloody 'compadre' you ever had if that's all you wanted."

We stared at each other across the room.

"For the love of God, say something," he said with a nervous laugh.

"You waited a whole bloody month?" I demanded. "All that time, and you—"

Then I was in his arms.

Chapter Seventeen
I DO

We walk down the stairs, hand in hand. Harry is in his sweaty shirt and stained jeans. I'm in burnt dress trousers and a urine-soaked dress shirt. I would have changed, but there is no time, and I'm more determined than ever that Harry and I are going to be married today. Come what may.

When we reach the ceremony room, all the guests turn to gape at us. My mother, Harry's parents, Siobhan and Ollie, Chloe, and Frank all stand up. Frank toasts me. Chloe shakes her head and wipes a little tear off her cheek. Siobhan looks like a Jackson Pollock painting—her makeup is all over the place from crying. Ollie has his arm around her. There's Maya beaming and waving excitedly. Bonnie and my mother are both in tears. Harry's dad smiles at Harry—more, I suppose, because he was right about his son than about what his son is about to do, but I'll take that over his previous attitude any day. Harry's work colleagues stare dumbfounded at the state of him.

We hold hands as we approach the front of the crowd, where, under a floral awning, the impatient registrar is standing.

"This is absolutely bonkers," Harry whispers to me.

It is the best day of my life.

The ceremony is blissfully short. I can barely hear the registrar for the blood rushing in my ears, and the awareness that this is happening after all. It's like a dream.

I repeat the registrar's words, and see Harry do the same, and all I'm thinking is, *He came back to me*. He will always come back to me. I knew he would. He's here. We're married. We'll be married forever. I just know we will. I sign the marriage certificate. Harry does the same.

And then, suddenly, as though waking from a dream, it's done. People are clapping. Harry is beaming. I beam back. He takes my face into his hands and kisses me. Siobhan is crying. My mother is crying. I realise I'm crying.

My vision is blurry from tears, but I discern Arabella at the other end of the room, waving at us. Amidst resounding applause (and has anybody deserved it more, I ask you?), we rush to a little anteroom. Arabella closes the door, and says, "There's some water here," she points at the table, stocked with a pitcher of ice water. "I will go and get you clothes. You stay here and chill for a minute. Okay?"

Then she leaves us. Harry and I are alone again.

"Oh my God," Harry says, giddy with laughter. "I can't believe we just did that. Look at the state of us."

"I can't believe it either."

He kisses me again and again, until suddenly he stops and says, "Can you take that shirt off?"

I do that. The smell of it is starting to impinge on the magic of the moment. I toss the shirt in a convenient bin.

"Dare I ask why you're covered in pee?" he says, amused.

"It's Siobhan's."

"Ah, say no more."

"No, really!" I laugh. "She took a pregnancy test in our bathroom and then we fell into each other and it just sort of happened. I don't know why these things keep happening to me."

"Hang on. Pregnancy test?"

"She's pregnant. Hence the meltdown."

"I thought that was about the wedding," he says. "Did you say she's pregnant? At last?"

I nod at the bin and say, "We have a urine sample of hers right here. Do you want me to test her again?"

We both laugh. How is it possible for a day that started so badly to end so well? I feel exhausted. Harry looks no less tired. I go to him and kiss him again, feeling so unspeakably glad to be able to do that.

"Do you know," I say, leaning my forehead against his. "For a moment there, I did think you went back to Kieran, in Sweden."

He pulls his head back, surprised.

"Kieran?" he asks, bemused.

I explain about Kieran—it turns out Harry had no idea Kieran was there. It was, after all, a crazy coincidence.

"The only reason I told you I was going there was because there was a flight to Malmö at around the same time my actual flight was leaving. I wanted to keep everything hush-hush. Like an idiot. It's the last time I try to do anything behind your back, I swear. Besides, do you know why Kieran's hopping around the globe so much these days?"

I shake my head.

"Because he's courting a male steward. He started his own security agency, remember, he told us. It was so he could have more flexibility. So that he could follow him around everywhere, like a lovesick puppy."

Right now it seems absurd that I should ever have worried about Kieran at all. In fact, I feel a little proud of myself for not having cancelled the wedding. For having trusted in him.

"What are they like?" I ask. "My birth parents." I didn't forget where Harry went and what he did this past week. But it is only now that I'm able to let it sink in, believe it, think about it. In fact, I'm a little excited.

"You really want to know?"

I nod. He takes out his phone and shows me pictures. My birth mother is short, stout, with dark, curly hair and a skin tone like my own. My biological father is a tall, loose-limbed black man with a grey beard and soft, brown eyes. They look like mine.

"They're friendly people," Harry says.

"They knew who you were?"

"I told them," he says. "Are you angry? I mean, I know I shouldn't have done it without your permission, but can you forgive me?"

I nod quickly, my eyes fixed on the picture of those two strangers. Having spent so much time imagining these people, I'm not sure now how to feel about it, seeing what they're really like. A part of me hoped childishly that they were special agents or some sort of royalty who had me illegitimately and thus had to give me up. It's sobering to see that they are just two ordinary people with alternative lifestyles. They look like nice people. They are both smiling in the picture.

"You should have told me," I say, staring at it. "I could have gone with you."

"I know. It was a stupid thing to do from start to finish."

"What did you tell them about me?"

"The truth," he says, smiling. "That you're a successful, award-winning artist; that you're engaged to me; and that you look like this." He shows me the picture of me he has on his phone. It's a flattering one, which is a relief.

"I have this for you, if you're interested."

He swipes his phone until he finds a video. I give another nod, though my mouth has gone dry. He presses Play.

My birth parents are standing close together, in front of a wall covered in a climbing plant. It's all green around them. My biological dad's arm is around my birth mother's. He says, "Hi, Joseph! How are you? Your boyfriend says that you will be getting married soon. We are so happy to hear you are doing well. So happy." His accent is still British, with only a mild Australian twang. "He tells us you're an artist! We would love to see your work one day."

My biological mother chimes in, "We hope you can come down here one day to see us. It would be so wonderful to meet you!" She tears up. "I want you to know that I have been thinking about you every single—" She chokes up. I blink hard, and Harry's arm snakes about my waist. "—every single day," she finishes, her voice now raspy with emotion. "It is so wonderful to hear you found a good family who loves you, and a boyfriend who loves you so much. It makes me so happy."

"Do come and visit," my biological father insists. "We can show you some beautiful spots here: there's great weather, wonderful nature, so much to do, you wouldn't be bored, I promise!"

"Yes, do come!" my birth mother says, and then she kisses her hands at me and waves, and the video ends.

For a moment, I am just blown away.

"I'm really sorry," Harry says, again, quietly. "I shouldn't have done it. I thought it would be—"

"No," I interrupt him. "No, I liked it. I'm sorry you had to go through so much trouble."

"In the future you will stick to being spontaneous, and I'll stick to the planning," he says.

"Okay."

He kisses my temple. Everything inside me goes calm.

Chapter Eighteen
THE AFTERMATH

The reception passes us by. Magically—perhaps because of Harry's presence—nothing goes wrong. I mean, of course, the ketchup-lettuce-caviar wedding cake collapses before we manage to cut it; and Siobhan is inconsolable/ecstatic about the pregnancy and therefore looks like Batman's Joker in all the pictures; and Harry's dad gives a really short speech, in which he basically gives up and concedes defeat to me, which is a bit odd, but equally kind of touching. But Arabella has colluded with the caterers so there's an extra cake for people to eat. And Siobhan doesn't care at all what she looks like. We're all happy for her and try to console her about all the alcohol she consumed while in France. Eventually, Chloe reminds her that in the history of the world, most people were drunk all the time, and bred like rabbits.

"It's thanks to alcohol, if you ask me, you got pregnant in the first place!" she says. For some reason, this does help Siobhan get over it.

Harry and I have our first dance to Bobby Darin's "Dream Lover," which the band kindly altered by exchanging all the *girl* in the lyrics to *boy* for us.

At some point late in the night, Harry falls asleep on my shoulder, and so I take him up to our room. He zombie-walks up the stairs while I support him on my arm. I deposit him on our fresh bed. The room's been cleaned while we were downstairs. The bed looks soft, white, and inviting. New curtains are up, the iron's been cleaned away. Suddenly I feel really bad about how I treated Arabella, because I'm pretty sure she's made all this happen.

I strip Harry of his clothes and tuck him in. Then I undress myself and lie beside him. A wave of weariness washes over me, and while the sounds of the party penetrate from downstairs, I feel so tired, so soothed by Harry's warm body next to me, that sleep takes me almost at once.

It's three in the afternoon by the time we wake up, shower, go back to bed, fool around, shower again, and then take another nap. We wake up a second time, and we're hungry. I order room service, while Harry stretches in bed, marvelling at how he doesn't even feel guilty for not getting up.

"We should do this more often," he says.

We have a three-course meal right there in bed. Harry is amazed that such a thing is even humanly possible. He can't decide whether it's really disgusting or bloody awesome. I convince him it's the latter by eating my dessert off him.

When the sun goes down, we're like John Lennon and Yoko. We spent the whole day in bed, and Harry decides that he likes it after all.

"It's so . . . decadent," he says. He's flushed and breathing hard, but the smile on his face shows complete satisfaction.

I crack a window. We've misted it up. Then I fall back onto my pillow and breathe in the fresh air now mingling with that of our sweat and exertion.

"Are you tired?" He rolls onto his side to face me.

I laugh. "Give me a minute."

"Do you know," he says with a wistful smile, "yesterday, I came here from the airport straight away?"

"What, you didn't stop at our flat first?"

"No."

"Why?"

"For the same reason, I imagine, that you didn't cancel the wedding."

"I don't know if I deserve credit for that," I say, putting my hands behind my head. "I had the worst week imaginable, and was paralysed with panic."

I tell him everything. About his mother's insane wedding cake (he barely registered it at the reception), his sister's disappearance in

France, and about my gym visits with Frank. I even tell him about my conversation with Kieran just before Harry turned up. I can't keep secrets from my husband, after all.

Then I remember how I bumped into Gabriella, and I tell him about the inscrutable conversation I had with her—how she claimed to love Frank but still thought it necessary to leave the continent and never see him again. Unlike me, though, Harry doesn't seem mystified by her words at all.

"Can you really not imagine what her problem was?" he asks, half-amused, half-astonished at my incomprehension.

"No," I say, indignant. "I warned her, before she married him, that Frank was as he was, and if this wore on her with time, then why not just say so? I mean, I get it, he can be a bit much, but it's not like she didn't know that. In fact, when I spoke to her before her wedding, she was gushing over how dreamy he was, and how flattered she was that someone like he should choose someone like her!"

"I don't think this is about Frank, love."

"What else, then?"

He sighs and puts his hand on my stomach.

"I only spoke to her about it once or twice," he says. "Far be it for me to speculate on her motivations on the basis of that. But I had the impression, when they were still together, that she wasn't being entirely honest with Frank."

"What do you mean? Did she cheat on him?"

"No, I think she was pretending to be wilder and more, you know, like Frank, in order to appeal to him. In reality, I think she's a calm, placid soul. At least that's how she struck me when Frank wasn't around. When he was around, she was straining to be what she probably thought Frank wanted. Wild and spontaneous."

"That's ridiculous!" I sit up, indignant. "Nobody would do that!"

"I'm just saying what I thought I saw," he says, leaning back. "I might be wrong. Probably I am."

I stew over this for a minute. Her words come back to me. She said she couldn't go on pretending. That it was frightening and tiring. I turn to Harry.

"She wouldn't, would she?" I ask, less certain now.

He shrugs. "I can tell you this much. You and Frank can be quite intimidating."

"What?"

"I'm just saying." He laughs. "You have this wild, artistic set of friends. Your anecdotes are full of incredible adventures. Like that time Frank lost his leg rescuing a guy from a burning car. Or that time you and he initiated a whole New Year's Eve street party that ended up in national newspapers. Or that time you flashed a whole pub as part of a card trick? Or in Dublin, when—"

"Okay, okay, thank you, I get it."

"Every time you go out, something weird happens. When you're just a boring old suit like me, or a grey little church mouse like Gabriella, it can be a little overwhelming."

"Hang on; you don't want to tell me that *you* feel that way?"

"I did for a time."

I can't believe him.

He lifts himself up onto his elbows. "When I first met you, you were this . . . this charismatic, charming pirate, and I—"

"Pirate!" I burst out. "What the— What do you mean, *pirate*?"

He reddens and laughs. "Well, with your long hair and your rings and earrings and bracelets, and your tanned skin tone, I liked to think of you as a little bit pirate-like. In a sexy way."

"And I'm finding this out now?"

"So it was intimidating," he continues despite my outrage, "and I felt like such a dweeb in comparison."

"Hang on," I say, because this really is too much. "I don't get it. Why then are you and I married now, and she's going to Brazil to teach the Bible in the jungle? This doesn't make any sense."

"Well, our stories are different," he says. "You and I didn't get married immediately."

I sink my head into my hands again. None of this is making any sense to me. "What are you saying?"

"As much as you'll hate to hear this, we did have Kieran to force us to confront what we felt." He puts his hand to my cheek. "They had no obstacles at all."

"I'm not thanking Kieran for anything."

He thinks this is funny. "You do realise that if it hadn't been for him, I might never have had the guts to go to you?"

I frown. "What?"

"After he and I split up that second time, and I was absolutely miserable, he was the one who encouraged me to go find you. I wanted to, but I thought you'd be too angry to look at me. I thought I'd messed up everything. You stopped responding to the invitations. I thought you were done with me."

I don't like thinking back to that time. It still makes my heart contract with pain.

"Pf," I say. "I'm not that fickle! Besides, you kept sending all these people to me, with offers of work and awards and what not. How could I possibly forget you? You didn't give me the chance to!"

"Okay, so I'm not subtle. But for all I knew, you had dozens of guys doing that for you."

"What did Kieran do?"

"He pointed out, none too gently I might add, that I had the infuriating tendency—a weakness of character, I suppose—to focus too much on what others want, and what's right and good and decent, and not enough on, well, on what *I* want. He didn't put it that way. He used words like 'pussy' and 'coward.' We were arguing at the time, and it wasn't pleasant to hear, but he hit the nail on the head. Repeatedly. That's how I ended up deciding that, though you might not want me back, you deserved to know the truth. Boring old suit though I am, I could at least tell you how I feel."

He must be joking. At this precise moment, he's lying before me propped up on one elbow, in the pose of a young Roman, with his gorgeous body, his sexy stubble, his sex-mussed hair, having just returned from Australia, of all places, after rescuing a pair of incorrigible hippies from jail. Boring old suit my arse.

But he's serious.

"So you think that Gabriella's as deluded as you?"

He rolls his eyes. "I think that Gabriella was similarly swept away by a larger-than-life character. But their story went differently. She married him straight away. Probably because she was afraid of losing him. I mean, you did say that Vegas had been her idea, right? I can totally understand the impulse, though it was terribly silly of her to have done it. And then she never understood that Frank loved her for who she was and not for who she pretended to be. At least"—here he wavers—"I think he does. Does he?"

"Yes!" I cry. "Oh my God. Haven't you seen him lately? He's like a shadow of his former self."

Harry shrugs helplessly. I digest his words, match them against my memories of Frank and Gabriella's marriage. I remember how stressed she got about Frank's birthdays. How convinced she had been she'd never live up to Frank's expectations. I thought it was funny at the time, because of course none of those "wild adventures" Harry spoke of were planned—stupid stuff just happened to us. We liked the Harries and Gabriellas of this world because they made everything actually go to plan. Our chaos was contained by their forces of order. I remember Frank's words. *She has a way of looking at me, and suddenly everything inside of me goes calm.*

In truth, Harry spent more time talking to her than I did. Maybe he does know. Maybe, though, he's only projecting his own ridiculous hang-ups on her (I mean, really, a *pirate*?).

"We have to do something," I say, at last.

Harry falls back onto his pillow. "Today?" he moans. "I thought we were staying in bed today."

"I can't believe *you* are saying this to *me*," I say, crawling out and hunting for our clothes. "We have to find Frank, and you have to explain this to him."

"We can do it tomorrow."

"At least call him, then," I say. "Tell him everything you told me, only leave the embarrassing bits out. And then he can find her and clear things up."

He sighs, "We really shouldn't meddle . . ."

I hand him his phone. Resigned, he finds Frank's number.

After a lengthy conversation with a hungover Frank, Harry and I return to our extended wedding night. I order us ice cream and strawberries, which we have with champagne. We shower together, and then, tired once more, we snuggle up and fall asleep again.

In the middle of the night, we're fast asleep, when Harry's phone rings.

"Hrhghello?" Harry says, putting a protective hand over my ear, as I lie with my head on his chest. I do hear him, though, and look up.

"It's Frank," he says to me. "I don't understand a word he's saying."

"Put him on speakerphone."

Harry fiddles with his mobile. Frank's voice comes through, sounding hoarse and panicked.

". . . flying out tonight! I don't know if I can get to her. Chloe's driving, but we're not even on the M25 yet and—"

"Frank?" I interrupt him. "Frank, it's me, Joe. What's going on?"

"Oh, Joe! I couldn't reach Gabriella, so I called her parents, and they wouldn't tell me where she was, so I called Rachel, and she told me that Gabriella was on her way to do mission work in Brazil. And she's flying out tonight!"

"Tonight!" This wakes me right up. "Shit."

"So Chloe and I are trying to get to the airport to catch her," Frank says. "But time's running out. Can you try and get hold of her or someone in that group and see if she could wait for me?"

"Yeah, sure," I say at once, although I've no idea how I could possibly do that.

"Is her phone off?" Harry asks. "Or is she just not picking up?"

"It's off," Frank says. "Rachel gave me the number of one of the people going with her, but I probably wrote it down wrong. There's no answer when I try."

"Okay, I'll find out," I say.

While Harry talks to Frank, I call Rachel. She picks up, irate.

"What?" she says.

"I need a number to reach Gabriella."

"Wha—"

"There's no time, I need a number! Frank's trying to get to her."

"Oh," she startles. "Is he? Okay, hang on a minute."

I hear her shuffling around on the other side. Harry says, "They're on the M4 now."

"What's the traffic like?"

"At this time of the night?" Harry lifts a shoulder. "Probably not too bad." He stands up and goes to the desk where his laptop is. "I'll check what time her flight is." He brings the laptop to bed.

Rachel gets back to me with a number, which I jot down on the hotel notepad.

"Do you know the people she's going with?" I ask her.

"No," she says. "It's a new group, I'm not familiar with them. The number is for her emergency contact, a girl called Katie. I tried to talk Gabriella out of this, by the way, but she wouldn't listen."

I thank her, ring off, and try the number. As I listen to the ringing, Harry tells Frank to avoid the stretch of the M4 past the Furnival Gardens, as they have building work going on. He navigates them to King's Road. Katie's phone isn't picking up.

"Nothing," I tell him. Harry relays the information to Frank.

"She's probably already gone," he cries, despairingly. "She's on the other side of the world. I'll never find her!"

"It's not that bad," Harry tries to calm him. "Even if she does fly off, in this day and age, you'll be able to track her down, email her or something."

"She'll meet some holier-than-thou wanker and marry him and it will be too late!"

Frank is in the bouts of full-on hysteria.

"Listen to me!" I shout at him. "Get a grip! She's not going to marry anybody else, because she loves you. Okay? She told me so herself. So hold it together. You don't want to scare her when you get to her."

"Did—did she say that?" he whimpers.

"Yes, so don't lose your cool," I tell him.

"Er, bad news," Harry says, quietly. He's on his laptop, looking at the Heathrow website.

"What?" I ask.

"Looks like her flight's already boarding."

"What!" Frank and I scream at the same time.

"Wait, wait," I say, my brain feverishly at work. "Didn't you say Kieran's dating a flight attendant?"

Harry frowns. "Yeah, and?"

"Well, maybe that guy knows someone on this flight and maybe they can tell Gabriella . . . I don't know, worth a shot?"

"You really want me to call Kieran at this time of night?" Harry asks wearily.

I take his phone and tell Frank, "We're going to hang up now. Keep driving to the airport. We'll get back to you shortly."

In the middle of his wailing reply, I hang up and then find Kieran's contact details.

"Do it," I say, handing it to Harry. "For Frank."

Harry, resigned, presses Kieran's contact, muttering something about Frank and mental institutions. While he's on the phone with Kieran, I ring Frank from my own phone and tell him about Kieran's new lover.

"It's too late!" Frank cries. "If they're boarding already, then it's too late. Even if you do reach him, there's no way . . . AAAH!"

"Oh my God! Frank?"

"It's all right," he says. "It was an owl. It's nothing. It's nothing. I thought we were going to die, that's all. Not that I wouldn't welcome the sweet release of death right now . . ."

I can hear Chloe groaning in the background.

I say, "Okay, I'm glad you're alive. Where are you right now?"

"We're joining the M4 again. Quarter of an hour away from the airport, Chloe says. That's unless she kills me before that, she says."

I glance at Harry, who's in muted conversation with Kieran.

"Well?" I ask him.

"He's in the shower," Harry says.

"Who is?"

"Ryan."

"Who's Ryan?"

"Kieran's boyfriend."

"The steward?"

"Yes, the steward," Harry says. "What's that?" this was to Kieran. "He's out," he says to me. "Okay, I'll wait."

Harry looks to me. "I can't believe that after everything we've been through, we have to do an actual chase to the airport."

"I tell you what!" Frank butts in. "When this all has failed, you're coming with me to drink it all away! Why didn't you tell me you saw her? Why didn't you tell me what she said to you?"

"I didn't know what to say!" It's useless to defend myself. "I didn't want to make you feel worse."

Harry makes a *sh* gesture with his finger, so I take Frank off speakerphone.

"I'm sorry," I tell Frank. "I should have told you. If I'd understood what she meant, I would've told you at once. But I didn't. And I didn't want you to rack your brain over it any more than you were already doing. It was a bad call. I'm sorry."

"And now it's too late! What's the status of the flight?"

I check Harry's laptop.

"Still boarding. Not yet taken off. There's still time."

"There isn't. You know there isn't. No way will I get a ticket in time, and then go through security and then find the right gate before they take off. It's too late. It's too late!"

I feel it too. It is too late. He's right. I look to Harry, who's nodding and saying okay to Kieran. He turns to me.

"Ryan's trying a few of his friends."

"He is?"

I can't believe it. It seemed like such a desperate idea.

"Frank?"

"Yes?"

"Ryan's making a few calls."

"Who's Ryan?"

"The air steward."

"Huh?"

"Kieran's boyfriend. The steward. Keep up."

"Oh. And?"

"And?" I turn the question to Harry.

But Harry has already gone off the phone. He's staring at the laptop. I, too, turn my attention to the laptop.

"I'm sorry," Harry says. I stare at the screen. The *Boarding* has changed to *Gate Closed*. I focus my eyes to see if I was reading the right line, but there is no mistaking it.

"Frank," I turn to my phone.

"Yeah?"

It breaks my heart to have to tell him.

"The flight's gone. She's gone."

There's silence on the other side.

"Frank?"

"It's not like I expected any different," he says in a low, subdued tone. "It's my own damned fault. I deserve this. I made her feel that way. It's on me." His voice trembles. I look to Harry, who puts his hand on my arm.

"I'm sorry too, Frank," he says into my phone. "It was a close one. But it's not lost yet. You can still find her. It's not the end of the world. We'll help you."

"He will," I say to Frank. "He just tracked down my birth parents in Australia. After that, finding Gabriella will be an afternoon's work. You'll see."

"That's all right, guys," Frank says after a deep sigh. "It's all right. Turn us around, Chloe. We can go back home. I'll speak to you later."

He hangs up before I can say anything more. Harry and I stare at the phone, lost for words.

"Somehow," Harry says at last, "I really thought we'd catch her in time."

I did too. Now I feel silly. And at fault too. I should have told Frank about seeing Gabriella, and about what she said . . . I should have done something. But hindsight being what it is (perfectly bloody useless), all I can do now is lie back and wonder how to repair this mess.

Harry lies down next to me.

"It's not your fault," he says, as though reading my thoughts.

I hold his hand.

And then my phone rings.

"Who is it?" I ask.

Harry hands it to me. "Unknown number."

I pick up. The voice on the other side is female and sounds timid. "Frank?"

"Gabriella?" I say, as recognition floods my brain.

"Joe?"

"Oh my God!" I cry.

"Oh my God!" cries Harry.

"Call Frank," I instruct him. And then, to Gabriella, I say, "Aren't you on a plane right now?"

"No," she says. "I—I thought . . . Oh dear, I thought you were Frank."

I can hear Harry telling Frank that I've got Gabriella on the line. It's like the CIA headquarters here.

"Why would you think I was Frank?" I ask, for want of a better thing to say. I feel like I'm negotiating a hostage situation and it's my role to not let her hang up.

"It's just . . ." Her voice wobbles, and she sniffs loudly. "I was just going to get on the plane, when my friend showed me all these missed calls from an unknown number, and I imagined . . . but of course it wasn't. It was you."

"What? No! Are you kidding me? Frank's on his way to the airport. He's been trying to ring you, and then, when he couldn't do it, I tried too. And then we called a Swedish flight attendant . . . well, he isn't Swedish, actually, but he's in Sweden now and . . . it's a *very* long story. Where are you right now?"

"Heathrow."

"Don't move," I say. "Frank is coming to get you."

Harry tells Frank, "Did you hear that? Joe just told Gabriella you're going to get her."

"What did she say?" It's Frank's voice on speakerphone. "Does she want me to come?"

I have the brilliant idea of putting my phone on speaker too.

"Gabriella?" I say, loudly. "Gabriella, can you hear Frank? Frank, speak up."

There's a moment's silence, as Harry and I stare at our phones.

"Gab?" says Frank's voice on Harry's phone.

"Frank?" says Gabriella on mine.

"I'm on my way to the airport," Frank says, eagerly. "I can come and pick you up if you want to."

"Oh, that's— That sounds lovely," she says. "I don't want to inconvenience you. I can take a cab."

"No! No, I'll be there in ten minutes. Wait for me!"

"Okay," she says. "I'll wait."

There's a pause.

"Why didn't you go on that plane, Gabriella?" I ask. "Why didn't you board?"

"I don't know what to say." She laughs and sniffs at the same time. "I'm so embarrassed."

"Don't be!" Frank exclaims. "Don't be embarrassed. I'm coming for you. I love you, lass!"

Gabriella is either laughing or crying; it's hard to tell by the sounds she's making. Harry says, "How about you call each other?"

Both Frank and Gabriella agree to this, and so, reluctantly, Harry and I ring off. The room feels oddly quiet now that the storm has passed. I go to the window and open it wider. The stress of all this is now wearing off, and I feel relief and renewed exhilaration.

In the light of the streetlamp outside, I can see Harry sitting up in bed smiling at me and shaking his head.

"What?" I say, defensively. I know what he's going to say.

Before he can, there's a pounding on our door. I wrap a bedsheet around me and go open it. It's Alan Yates, hotel manager and firm anti-Joe-ite, looking very disapproving.

"Hello, Mr. Kaminski," he says, as though we were old enemies. "Do you know, by any chance, what time it is?"

I have been so wrapped up in the airport chase, I'm a little confused. But he's right: it's the middle of the night.

"Uh-oh," I say. "Have we been loud?"

"Let us just say," he says, magnanimously, "that our explanations to other guests that this is your wedding night are wearing exceedingly thin. Will I be able to convince you to keep it down?"

"Absolutely," I say.

Harry, wrapped in another bedsheet, comes to my aid. "What's the problem? Are we too noisy?"

"Ah, Mr. Byrne," Alan says, sounding very disappointed—like a school principal who has found, to his dismay, that his star pupil has now befriended the school clown. "Yes, it just so happens that cries of 'He's in the shower!' and 'Aaah, it's an owl!' are growing somewhat tiresome to our other guests."

"We understand," says Harry. "We're done now. We'll be quiet, we promise. We're really sorry. How about you treat everyone to a champagne breakfast tomorrow morning, on us?"

"That's very gentlemanly of you," he concedes, mollified.

Harry grins. "It's settled, then. Good night."

Alan sends me another reproachful look, as though to say *I have my eye on you*, and then retreats.

We close the door.

"I don't know what his problem is," I tell Harry, as we return to bed. "There are no dogs in the bathroom, nobody got sprayed with urine, and nothing's on fire. And does he thank me? No!"

Harry throws his head back and laughs.

"Oh God," he says. "If this is the first day of our marriage, Joe, I can't wait to see what the rest of them are going to be like."

"Come to bed, husband," I say with a grin. "I'll show you."

How to get married in eight easy-peasy steps:
1. Meet a guy you hate.
2. Sleep with the guy on a whim.
3. Lose the guy to his ex.
4. Take him to Dublin.
5. Shave your head and scare the bejeezus out of his cousins.
6. Propose to him anyway.
7. Tell his father to stop being a fuckweasel or else.
8. Marry him.

How to get married in eight easy-peasy steps, as revised by Harry:
1. At the lowest point in your life, and at the worst possible moment, meet a real-life, twenty-first-century pirate and rogue.
2. Ignore all your better instincts. Fall inexplicably in love with him.
3. Dump everything and roll the dice on your inexplicable attraction to twenty-first-century pirate and rogue.
4. Ruin his career by threatening to sue the entirety of the Dublin art world for imagined harm done to your very own twenty-first-century pirate and rogue.
5. Accept proposal from him. Naturally.
6. Track down his birth parents in attempt to be cute.
7. Return with barely any time to spare, only to find that regardless of how much you fucked up, your very own twenty-first-century pirate and rogue wants you anyway.
8. Marry him.

Dear Reader,

Thank you for reading Marina Ford's *Marry Him*!

We know your time is precious and you have many, many entertainment options, so it means a lot that you've chosen to spend your time reading. We really hope you enjoyed it.

We'd be honored if you'd consider posting a review—good or bad—on sites like **Amazon, Barnes & Noble, Kobo, Goodreads, Twitter, Facebook, Tumblr,** and your blog or website. We'd also be honored if you told your friends and family about this book. Word of mouth is a book's lifeblood!

For more information on upcoming releases, author interviews, blog tours, contests, giveaways, and more, please sign up for our weekly, spam-free newsletter and visit us around the web:

Newsletter: riptidepublishing.com/newsletter
Twitter: twitter.com/RiptideBooks
Facebook: facebook.com/RiptidePublishing
Goodreads: tinyurl.com/RiptideOnGoodreads
Tumblr: riptidepublishing.tumblr.com

Thank you so much for Reading the Rainbow!

RiptidePublishing.com

Acknowledgements

A massive thank-you to Carole-ann Galloway, the acquisitions editor whose patient work has made this novel better in innumerable ways, and whose attention to detail and craftsmanship have taught me a great deal about writing.

Thank you to Grace Stack at Riptide for reaching out to me after this book's short-lived release with its previous publisher.

And thank you to the whole Riptide team for making me feel so welcome!

Ten years ago, when my husband took me for a surprise visit to Ireland with the intention of proposing to me, everything went wrong: security at the airport stopped to search his bag, because he accidentally forgot to take out a pair of scissors, nearly exposing the ring he had hidden there (a shout-out to the security people at Leeds Bradford airport who handled this without laughing at my husband though they so clearly wanted to); we'd left for Dublin at four in the morning, so during the traditional Irish dancing performance at the lovely pub he took me to later that day, I fell asleep. When we got to the truly romantic Ha'penny Bridge, it was raining, and when finally he conquered his nerves, he decided to go down on one knee in front of a group of tourists he didn't even notice. I want to thank my ridiculous, disorganised chaos prince of a husband for planning something for the first time in his life. And for every single day since. This, and everything else I do, is for you.

Also by Marina Ford

Lovesick
Twelve Dates of Christmas